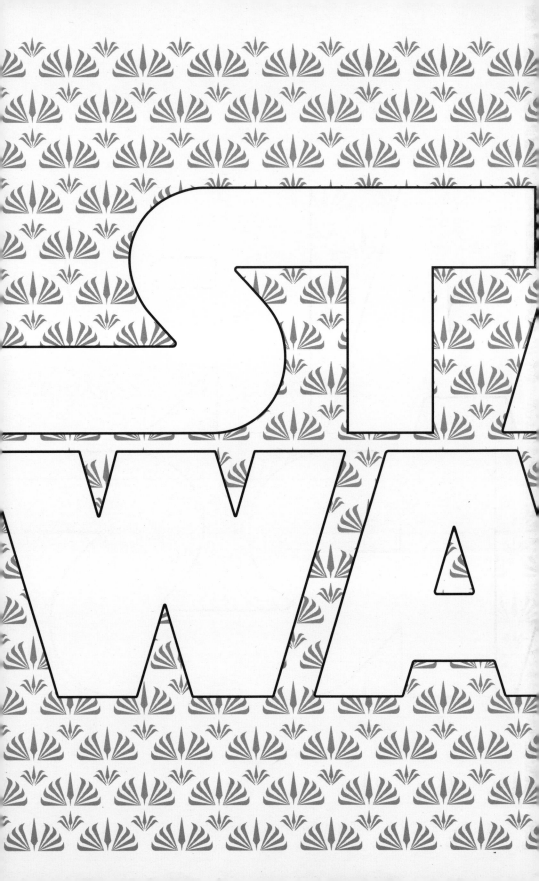

THE BATTLE OF JEDHA

THE BATTLE OF JEDHA

George Mann

1 3 5 7 9 10 8 6 4 2

Del Rey
20 Vauxhall Bridge Road
London SW1V 2SA

Del Rey is part of the Penguin Random House group of companies
whose addresses can be found at global.penguinrandomhouse.com.

Star Wars: The High Republic: The Battle of Jedha is a
work of fiction. Names, places, and incidents either
are products of the author's imagination or are used
fictitiously. Any resemblance to actual events, locales,
or persons, living or dead, is entirely coincidental.

First published in the United States by Random House Worlds in 2023
First published in the UK by Del Rey in 2023

www.penguin.co.uk

A CIP catalogue record for this book is available from the British Library.

Hardback ISBN 9781529907803
Trade paperback ISBN 9781529907810

Printed and bound in Great Britain by Clays Ltd, Elcograf S.p.A.

The authorised representative in the EEA is Penguin Random House Ireland,
Morrison Chambers, 32 Nassau Street, Dublin D02 YH68

www.greenpenguin.co.uk

Penguin Random House is committed to a
sustainable future for our business, our readers
and our planet. This book is made from Forest
Stewardship Council® certified paper.

For Cavan Scott

THE **STAR WARS** NOVELS TIMELINE

THE HIGH REPUBLIC

Convergence
The Battle of Jedha
Cataclysm

Light of the Jedi
The Rising Storm
Tempest Runner
The Fallen Star

Dooku: Jedi Lost
Master and Apprentice

I | THE PHANTOM MENACE

II | ATTACK OF THE CLONES

Brotherhood
The Thrawn Ascendancy Trilogy
Dark Disciple: A Clone Wars Novel

III | REVENGE OF THE SITH

Inquisitor: Rise of the Red Blade
Catalyst: A Rogue One Novel
Lords of the Sith
Tarkin
Jedi: Battle Scars

SOLO

Thrawn
A New Dawn: A Rebels Novel
Thrawn: Alliances
Thrawn: Treason

ROGUE ONE

IV | A NEW HOPE

Battlefront II: Inferno Squad
Heir to the Jedi
Doctor Aphra
Battlefront: Twilight Company

V | THE EMPIRE STRIKES BACK

VI | RETURN OF THE JEDI

The Princess and the Scoundrel
The Alphabet Squadron Trilogy
The Aftermath Trilogy
Last Shot

Shadow of the Sith
Bloodline
Phasma
Canto Bight

VII | THE FORCE AWAKENS

VIII | THE LAST JEDI

Resistance Reborn
Galaxy's Edge: Black Spire

IX | THE RISE OF SKYWALKER

Dramatis Personae

OF THE JEDI

Creighton Sun: Human, Jedi Master, on a diplomatic mission to Jedha

Aida Forte: Kadas'sa'Nikto, Jedi Knight, on a diplomatic mission to Jedha

Silandra Sho: Human, Jedi Master, on a pilgrimage to Jedha

Gella Nattai: Human, Jedi Knight

Xinith Tarl: Bith, Jedi Master, Jedi Council member

Har'kin: Gran, Jedi Master

Vohlan: Human, Jedi Master

B-9H0: Creighton and Aida's protocol droid

GT-68: Creighton and Aida's astromech droid

OF THE CHURCH OF THE FORCE

Keth Cerapath: Human, adjunct of the Church of the Force

P3-7A: Keth's often-sarcastic droid

Prefect Saous: Human, prefect of the Church of the Force

OF THE GUARDIANS OF THE WHILLS

Mesook: Human, Guardian of the Whills

Selik: Iridonian Zabrak, Guardian of the Whills

OF THE PATH OF THE OPEN HAND

The Mother: Human, also known as Elecia, leader of the Path of the Open Hand

Marda Ro: Evereni, Guide of the Path of the Open Hand

The Herald: Nautolan, Herald of the Path of the Open Hand

Naddie: Human, mischievous Little of the Path of the Open Hand

Tromak: Gran, tremulous Little of the Path of the Open Hand

Mylas: Duros, inquisitive Little of the Path of the Open Hand

Pela: Togruta, Disciple of the Path of the Open Hand

Qwerb: Human, bodyguard to the Mother

Jukkyuk: Wookiee, bodyguard to the Mother

Elder Delwin: Weequay, Elder of the Path of the Open Hand

Path disciples

OF ENLIGHTENMENT

Kradon: Villarandi, owner and impresario of Enlightenment tapbar

Piralli: Sullustan, dockworker

Moona: Twi'lek, barfly

Camille: Gloovan, monosyllabic bouncer of Enlightenment, twin sister of Delphine

Delphine: Gloovan, monosyllabic bouncer of Enlightenment, twin sister of Camille

OF EIRAM

Ambassador Cerox: Human, ambassador to the peace conference

Eirami guard: Ambassador Cerox's personal guard

Eirami sergeant

Eirami troopers

Enforcer droids

OF E'RONOH

Ambassador Tintak: Human, ambassador to the peace conference

Lesser Councilor Linth: Human, sycophantic aide to Ambassador Tintak

E'roni guard: Ambassador Tintak's personal guard

E'roni sergeant

E'roni troopers

Mining loader pilots

OF JEDHA

Mytion: Human, disciple of the Brotherhood of the Ninth Door

Inoke: Kel Dor, disciple of the Brotherhood of the Ninth Door

Baarla: Mournish, disciple of the Brotherhood of the Ninth Door

Tarna Miak: Human, Sorcerer of Tund

Street traders, civilians, rioters, pilgrims, tourists, droids

OTHER PLAYERS

Morton San Tekka: Human, mediator at the peace conference, representative of the famed hyperspace prospecting family

Tilson Graf: Human, traveler, representative of the famed hyperspace prospecting family

Chairperson Meldan: Pantoran, Republic representative on Jedha

THE BATTLE OF JEDHA

ANNOUNCER:
A long time ago, in a galaxy far, far away. . . .

CUE THEME

ANNOUNCER:
Star Wars: The High Republic

The Battle of Jedha

By George Mann

SCENE 1. INT. JEDHA—THE SECOND SPIRE— MEETING CHAMBER

ANNOUNCER:
Time until the battle begins: zero hours.

ATMOS: We're in the Second Spire on Jedha, an old, previously abandoned temple that has been recently refitted for the peace conference. We're in a large meeting chamber on the lower level of the spire. A small group of people has gathered, but the mood is subdued as everyone waits for proceedings to begin.

From outside, we can hear the general murmur of distant crowds. As the scene progresses, however, the sounds of angry people should grow louder in the background, as a riot is heading this way . . .

FX: Tilson Graf, the serving mediator, is rapping his fingertips nervously on the pedestal before him.

TILSON GRAF:
(NERVOUS)

Right, then.

It's almost time to begin.

AMBASSADOR TINTAK:
Indeed. Let's get it over with. I'm eager to return to E'ronoh to help with the reconstruction efforts, just as, I'm sure, Ambassador Cerox wishes to return to her people on Eiram.

TILSON GRAF:
(HESITANT)

Yes, Ambassador Tintak. If you could just give me a moment . . .

CREIGHTON SUN:
Is everything all right, Mediator Graf?

TILSON GRAF:
(DISTRACTED)

What? Yes, yes. Of course, Master Sun.

(PULLING HIMSELF TOGETHER)

Everything's fine. I just need a minute to compose myself. This is, after all, a momentous affair. The signing of this peace treaty is a key moment in galactic history. Eiram and E'ronoh have been at war for over *five years*. And now, following the marriage of their heirs, the worlds have finally come together in peace. We're gathered here in the Second Spire on historic Jedha to—

AMBASSADOR CEROX:
(INTERRUPTING)

Mediator Graf?

TILSON GRAF:
(PUT OUT)

Yes, Ambassador Cerox?

AMBASSADOR CEROX:
(IMPATIENT)

With the greatest respect, we are all aware of the reasons why we're here. Please, get on with it before—

FX: Ambassador Cerox is drowned out by the sudden, surging sounds of the riot just outside the building.

AMBASSADOR TINTAK:
(ANGRY, BARKING FRUSTRATION)

Oh, what *now*?

TILSON GRAF:
Umm ...

CREIGHTON:
Aida. What's going on outside?

AIDA FORTE:
There's a crowd of people approaching the spire, Creighton. They're ...

FX: A thrown rock puts out a window. The bellowing from outside grows louder. The crowd is angry.

AIDA:
(SHOCKED)

It's a *riot*!

CREIGHTON:
(WORRIED)

Get back, everyone. Away from the windows.

FX: A lightbow fires, somewhere else in the building.

MUFFLED SHOUT:
(FROM "OFF-SCREEN")

Stay back! All of you!

FX: More banging and clanging. The riot is spilling into the building close by. A door bursts open into the meeting chamber. It's Mesook, a Guardian of the Whills.

MESOOK:
(DESPERATE)

It's the civilians. They're rioting. They're swarming the building. We can't hold them back without a massacre.

FX: There are sounds of brutal close-quarter fighting from behind him. The Guardians aren't firing on the civilians unless they must.

TILSON GRAF:
(QUIETLY, AS HE RETREATS)

I . . . ummm . . . I think we'd better make for safety.

CREIGHTON:
(COMMANDING)

Ambassadors, to me.

FX: There's a massive crash as a speeder bike bursts through the plate-glass window, splintering shards everywhere. A man screams in pain as he's speared and killed by a ragged shard.

CREIGHTON:
Get down!

CUT TO:

Part One
PILGRIM

SCENE 2. INT. THE SECOND SPIRE—ANTEROOM—DAY

ANNOUNCER:
Time until the battle begins: seventy-two hours.

ATMOS: We're in an anteroom in the Second Spire attached to where the Jedi are staying. We can hear the gentle murmur of the city from outside. In the distance is the soft ringing of bells.

CREIGHTON:
I never thought I'd see the day when military transports hung in the skies over Jedha. It seems . . .

(SIGHS)

Well, it feels wrong.

All the work we've done. All the efforts Princess Xiri and Prince Phan-tu have made toward peace . . . and their worlds still send military ships to the signing of a treaty.

FX: There's no reply. The moment stretches, and then:

CREIGHTON:
Aida?

FX: Jedi Knight Aida Forte walks over to join him by the window. She pauses for a moment while she takes in the sight.

AIDA:

War casts a long shadow, Master Sun. Perhaps, after all this time, the people of Eiram and E'ronoh are finding it hard to trust one another.

CREIGHTON:

I suppose it's to be expected. The old royals were mired in hatred for so many years before the war, their trust for one another is tenuous at best.

AIDA:

Particularly as Queen Adrialla was found to be manufacturing poisoned weapons even after the cease-fire had been called.

CREIGHTON:

And despite the fact such weapons have been destroyed and the war is officially at an end, they still insist on sending military escorts to Jedha. Their minds and hearts remain gripped by fear and loss.

Thank the Light for the new generation and the hope they bring.

AIDA:

The heirs are the future, Creighton. Xiri and Phan-tu will unite their people, given time. The horrors of the past will be forgiven, if not forgotten. And people will look back at their union as the turning point. The moment that peace finally won out over war.

CREIGHTON:
(THOUGHTFUL)

You're right. We're so close.

No more needless death. No more hatred. The new generation will lead the old toward a better future. I truly believe that.

FX: Somewhere outside, we hear a commotion—the distant sound of raised voices, too far away to make out what's being said, but it sounds like a fractious argument between several people or groups.

CREIGHTON:
But seeing those ships up there . . . I worry what message it sends.

AIDA:
To whom?

CREIGHTON:
The locals. The pilgrims. This new "Convocation of the Force."

What if they think we've brought the conflict to their door?

AIDA:
The conflict's over. Everyone knows that. The cease-fire has held for over a month. This is a celebration of *peace.*

The transport ships are nothing but posturing. A last show of pomp before the treaty is finalized and all those military commanders are out of a job.

CREIGHTON:
Yes, you're right.

AIDA:
Soon the chancellors will arrive, and the treaty can be written into law.

CREIGHTON:
Ah, about that. I received a transmission from Chancellor Mollo just before we arrived. It seems that, despite both his and Chancellor Greylark's insistence, Republic security have put their foot down. Chancellor Mollo is to remain with Xiri and Phan-tu, to help them oversee the rebuilding of their worlds, while Chancellor Greylark returns to Coruscant.

AIDA:
So who will serve as mediator to oversee the signing of the treaty?

CREIGHTON:
Morton San Tekka.

AIDA:
(SURPRISED)

A *San Tekka*?

CREIGHTON:
You know Chancellor Mollo. He's a politician through and through. A chancellor of the people. He thought it best to appoint someone with connections to the frontier, rather than another elected official. Since Eiram and E'ronoh aren't part of the Republic he wants to tread carefully, so it doesn't appear that the Republic are overstepping in their role as neutral advisors. I gather that Chairperson Meldan, the head of the committee that oversees Republic affairs on Jedha, is a little put out at being overlooked, but Chancellor Mollo's decision *does* make sense. This way, the Republic won't be seen to be unduly interfering in the business of non-member worlds.

AIDA:
I see.

CREIGHTON:
Besides, it's an honorary role at best. There's no mediation needed. The ambassadors have been ordered to sign by the heirs.

We'll meet Morton San Tekka at the reception this evening.

AIDA:
I'm sure it's the right call. But I still think it's a shame that Phan-tu and Xiri couldn't attend the signing themselves.

CREIGHTON:
The heirs have plenty to do overseeing the reconstruction efforts. Starting with building a new array of communication buoys. So many were destroyed in the war that long-range communications with both Eiram and E'ronoh are near impossible at present—and that's even before the local comms on Jedha started acting up.

(Beat)

Besides, the two of them deserve some time together as newly-weds, after all they've been through.

AIDA:
(LAUGHS WARMLY)

I didn't have you down as a romantic, Creighton.

CREIGHTON:
(TEASING)

We all have hidden depths, Aida. Even a tired old master like me.

AIDA:
Old!

CREIGHTON:
Well, tired, then.

AIDA:
The road has been long and the journey hard. Have you taken time to reflect? To enjoy the city while we're here?

CREIGHTON:
You know I haven't. The preparations—

AIDA:
(INTERRUPTING HIM)

—have been all-consuming. Yes, yes. But we're on *Jedha*. At the very least, you should consider visiting the Kyber Mirrors, to pause and take a few moments to—

FX: The door whooshes open and a protocol droid enters, cutting Aida off. This is B-9H0.

B-9H0:
A thousand apologies, masters, but I thought you would wish to know immediately—Jedi Knight Gella Nattai is ready for you.

CREIGHTON:
(RELIEVED)

About time. Have we established what's affecting the city's communication network so badly?

B-9H0:
It is posited to be a result of the desert storms, Master Sun. Vast clouds of sand particles have entered the upper atmosphere and are interfering with local transmissions. Establishing long-range communications remains possible, but is nevertheless proving challeng—

CREIGHTON:
(INTERRUPTING)

Yes, Bee-Nine. I understand.

B-9H0:
Excellent, sir. Then, if you would care to follow me . . . ?

FX: Creighton and Aida begin to follow the droid out of the room.

AIDA:
(QUIETLY, TO CREIGHTON)

All I'm saying is—think about it. It'll do you good.

CREIGHTON:
(QUIETLY, TO AIDA)

I will. I promise. Just . . . *after* the briefing, okay?

CUT TO:

SCENE 3. INT. THE SECOND SPIRE—BRIEFING ROOM—MOMENTS LATER

ATMOS: The soft hum of computers, punctuated by the occasional beep.

GT-68:
(ANXIOUS)

Bee-da-doo-waah.

B-9H0:
Yes, thank you, Geetee-Sixtyate. Master Sun knows that the signal is intermittent.

CREIGHTON:
Where is—

FX: The holoprojector whumps back to life with a hum and crackle. The signal is poor, so let's add a bit of static under Gella's speech.

GELLA NATTAI:
(VIA HOLO)

Ah! There you are.

CREIGHTON:
Greetings, Gella. It's good to see you.

GELLA NATTAI:
(VIA HOLO)

And you, Master Creighton. Aida. Well, as much as this terrible signal allows.

CREIGHTON:
I was pleased to hear the Jedi Council approved your petition to become a Wayseeker. How do you feel now that it's real?

GELLA NATTAI:
(VIA HOLO)

I feel . . .

(Beat, then MORE ASSURED)

I feel *good.* For the first time, it's as though I truly understand my calling. I'm going where the Force leads me. And my journey is only just beginning.

CREIGHTON:
I'm pleased for you. Truly.

GELLA NATTAI:
(VIA HOLO)

Thank you, Master Sun.

But more to the point, how's Jedha?

CREIGHTON:
Cold. And sandy.

GELLA NATTAI:
(VIA HOLO)

(LAUGHS)

AIDA:
Tensions here are running high, Gella. The Convocation is preparing for their Festival of Balance, and it's proving a little . . . *controversial.*

GELLA NATTAI:
(VIA HOLO)

The Convocation?

CREIGHTON:
The new, non-partisan council here on Jedha, designed to bring all the disparate sects and religions together. They're co-opting the Season of Light to make a point.

AIDA:
(TUTS)

They're doing no such thing.

Well, technically they *are,* but lots of different groups observe celebrations and periods of reflection around this time of year, not just the Jedi. It makes sense. They're throwing a party.

GELLA NATTAI:
(VIA HOLO)

I think we're all entitled to a party when that peace treaty is finally signed.

AIDA:
Indeed. We're meeting with the ambassadors this evening. And Morton San Tekka, the mediator appointed by Chancellor Mollo to oversee the signing.

GELLA NATTAI:
(VIA HOLO)

Well, just remember—the last time we tried to oversee a peace deal between Eiram and E'ronoh . . .

CREIGHTON:
. . . things didn't go so well. I've briefed Aida on what happened.

AIDA:
The repeated assassination attempts. Yes.

GELLA NATTAI:
(VIA HOLO, A LITTLE PAINED)

And the betrayal of Axel Greylark and the Ferrols. The fallout from that almost set the entire peace process back to the start.

CREIGHTON:
The Ferrols I can almost understand. An old family of E'ronoh, too hurt and set in their ways to compromise and seek peace. But Axel Greylark? The chancellor's own son. It's still hard to believe, even now.

(Beat)

How are you, Gella? I know the two of you had formed a bond.

GELLA NATTAI:
(VIA HOLO)

It's . . . complicated. I thought he was an ally, a *friend.*

(Beat)

His betrayal felt personal.

And I'm still at a loss as to why he did what he did.

CREIGHTON:
We're still no closer to understanding his motives, then?

GELLA NATTAI:
(VIA HOLO)

No. We're no closer to understanding *any* of it. I visited Axel before the prison transport took him away, but he was still refusing to talk.

I don't know . . . despite the fact he and the Ferrols were responsible for the sabotage and assassination attempts, something still doesn't feel right. It's like we're missing something important. We know there was another person involved, but so far, we've been unable to figure out who. I don't think we'll understand Axel's true motivations until we do.

CREIGHTON:
And you have no inkling?

GELLA NATTAI:
(VIA HOLO)

Only that you should remain alert and mindful. It's a sad truth that there are people who would be *happy* to see the war continue between Eiram and E'ronoh. Entire factions who are actively seeking to reignite the war, despite the wishes of the heirs. People who hate what Xiri and Phan-tu are doing and wish to undermine it. I suspect that's the real reason why they're not with you there on Jedha. Yes, there's rebuilding to be done, but more importantly, they need to work to quell the dissent of those factions who seek to undo their good work.

CREIGHTON:
There are ever profits to be made from conflict, and plenty of unscrupulous politicians happy to line their own pockets. I suspect those dissenting voices will find support amongst the ruling classes of both worlds. The Ferrols will not be alone in that.

AIDA:
Yes, but this is *Jedha.* And with the newlywed heirs so committed to peace, surely that's all behind us. Once the treaty is signed into law, such protests become moot.

GELLA NATTAI:
(VIA HOLO)

All the same . . . Just be wary.

And know that I'm just a call away if you need me.

AIDA:

We'll let you know how the signing goes, just as soon as we can.

GELLA NATTAI:

(VIA HOLO)

All right. Thanks, Aida. And good luck to you both.

May the Force be with you.

FX: The holo shuts off.

CUT TO:

SCENE 4. INT. TRANSPORT SHUTTLE—JEDHA ATMOSPHERE

ATMOS: The background churn of the air recyclers on the ship. The turbulence of the ship cutting through Jedha's atmosphere. The muttering of other passengers.

FX: A loud digital chime indicating an announcement:

PILOT DROID:
(VIA SPEAKER)

We are now entering Jedha atmosphere. Please prepare for turbulence.

I repeat: We are now entering Jedha atmosphere. Please prepare for turbulence.

FX: The turbulence increases. One of the passengers, a man called TILSON GRAF, stumbles into a woman, SILANDRA SHO.

SILANDRA:
(GRUNTS, BUT NOT UNKINDLY)

TILSON GRAF:
Oh, I'm sorry. I didn't—

I mean, I wasn't expecting—

(SIGHS)

My apologies.

SILANDRA:
Here. There's a spare handhold. I've been told this approach can be quite the ride. Especially with the recent sandstorms. You might want to follow the droid's advice and hang on.

TILSON GRAF:
Thank you.

FX: They stand in companionable silence for a moment as the ship drops deeper into the atmosphere, which we can hear rumbling outside. The rumbling begins to increase.

TILSON GRAF:
So, first time?

On Jedha, I mean.

SILANDRA:
(AMUSED)

What gives you that idea?

TILSON GRAF:
(LAUGHS)

Only that you said you'd "been told" about the approach from orbit.

SILANDRA:
Ah, yes. I did, didn't I?

Well then—no, it's not my first time here.

But it *is* my first time for many years.

TILSON GRAF:
And you're a *Jedi.* Presumably making a pilgrimage to honor the Season of Light.

SILANDRA:
Presumably.

(LAUGHS)

I suppose it was the robes that gave it away.

TILSON GRAF:
Well, that and the lightsaber fixed to your belt . . . Although I've never seen a Jedi carry a *shield* on their back before . . .

SILANDRA:
(AIRILY)

No. I don't suppose you have.

I'm Silandra. Silandra Sho.

TILSON GRAF:
Tilson Graf.

SILANDRA:
(SURPRISED)

Graf? As in the ubiquitous hyperspace prospecting dynasty?

TILSON GRAF:
Ah. I see the family reputation precedes me.

Pity.

Yes. I'm one of *those* Grafs.

FX: In the background, the noise of the turbulence is getting louder. We can hear the patter of blown sand against the hull of the ship.

SILANDRA:
Then forgive me for asking, but why are you here, on a third-class public transport shuttle to Jedha? Surely one of the richest prospecting families in the galaxy has plenty of their own ships. Fleets of them, in fact.

TILSON GRAF:
Oh, they do. They do.

But I, alas, am something of a poor relation, cast out from the bosom of the clan for a somewhat regrettable series of youthful misdemeanors.

SILANDRA:
I'm sorry.

TILSON GRAF:
I'm not. Not really. It meant I was able to escape all those dreary family meetings and responsibilities. And anyway, I've turned over something of a new leaf, these days.

SILANDRA:
So, you're making a pilgrimage, too?

TILSON GRAF:
(AMUSED)

Of a sort. I'm here to witness the signing of the peace treaty between Eiram and E'ronoh. You could say I'm something of a "collector" of historic events. And I have a sense this is going to be really quite a momentous occasion.

SILANDRA:
I hope you're right.

TILSON GRAF:
(REASSURING TONE)

Oh, I'm certain of it.

FX: In the background, we hear the pitch of the ship's engines change to a high whine. One of the engines starts to pulse and choke. We can now hear a full sandstorm striking the hull of the ship. The hubbub of other passengers increases as they grow nervous.

FX: Another digital chime.

PILOT DROID:
(VIA SPEAKER)

Please remain calm. We are currently experiencing extreme turbulence as we pass through a temporary atmospheric disturbance.

TILSON GRAF:
(UNCERTAIN)

This doesn't sound good . . .

SILANDRA:
I'm sure it's noth—

FX: One of the shuttle's engines stutters, clogs, and explodes, cutting Silandra off. The ship lists dramatically. People begin to scream.

SCARED PASSENGERS:
(SCREAMS)

TILSON GRAF:
(WORRIED)

The starboard engine! It's blown!

FX: The shuttle wavers as it's buffeted by the storm. The single remaining engine grinds on.

SILANDRA:
(SHOUTING)

Everyone—stay calm.

FX: The remaining engine begins to whump and grind as it, too, clogs with sand.

SCARED PASSENGERS:
(SCREAMS)

TILSON GRAF:
(INCREASINGLY WORRIED)

And now the portside engine is failing . . .

FX: Another digital chime.

PILOT DROID:
(VIA SPEAKERS)

Please remain calm and adopt bracing positions.

I repeat: Please remain calm and adopt bracing positions.

FX: The second engine blows. The shuttle goes into a dive.

SCARED PASSENGERS:
(MORE SCREAMING)

TILSON GRAF:
(PANICKED)

We're going to crash!

SILANDRA:
(CALM, DETERMINED)

No. We're not.

(Beat, then STRAINED)

Just . . . give . . . me . . . a . . . minute . . .

FX: Slowly, the shuttle begins to level out. The storm continues to rage, but the shuttle holds steady as it cruises through the churning sand.

TILSON GRAF:
(RELIEVED, IMPRESSED)

What—are *you* doing that?

You're doing that Jedi thing, aren't you? You're keeping the shuttle from falling!

SILANDRA:
(THROUGH GRITTED TEETH)

Concentrating here . . .

FX: The shuttle dips lower, out of the storm. The whipping sand stops striking the hull. The other passengers are beginning to calm. Everything is quiet, subdued.

FX: A digital chime.

PILOT DROID:
(VIA SPEAKER)

Deploying landing gear.

FX: The landing gear whines as it unfolds. After a moment, the shuttle touches down.

SILANDRA:
(EXHALES IN RELIEF)

There.

FX: A round of relieved applause and cheering goes up inside the shuttle.

RELIEVED PASSENGERS:
(CHEERS)

FX: A digital chime.

PILOT DROID:
(VIA SPEAKER)

Welcome to Jedha.

FX: The shuttle door sighs open, and people begin rushing out.

TILSON GRAF:
Now, that was *seriously* impressive.

SILANDRA:
(BREATHLESS)

It should never have been necessary.

TILSON GRAF:

It's as you said: There's been a lot of sandstorms rising in the desert recently. We're just lucky you were here.

(Beat, then CONCERNED)

Do you need anything?

SILANDRA:

No. Thank you. I'm fine. I'm meeting a friend.

TILSON GRAF:

Well, it's been an honor to meet you, Silandra Sho.

And thank you.

SILANDRA:

May the Force be with you, Mr. Graf.

FX: They both leave the shuttle, into the bustling crowds of the shuttle docks.

CUT TO:

SCENE 5. EXT. JEDHA—SHUTTLE DOCKS

ATMOS: The bustle of crowded docks. The distant ringing of bells. The sound of another shuttle struggling in through the storm to land.

SILANDRA:
Mesook!

Is that really you?

FX: Silandra hurries over to meet Mesook, her old friend and Guardian of the Whills.

MESOOK:
(DELIGHTED)

Silandra Sho!

FX: They embrace.

SILANDRA:
It's good to see you. And this is?

MESOOK:
My fellow Guardian, Selik.

SELIK:
(WARMLY)

Well met, Master Sho.

SILANDRA:
And you, Selik.

MESOOK:
And what about this Padawan I've heard about? Where's Rooper?

SILANDRA:
Back on Batuu. After our recent experiences on the frontier, I thought some quiet meditation at the temple would do her good.

MESOOK:
It would do us *all* some good. Especially after *that* landing.

(SERIOUS NOW)

For a moment there, I wasn't sure you were going to make it.

SILANDRA:
We nearly didn't. The storm took out the engines on the final approach.

SELIK:
It's about time they upgraded those hunks of junk they use for the pilgrimage routes. It's not like they don't charge enough to fly people in on better ships.

SILANDRA:
Hmmm.

Well, no one was hurt. And I'm here now.

How long has it been, Mesook?

MESOOK:
(AMUSED)

A long time. So long I've lost count.

SILANDRA:
Too long. You look well! And the lightbow suits you.

MESOOK:
(PLEASED)

It does, doesn't it.

Not that I ever have cause to use it. The temple is a peaceful place, and the Guardians of the Whills have little jurisdiction out in the wilds of the Holy City.

SILANDRA:
(WITH DISBELIEF)

The wilds, of Jedha?

MESOOK:
(LAUGHING)

You'd be surprised.

SELIK:
We've even had to get special dispensation to oversee the security at the peace conference. The captain isn't happy about it at all.

SILANDRA:
And you?

MESOOK:
A change is as good as a rest. Or so we're told.

And as I understand it, they've had some ... *difficulties* with security before now. We're just happy to play our part, however small, in bringing peace to the galaxy. Isn't that right, Selik?

SELIK:
(LAUGHING)

So you keep telling me.

MESOOK:
(CHUCKLING)

I'm meeting with Master Creighton Sun later to run over the arrangements again.

SILANDRA:
Creighton? He's here?

MESOOK:
Yes. He and Jedi Knight Aida Forte are part of the delegation assigned to oversee the signing of the treaty.

SILANDRA:
And here I was thinking it would be a peaceful trip, full of quiet contemplation.

MESOOK:
(LAUGHING)

There'll be plenty of time for that. First, I'm going to take you on a stroll.

SELIK:
I'll cover for you. See you back at the temple later.

MESOOK:
You're a good one, Selik.

SELIK:
You'd better believe it.

May the Force be with you, Master Sho.

SILANDRA:
And you, Selik.

FX: Selik leaves. Mesook claps his hands together.

MESOOK:
Right! Come along. I want to show you the ancient statue that stands guard over the city.

SILANDRA:

The Protector! I can't wait.

FX: They start walking away, toward the crowds, under:

MESOOK:

The statue is one of the oldest images of a Jedi anywhere in the galaxy. If not *the* oldest. It is a sight to behold. It's a symbol to the people of Jedha. An ever-vigilant guardian. A reminder that they're always protected.

SILANDRA:

And are they? Always protected?

FX: Their voices fade out as they walk away.

MESOOK:

(LAUGHING)

Of course! They have me. And Selik.

SILANDRA:

(LAUGHING)

Well, that's all right then. Nothing could ever go wrong where *you're* involved . . .

CUT TO:

SCENE 6. EXT. JEDHA STREET—OUTSIDE ENLIGHTENMENT TAPBAR

ATMOS: The bustle of crowded streets. The distant ringing of bells. The occasional bellow of a salesperson touting their wares.

FX: A set of footsteps trudging toward us. A droid buzzes alongside the walking person, hovering. They stop.

KETH:
You'd better wait here, Pee-Three. You know how some of the Enlightenment regulars get when they think you're being preachy.

P3-7A:
(BEEPS IN ANNOYANCE)

(Brief beat, AND THEN)

KETH:
(SIGHS)

Don't be like that. You *know* what I mean.

P3-7A:
Those whose beliefs are thin will ever attempt to justify their actions. Only the truly pious know the sanctity of silence.

KETH:

See! That's exactly what I'm talking about.

Look, I'm only going to be a few minutes. Just ... a quick drink to settle my nerves, okay?

P3-7A:

Only the Force can judge our worth. We are all but wretches before its glory.

FX: Keth starts to walk off, calling back to the droid as he goes.

KETH:
(CALLING BACK)

Just because I work for the Church of the Force doesn't mean *I* have to be a paragon of virtue, you know.

(MOCKING)

"Keth Cerapath the Holy"!

P3-7A:

We must see ourselves in the light of the Force to know who we truly are.

KETH:
(CALLING BACK, TRAILING OFF)

I'm starting to wish I'd never paid those Bonbraks to fix you up. You know I can hand you back at any point, don't you ... ?

CUT TO:

SCENE 7. INT. JEDHA—ENLIGHTENMENT TAPBAR—CONTINUOUS

ATMOS: The dull chatter of a tapbar that's only half full at this time of day. The strains of an electric harp, playing a tune.

FX: The door opens. Keth walks in. The door swings shut behind him.

KRADON:
Keth! How are you, my boy?

FX: Keth approaches the bar. The chink of glasses being lined up on the beaten metal surface.

KETH:
Hi, Kradon. I'll take a shot of Retsa, please.

KRADON:
Mmmm. Like that, is it? Kradon worries about you, Keth.

FX: The chink of bottles, followed by the glug of liquid being sloshed into a glass. Keth picks it up and downs it.

KETH:
(THE RETSA BURNS LIKE WHISKEY)

Busy day, that's all.

KRADON:
So it seems. Another?

FX: Keth places the empty glass back on the bar.

KETH:
Why not?

FX: Kradon fills the glass again.

MOONA:
What's troubling you, kid?

KETH:
Oh, hi, Moona.

It's nothing. Not really. Like I said, I'm just busy.

FX: In the background, the door swings open again as someone else enters.

MOONA:
Well, just you remember—this is *Enlightenment.* The only tap-bar on Jedha where it's a prerequisite that you leave your troubles at the door.

PIRALLI:
And your droids, apparently.

You know, if that tin can of yours wasn't so damn pious, I'd swear it was being sarcastic.

FX: Keth almost chokes on his drink.

KETH:
(SPLUTTERS)

I'm sorry, Piralli. I swear, he'll be the death of me one day.

PIRALLI:
You're not wrong.

Kradon—I'll take a Blue Mappa.

KRADON:
Kradon shall oblige.

FX: Piralli pulls out a stool at the bar.

PIRALLI:
What are we talking about?

MOONA:
Keth's having a bad day.

PIRALLI:
(GRUNTS)

Aren't we all? Orbital traffic is a bleedin' nightmare, what with all those military freighters just hanging there like a damn blockade. Over *Jedha*.

Sooner this peace treaty business is over with, the better.

MOONA:
Yeah. And this so-called Festival of Balance everyone seems to be preparing for, too. Only thing it's doing is *un*balancing my regular business. And it hasn't even started yet.

The streets are nothing but a constant stream of parades and religious demonstrations, trapped in an endless, yawning cycle . . .

FX: Keth puts his glass back on the counter.

KETH:
Well, thanks, both. You've really cheered me up.

FX: Everyone is silent for a moment. Even the harp stops playing. And then they all burst out laughing.

ALL:
(LAUGHTER)

FX: Piralli slaps Keth on the back. The harp starts up again.

PIRALLI:
(STILL CHUCKLING)

Nice one, Keth.

MOONA:
So, what *has* got you all worked up?

KETH:
Oh, it's nothing. It's just . . . I've been put on babysitting duty for the duration of the peace conference.

KRADON:
Babysitting? As in, looking after the church's younglings?

KETH:
Worse.

I'm chief liaison between the church and the Republic-appointed mediator, Morton San Tekka.

PIRALLI:
(CONFUSED)

But . . . isn't that a *good* thing?

KETH:
No!

Well, yes. I suppose. It's just . . . it's a lot of responsibility. The San Tekkas are—

KRADON:
—good tippers. You must bring him along to Enlightenment for an evening of entertainment and frivolity!

KETH:
I'm not sure frivolity is going to be foremost in his mind, Kradon.

But it's not an *entirely* bad idea . . .

MOONA:
Anyway, I thought the Jedi were the ones doing the babysitting? They love all that pomp and ceremony, don't they? I've never known a Jedi to knowingly avoid the limelight.

KETH:
The Jedi are overseeing the signing of the treaty and escorting the ambassadors from Eiram and E'ronoh, but the San Tekkas were chosen to provide an impartial mediator. Someone who has no vested interest in the outcome of the conflict.

MOONA:
And what's it got to do with you?

KETH:
The San Tekkas have close ties to the Church of the Force.

PIRALLI:
And so, you—

KETH:
—find myself at his every beck and call. As of this evening.

MOONA:
Well, the answer's clear, isn't it?

KETH:
It is?

MOONA:
Yeah.

Just leave him alone with that droid of yours for a few minutes and he'll want nothing more to do with you.

FX: Moona, Piralli, and Kradon all laugh heartily.

KETH:
(GROANS)

Don't. Pee-Three is a liability.

MOONA:
You realize how *creepy* that thing is, too, don't you?

KETH:
(SURPRISED)

Creepy?

MOONA:
Yeah, with all that weird gilding on its big floating core—

KETH:
He started off as a ceremonial droid from the church, remember.

MOONA:
And all those twitching legs, like mandibles—

KETH:
Taken from a probe droid so he can help around the place.

MOONA:
Not to mention that ghoulish "head in a box" you've had mounted on top. It looks like a skull with bug eyes, and that horrible grille for a mouth . . .

KETH:
(EXASPERATED)

All right! All right! I get the point. He looks a bit unusual. But that was all the Bonbraks had. Or at least, all I could afford.

(SIGHS)

That head was part of a processional droid once. A highly prized protocol model. You realize how hard it is to get parts around here that *haven't* come from the church or one of the temples?

MOONA:
Hmmm.

PIRALLI:

Face it, Keth. You'd be better off junking the thing like any other sane person would. I mean, it was destined for scrap before you saved it, anyway.

KETH:

Piralli, Pee-Three is my *friend.* And no matter how difficult someone can be, a friend is still a friend, aren't they?

FX: Piralli glugs down the rest of his drink.

KETH:
(EXASPERATED)

Right?

PIRALLI:

All I'm saying is you're a better man than me.

MOONA:

And Piralli isn't even a man.

FX: More laughter, including Keth this time.

KETH:

The thing is—I thought this peace conference might be my chance.

MOONA:

Your chance at what?

KETH:

At finally doing something *meaningful.*

I mean—nothing ever happens around here, does it? At least, not to me. All I want is a bit of *excitement.* Something *new* and *different,* aside from sweeping floors and lighting candles. A story of my own. The sort of tale I could tell in a place like this, regaling friends over a few drinks.

But instead . . .

Well, it's babysitting and running errands while all the exciting stuff happens to other people.

MOONA:
(CLICKS HER TONGUE)

You worry too much, kid. Who needs excitement? Or stories?

PIRALLI:
(SARCASTIC)

Yeah! You've got us! And a weird droid! Who needs anything else?

MOONA:
(LAUGHS)

KETH:
Yeah. I guess you're right.

FX: Keth's stool scrapes back as he gets down from his place at the bar.

KETH:
Well, I suppose I'd better be off.

KRADON:
(SERIOUS NOW)

Kradon believes everything will be fine, boy.

KETH:
Thanks, Kradon.

KRADON:
And that'll be eighteen zukkels for the drinks.

KETH:
(LAUGHING)

I'll get away with it one of these days.

FX: Keth tosses some zukkels on the bar.

KRADON:

And then, sadly, you would have the Twinkle sisters to answer to.

Now go. Go!

KETH:

I'm going! I'm going!

KRADON:

(CALLING AFTER HIM, AMUSED)

And do not forget to bring the San Tekka around here with all his fine zukkels, either . . .

CUT TO:

SCENE 8. EXT. JEDHA MARKETS—STREET

ATMOS: A busy marketplace. Traders touting for business. Animals being led through the streets, making a variety of barks, hoots, and chirps. People chattering in a general hubbub. The distant strains of someone playing music. Hovering vehicles gliding by.

TIRED TRADER:
(IN BACKGROUND)

Whole roast tip-yip.

Get your whole roast tip-yip.

PUSHY TRADER:
(IN BACKGROUND)

Spiced ranga! Best spiced ranga on Jedha!

MESOOK:
And here we are. Back in the markets of Jedha after all these years.

SILANDRA:
It's . . . not what I remember.

MESOOK:
(UNCERTAIN)

You're disappointed.

SILANDRA:
No. Quite the opposite. It's *perfect*.

But it's changed. It's like seeing it with new eyes.

MESOOK:
Nothing is still forever. Even the desert sands shift to make the landscape anew.

SILANDRA:
Yes, and I suppose that's true of us all. Although some things *don't* change.

(Beat, then TEASING)

For example—you're still sporting a *most* impressive beard.

MESOOK:
(LAUGHING)

And you're still carrying that old shield around on your back like a talisman.

SILANDRA:
(LAUGHING)

Perhaps that's exactly what it is.

But it has saved my life a few times.

MESOOK:
And plenty of other lives, too, if the stories are anything to go by.

SILANDRA:
Stories! Now I know you're having me on.

MESOOK:
(LAUGHING)

As if I would. Remember—us Guardians of the Whills are all-knowing.

SILANDRA:
(LAUGHING)

It's good to see you, Mesook.

MESOOK:
(WITH MOCK GRAVITY)

See—I knew you were going to say that.

FX: Low in the background, but growing louder, we begin to hear a procession moving through the markets, chanting:

PATH DISCIPLES:
(IN BACKGROUND)

The Force will be free! The Force will be free!

ELDER DELWIN:
(IN BACKGROUND)

The Force *will* be free! Free from all manipulation! Free from the shackles of those who bend it to their will!

The Force must be allowed to find its *balance*. Only then can we truly know peace. Only then will we *all* be free!

SILANDRA:
This is new.

Protestors?

MESOOK:
Be on your guard, Silandra.

SILANDRA:
(CONFUSED)

On my guard?

FX: The procession is getting nearer, their chanting louder.

PATH DISCIPLES:
The Force will be free! The Force will be free!

MESOOK:
There are people here on Jedha who feel ambivalent toward the Jedi. Ambivalent at *best.*

SILANDRA:
There are *always* people who feel ambivalent about the Jedi. It keeps us humble.

FX: A female child comes running over to Silandra and Mesook.

NADDIE:
Here. A gift freely given.

SILANDRA:
A gift? For me? Oh, that's a pretty flower.

Thank you. It smells lovely.

NADDIE:
(GIGGLES)

SILANDRA:
What's your name, little one?

NADDIE:
I'm Naddie—

FX: An adult disciple of the Path comes running over. This is Marda.

MARDA:
Naddie, *no*!

To me, now!

NADDIE:
(CONFUSED)

But Marda, I was just giving out the flowers as you asked.

MARDA:
Yes, Naddie. I know. But you must remember what I told you. There are *dangerous* people here on Jedha.

FX: Naddie whimpers. She's upset and doesn't really know what she's done wrong.

SILANDRA:
It's all right. The child meant no harm.

MARDA:
(TIGHT)

It is *not* all right.

Naddie, this woman is a *Jedi.*

NADDIE:
(CRIES)

I'm sorry, Marda!

SILANDRA:
I think there's been some sort of misunderstanding. Naddie—I thank you for your gift.

NADDIE:
(WAILS)

MARDA:
That's *enough.*

(KINDLY, TO NADDIE)

Come along, Naddie. Back to Elder Delwin and the others. Everything will be fine. All is as the Force wills it.

FX: Marda and Naddie start to leave.

SILANDRA:
Hold on a moment. If I could just speak with the child—

MARDA:
You've said enough. I will not have her corrupted by one who bends the Force to their own will.

SILANDRA:
But . . .

MESOOK:
Silandra—I think you should let them go.

SILANDRA:
(SIGHS)

FX: Marda and Naddie's footsteps are lost in the crowd. The chanting begins again, in the background.

PATH DISCIPLES:
The Force will be free! The Force will be free!

FX: The procession moves off, deeper into the market. The sound of their chanting fades, under:

SILANDRA:
Ambivalent, you say?

MESOOK:
Well, I was trying to be diplomatic.

SILANDRA:
Do you know who they were?

MESOOK:
A religious sect and protest group known as the Path of the Open Hand. They arrived soon after the Convocation was formed, and they pass through the markets most days, giving out those flowers and chanting their creed. They seem harmless enough—despite their evident dislike of Jedi.

You'll see them about—you can tell who they are by the pale robes and the three blue lines they paint on their faces.

SILANDRA:
"The Force will be free." Interesting.

MESOOK:
We are on Jedha. There are nearly as many different ideologies as there are pilgrims.

SILANDRA:

I suppose that's why this new Convocation is a good thing. If it can help to bring people together . . .

MESOOK:

Time will tell.

(Beat, then BRIGHTER)

Anyway, I think it's time we found something to eat.

SILANDRA:

Good idea. And then you can tell me what you've been up to since I last saw you.

MESOOK:

(AMUSED)

I fear it'll be a short conversation . . .

FX: Their footsteps move away into the crowd.

MESOOK:

(FADING OUT AS THEY WALK OFF)

. . . nothing exciting ever happens on Jedha . . .

CUT TO:

SCENE 9. INT. JEDHA—THE PATH'S ALMSHOUSE

ATMOS: It's quiet here. Just the low murmur of a few people speaking in hushed tones in the background.

FX: Marda is shepherding a still-whimpering Naddie into a building.

NADDIE:
(SNIFFLING)

MARDA:
Come along now, Naddie. Let's get you inside. The rest of the Littles will be along shortly, too.

NADDIE:
(COMING OUT IN A RUSH)

I'm sorry, Marda. She had a nice smile. I didn't realize . . .

FX: Marda bundles Naddie up into a hug.

MARDA:
There, there. That's right. You can squeeze me as hard as you like.

(WITH A GRUNT)

Ooph! Well, maybe not *quite* so hard! My, you're getting big and strong.

FX: Naddie's sniffling stops.

MARDA:
There, is that better?

NADDIE:
Yes. Thank you, Marda.

MARDA:
You didn't do anything wrong, Naddie.

NADDIE:
(CRYING AGAIN)

But I gave her a flower! And I talked to her. And she was a *Jedi*!

And . . . And . . .

MARDA:
What is it, Naddie?

NADDIE:
It's just . . . Kevmo was a Jedi, wasn't he? And he was your friend. He wasn't a bad person, was he?

MARDA:
It's all right, Naddie.

You're right. Kevmo wasn't a bad person. But he *was* misguided.

You see, it's what the Jedi *do* that's bad. You understand that the Force will always find balance. *Always.*

NADDIE:
Yes.

MARDA:
When people like the Jedi twist the Force and use it in ways that it was never meant to be used, they disrupt that balance.

They might use its power to save a life, and for a while, everyone will think they've done a good thing. A *kind* thing. But if they save a life here . . .

NADDIE:
(PARROTING DOCTRINE)

. . . someone else must die to restore the balance.

MARDA:
Precisely. That's how it works, you see. *Balance.*

NADDIE:
(SCANDALIZED)

And that's why Kevmo died? Because he used the power of the Force?

MARDA:
Yes, Naddie. That's why Kevmo died. You see, the Force had to find a way to balance itself again.

NADDIE:
Then what about the Jedi woman in the market?

MARDA:
You did the right thing, giving her your flower. Everyone should have the chance to understand the true nature of the Force. To see the error of their ways.

You gave her that chance, do you see? By offering to welcome her into the Path of the Open Hand. Showing her the way to forgiveness and peace.

NADDIE:
But what if she didn't understand?

FX: Two sets of footsteps enter the room.

THE MOTHER:
Then the Force will find a way to balance her crimes, too. To *level* itself.

HERALD:
The Force will be free.

MARDA:
Mother. Herald.

Naddie was just telling me about a Jedi she met in the market-place today.

THE MOTHER:
We heard.

And you, child, must listen to Marda, for she is our Guide, and she is wise.

NADDIE:
Yes, Mother.

FX: More children can be heard arriving, back from their time at the markets. They chatter excitedly.

MARDA:
Now, the other Littles are back from the market, too. Why don't you go ahead and join them?

NADDIE:
The Force will be free!

MARDA:
The Force will be free.

FX: We hear Naddie heading off, Naddie's voice, now much chirpier, fading as she hurries off.

NADDIE:
(FADING)

Mylas! Tromak! Did you give out all your flowers, too?

HERALD:
The resilience of youth. It is something to behold.

MARDA:

Naddie and the other Littles are the future of the Path. They must be protected.

HERALD:

(A STATEMENT, NOT A QUESTION)

From the Jedi.

THE MOTHER:

And *all* those like them who would abuse the Force.

HERALD:

This place—this *sacred* place—is infested with them, and the problem grows worse with every passing day. The peace talks and the festival seem to draw them in like moths circling a flame.

THE MOTHER:

And that is why we are here. So that we might make our voices heard. So that we might help them to understand the disaster they court every day.

MARDA:

And the Leveler?

THE MOTHER:

The Leveler will have its time.

(Brief beat)

MARDA:

(TO HERALD)

When will you petition the Convocation?

HERALD:

Soon.

MARDA:

They will see sense and admit us into their circle. I know it. The Path of the Open Hand *will* have a say in the guiding of the Force.

THE MOTHER:
I do not doubt it, Marda.

Not for a single moment. And then we shall show this so-called Convocation the truth of who the Jedi really are . . .

CUT TO:

SCENE 10. INT. THE SECOND SPIRE—RECEPTION PARTY

ANNOUNCER:
Time until the battle begins: sixty-four hours.

ATMOS: Tinkling piano music. The hubbub of murmuring voices. The chinking of glasses. We're at a party. A posh one.

CREIGHTON:
(SIGHS)

Oh, joy. Another party.

AIDA:
(LAUGHS)

Cheer up, Creighton. You might enjoy it.

CREIGHTON:
Aida—in all my considerable years, I've yet to attend a single party I could say that I've *enjoyed.*

And besides, the last party I was at hardly went according to plan, did it?

AIDA:
(CHIDING)

My, we are in good form this evening. I hardly think you can blame yourself for what happened at Xiri and Phan-tu's wedding reception.

CREIGHTON:
(LAUGHS)

You know what I mean. Events like this have never been my strong suit.

AIDA:
You do yourself a disservice. Don't forget, I've seen your full charm offensive more times than either of us would care to admit. You're *made* for missions like this, and you know it.

CREIGHTON:
(CHARMING)

You say all the right things.

AIDA:
(AMUSED)

See! Exactly my point.

FX: They both laugh. A protocol droid walks over.

PROTOCOL DROID:
Honored guests! May I offer you some refreshment this evening?

CREIGHTON:
No, I—

AIDA:
(INTERRUPTING HIM)

Yes. Thank you. We'll take a glass each of the sparkling roseka.

PROTOCOL DROID:
An excellent choice, ma'am.

FX: The protocol droid shuffles away.

AIDA:
Here. Try this.

CREIGHTON:
Aida, we're not here to have a good time.

AIDA:
But we *are* here to fit in. To put the other guests at ease. Drink up.

FX: They clink glasses and drink.

CREIGHTON:
(SURPRISED)

That's actually . . . not bad.

AIDA:
I do believe that was a smile.

You know, perhaps this will be the first.

CREIGHTON:
First what?

AIDA:
The first party you actually enjoy.

CREIGHTON:
(SLYLY)

Don't you believe it. With the ambassadors from Eiram and E'ronoh both in the room, something's bound to spoil the fun.

AIDA:
I'm sure they're doing their best, given the circumstances. It can't be easy.

CREIGHTON:

No. Especially as, up until a month ago, neither Eiram nor E'ronoh *had* any ambassadors.

AIDA:

So they weren't part of the original settlement talks?

CREIGHTON:

No. Both planets have been on a war footing for so long, their political classes had been folded into their military structures.

Lifelong politicians becoming generals. Taking up arms against their neighboring world.

AIDA:

It hardly bears thinking about. Imagine if that happened to the Republic. If *the senators* were forced to become soldiers.

CREIGHTON:

It could *never* happen to the Republic. They stand for peace and unity, not division.

AIDA:

I bet that's what the politicians of Eiram and E'ronoh said, before they were forced to take up arms.

So, where did Ambassadors Cerox and Tintak come from, then? Are they ex-military, too?

CREIGHTON:

I don't believe so. Chancellor Mollo said they were chosen from the noble families of each world. Cerox from Eiram, Tintak from E'ronoh. Two representatives of equal standing, who would best represent the will of their people—and of the heirs.

AIDA:

And you believe that they do? Represent the will of the heirs.

CREIGHTON:

I believe that they understand their duty. Whether they entirely like it . . . that remains to be seen. As Gella said, there are those on both Eiram and E'ronoh who are finding it hard to forgive and forget. But it's early days, and I remain confident that peace will be enshrined here on Jedha. The ambassadors will do their duty, to their people, and to their rulers.

AIDA:
I'm glad to hear it.

Well, I suppose we should pay our respects.

CREIGHTON:
Yes, I suppose we should. Which one do you want? Left or right?

AIDA:
Left. Definitely left. I couldn't deprive Ambassador Cerox of her favorite, now, could I?

CREIGHTON:
(SIGHS)

See? I told you something would spoil my evening. I just didn't think that something would be *you*.

AIDA:
(LAUGHING)

Tell her I said hi.

FX: Aida walks away.

CREIGHTON:
(TO SELF)

Oh, well. Bottoms up.

FX: Creighton drains his glass. Two people approach.

MORTON SAN TEKKA:
Ah, Master Sun. Good evening. I was hoping to speak with you for a moment.

CREIGHTON:
Mediator San Tekka. Good evening. It's good to make your acquaintance.

MORTON SAN TEKKA:
Morton, please.

CREIGHTON:
Morton. And this is?

KETH:
Keth Cerapath.

MORTON SAN TEKKA:
An adjunct from the Church of the Force. He has kindly offered to assist me with proceedings here on Jedha.

CREIGHTON:
Well met.

KETH:
Umm. Likewise.

CREIGHTON:
I trust Chancellor Mollo has provided you with a full and frank briefing?

MORTON SAN TEKKA:
(LAUGHING)

Let's just say that he was more than thorough, and leave it at that, shall we?

CREIGHTON:
(LAUGHING)

I quite understand.

MORTON SAN TEKKA:
It's quite an honor for a San Tekka to be chosen to oversee such a key matter. I admit to feeling a little ... well, *apprehensive.* Silly, really. But I'm no politician.

CREIGHTON:
And that's precisely why Chancellor Mollo chose you, rather than an elected official such as Chairperson Meldan.

MORTON SAN TEKKA:
Ah, yes. The head of the Republic contingent on Jedha. I gather her nose was a little out of joint at the perceived snub.

CREIGHTON:
Even more of a reason for Chancellor Mollo to choose *you*. This isn't a game of personalities, but one of diplomacy. Jedha is part of the Republic. Chairperson Meldan has her hands full dealing with everything that comes with that. Eiram and E'ronoh are independent worlds, and as such, the Republic cannot be seen to interfere unduly with their affairs. That's why your independent perspective is so valuable. Rest assured, the chancellor made the right choice.

MORTON SAN TEKKA:
And the chancellor himself—he remains in the Eiram-E'ronoh sector?

CREIGHTON:
I believe so. Helping the newlywed heirs to oversee their reconstruction efforts on both worlds.

MORTON SAN TEKKA:
Their efforts are going well, I take it?

CREIGHTON:
I can only presume. The war caused untold damage to the communication relays in the surrounding system—long-range transmissions aren't getting through.

MORTON SAN TEKKA:
And now the sandstorms have taken down the local network on Jedha, too. Let's hope it's not a portent.

CREIGHTON:
I have every faith that things will go as planned.

MORTON SAN TEKKA:
You're not anticipating any . . . *difficulties* with tomorrow's proceedings, then, I take it?

CREIGHTON:
(CAUTIOUS)

Tensions are running high, as I'm sure Chanceller Mollo has explained.

But the agreements are in place, and I believe the two ambassadors both intend to play their parts. They've received strict instructions from the heirs of Eiram and E'ronoh. I know Phan-tu and Xiri regret their absence, but in truth the signing of the treaty should be a simple formality.

MORTON SAN TEKKA:
Hmmm. And the military transports that both planets have parked in orbit? Are *they* part of that formality?

CREIGHTON:
Yes. Hard to avoid, aren't they?

MORTON SAN TEKKA:
You might say that. The chancellor assured me that my role here would be purely ceremonial. Yet now I find myself feeling somewhat uncertain. Should we be concerned?

CREIGHTON:
Not at all. I'm assured that any military presence is simply a precaution, to dissuade any would-be saboteurs from trying their hand.

Sadly, recent experience has taught us there are those who would rather the war had never come to an end.

MORTON SAN TEKKA:
So I understand.

Let us hope, then, that matters here are resolved swiftly and smoothly, and that my services as mediator will not be required.

CREIGHTON:
Force willing, the treaty will be signed without incident.

MORTON SAN TEKKA:
(LOWERS VOICE)

But not without pomp and ceremony, if my reading of the ambassadors is anything to go by . . .

CREIGHTON:
(CHUCKLES)

I couldn't possibly comment.

MORTON SAN TEKKA:
(LAUGHING)

No. I don't suppose you could.

Nevertheless, it's reassuring that you're here, Master Sun. The galaxy owes you and the Jedi Order a grave debt for the work you've done here.

CREIGHTON:
Oh, I can hardly take any credit for—

MORTON SAN TEKKA:
(INTERRUPTING)

Now, now, Master Sun. A Jedi must be humble before the Force, as must we all—but credit must also be given where it is due. Without the work of you and your fellow Jedi, this needless war would still be raging, with no end in sight.

(SINCERE)

The San Tekkas—and those of the Church of the Force—thank you for all you have done and will yet do.

Isn't that right, Keth?

KETH:
(CAUGHT OUT DAYDREAMING)

What? Yes! Absolutely!

The Jedi Order has the full confidence of the church.

CREIGHTON:
(AMUSED)

Well, I'm pleased to hear *someone* on Jedha still approves.

MORTON SAN TEKKA:
Come now, it's not that bad, is it? The Jedi have a seat on the Convocation, do they not?

CREIGHTON:
Yes, yes. Of course. Forgive me. It's just, there are rumors—

MORTON SAN TEKKA:
—that are greatly exaggerated, I'm sure. The Jedi are as welcome in the Holy City as any other order, sect, or creed.

CREIGHTON:
And that is surely all we can ask for.

Now, if you'll forgive me, I really should check on our other honored guests . . .

MORTON SAN TEKKA:
Ah, yes. Of course.

Then I bid you a successful evening, and we can both look forward to this unsavory chapter of galactic history being closed by this time tomorrow.

CUT TO:

SCENE 11. INT. THE SECOND SPIRE—RECEPTION PARTY—CONTINUOUS

ATMOS: As before.

LESSER COUNCILOR LINTH:
(CLEARS THROAT)

FX: The hubbub in the immediate area quiets.

LESSER COUNCILOR LINTH:
I would like to propose a toast, if I may be so bold, to our very own Ambassador Tintak of E'ronoh, without whom none of us would be here, on the eve of this momentous occasion, ready to usher in a new era of peace and prosperity for our world.

AMBASSADOR TINTAK:
Oh, no. Please. You exaggerate, Councilor Linth, really you do. Any role that I played in establishing this newfound—and most welcome—peace, was minor, to say the least. My appointment to the role recently . . . (ahem) *vacated* by Viceroy Ferrol means that I find myself here on Jedha in unprecedented waters. If it were not for the assistance of my team—including yourself—I would indeed be at sea. This is a team effort, in every sense.

LESSER COUNCILOR LINTH:

A team effort in which you, sir, lead the way. Without your dedication, the good people of our fair world would still be facing endless months—no, *years*—of conflict. Please, raise your glasses!

Ambassador Tintak!

ALL:

Hear, hear!

FX: Glasses chink, and people down their drinks.

AMBASSADOR TINTAK:

Now, now, my friends. If we must raise our glasses to anything this fine evening, it should be in memory of the fallen—those on *both* sides of this terrible war, who have given their lives to protect their people and their homes.

To those lost on the way!

ALL:

(A LITTLE LESS ENTHUSIASTICALLY)

The fallen!

FX: More glasses chinking, and more drinks being drunk. The merriment fades a little into the background under:

AIDA:

Nicely put, Your Honor.

AMBASSADOR TINTAK:

Ah, Jedi Knight Forte. I didn't see you there.

You're not partaking in the toasts?

AIDA:

One glass was enough for me, Ambassador.

AMBASSADOR TINTAK:

Yes, probably wise. You never know what trouble's lurking . . .

AIDA:
(LAUGHS)

There's nothing to fear here, Your Honor. The security arrangements are all in place. We have Guardians of the Whills patrolling the building and—

AMBASSADOR TINTAK:
—two Jedi in our midst. I know, I know. And yet I also know what's at stake here. It wouldn't do to be lax. Not now. Not *yet*.

FX: Another cheer goes up from the gathered revelers.

AIDA:
Your people seem in good spirits.

AMBASSADOR TINTAK:
Yes. They do, don't they.

(LOWERS VOICE CONSPIRATORIALLY)

It's a touch, umm, embarrassing, to tell you the truth. Councilor Linth has a habit of exaggerating one's role in events. As you're no doubt already aware.

AIDA:
Not at all. It's *good* to see them so warmly embracing the notion of peace.

AMBASSADOR TINTAK:
Yes. It *is* something of a novelty, isn't it, these days.

AIDA:
This time tomorrow the celebrations will reverberate throughout the entire sector. You must be very proud.

AMBASSADOR TINTAK:
Hmmm. While I know that our two worlds have been united through marriage, and that everyone is saying all the right things, I cannot yet bring myself to entirely trust our new "al-

lies" from Eiram. Not yet. Not after everything that's passed between us.

There's still time before the words on that treaty become law. I shall celebrate when both parties have signed, and not before.

FX: A droid trundles past.

DROID:
Can I interest the esteemed guests in some pickled bushka root?

AMBASSADOR TINTAK:
Pickled *what*?

DROID:
Bushka root, sir. A fibrous tuber that grows in the deserts here on Jedha. I'm told it is most delicious—once it's been seared, boiled, and jarred for several years, and presented on baked flatbreads such as this.

AMBASSADOR TINTAK:
I think I'll pass.

AIDA:
I think you're wise.

DROID:
Then I shall return presently with a selection of other local delicacies with which to tempt your distinguished palates.

FX: The droid trundles off again.

AMBASSADOR TINTAK:
I'm assured there *is* good food to be had on Jedha.

AIDA:
(CONSPIRATORIALLY, AS IF TAKING HIM INTO HER CONFIDENCE)

There is—if you promise you can keep a secret.

AMBASSADOR TINTAK:
(DRAWN IN)

Of course! You can trust me implicitly, my dear!

AIDA:
In the markets. All the best stuff is made by the locals. Perhaps tomorrow we can arrange to have someone fetch you some Gnunga Weed Hoppies. You really should give them a try before you leave.

AMBASSADOR TINTAK:
I knew I liked the Jedi. Thank you, Jedi Forte.

FX: Another cheer goes up from the gathered representatives of E'ronoh.

AIDA:
(LAUGHS)

AMBASSADOR TINTAK:
(JOLLY)

Now go! Enjoy the party. Or meditate, or whatever it is you Jedi do. I need to keep an eye on this lot before things get unruly.

AIDA:
Very well. My thanks to you, Ambassador. Tomorrow will be a great day.

AMBASSADOR TINTAK:
I do believe it shall.

CUT TO:

SCENE 12. INT. THE SECOND SPIRE—RECEPTION PARTY—CONTINUOUS

ATMOS: As before.

AMBASSADOR CEROX:
(CALLING FROM ACROSS ROOM)

Ah! Creighton! There you are!

FX: Creighton sighs almost inaudibly beneath his breath.

CREIGHTON:
Ambassador Cerox. I was just on my way over to say hello.

AMBASSADOR CEROX:
You were talking with that San Tekka chap, weren't you?

CREIGHTON:
Morton San Tekka, yes. The independent mediator appointed to oversee tomorrow's signing.

AMBASSADOR CEROX:
(AMUSED)

Signing? Is that what we're calling it now? As if we're all friends again and none of that nasty *war* business ever happened.

CREIGHTON:
If only that were so.

Forgive me—I didn't intend to sound flippant. It's just . . .

AMBASSADOR CEROX:
(SOFTENING AGAIN)

The diplomats are rubbing off on you. You were trying to be sensitive. I know.

It's me who should apologize.

CREIGHTON:
Not at all. These have been trying times.

AMBASSADOR CEROX:
(LAUGHS AGAIN)

My, you have been practicing the art of understatement.

CREIGHTON:
(LAUGHS TOO)

I trust you and the other delegates from Eiram are being well looked after?

AMBASSADOR CEROX:
The facilities are . . . most adequate. Although I must admit, the number of intimidating guards standing beside every exit is somewhat off-putting.

CREIGHTON:
Guardians of the Whills. A necessary precaution, I'm afraid. They'll be overseeing the security arrangements for tomorrow's signing, too.

AMBASSADOR CEROX:
I thought that's what the Jedi were here for?

CREIGHTON:
We're here to see that everything goes smoothly, just as we have been since the very beginning of the peace process. The assis-

tance of the Jedi was requested by both the monarchs of Eiram and E'ronoh, and the Republic. I am duty-bound to see the negotiations through.

Indeed, if I have need to activate my lightsaber, Ambassador, then I fear things will have already gone badly wrong.

AMBASSADOR CEROX:
(CONCERNED)

But you're anticipating trouble?

CREIGHTON:
Not at all. As I said, the Guardians of the Whills are a *precaution.* They're here to provide security, nothing more.

AMBASSADOR CEROX:
I wish I shared your confidence, Master Jedi. Yet I cannot bring myself to trust the intentions of the delegates from E'ronoh. For the last five years they *were* trying to kill us, after all.

CREIGHTON:
And were you not attempting to do the same?

AMBASSADOR CEROX:
(NONCHALANTLY)

Oh, yes, but that's different, isn't it?

CREIGHTON:
It is?

AMBASSADOR CEROX:
Well, of course it is. *They* started all of this, after all. E'ronoh were the first to drop bombs on our civilians. They *wanted* this conflict all along, and they provoked us into retaliating. Their martial traditions mean they've always been hungry for conquest. They even manufactured a diplomatic crisis when their prince was apparently "murdered" by Eirami agents so that they could justify their attempted invasion of our world. If it

weren't for them, there wouldn't even be a war, and therefore no need for a peace treaty in the first place.

CREIGHTON:
Madam Ambassador. While I'm certain the E'ronoh contingent would see things *quite* differently, I can assure you they fully intend to abide by the articles of your agreement. This is not something either of you are entering into lightly.

And need I remind you, once the treaty is signed tomorrow, any transgressions of the agreed terms shall become a matter of law.

This treaty marks the *end* of the war. Once and for all.

AMBASSADOR CEROX:
Hmmm. Well yes, of course, we all want an end to this nightmare, don't we? *Especially* Tintak, who knows his people were losing . . .

CREIGHTON:
(A NOTE OF GENTLE WARNING)

Ambassador . . .

AMBASSADOR CEROX:
(DISMISSIVE)

Yes, yes. I know! We're at a party.

And look—you don't even have a drink in your hand.

(CALLING TO DROID)

Here! You! Droid!

CREIGHTON:
No, I really don't—

AMBASSADOR CEROX:
(CUTTING HIM OFF)

—Nonsense. You said it yourself, we're supposed to be celebrating.

CREIGHTON:
(AWKWARD)

That's not exactly what I said . . .

FX: The protocol droid from earlier walks over.

PROTOCOL DROID:
Madam Ambassador. You require refreshment?

AMBASSADOR CEROX:
Not I. *Him.*

PROTOCOL DROID:
Master Jedi?

CREIGHTON:
No, I'm fine, thank you.

AMBASSADOR CEROX:
He'll take one of those. No, wait—two of those.

PROTOCOL DROID:
Very good. Sir?

CREIGHTON:
(SIGHS)

Yes, all right.

FX: The protocol droid leaves.

AMBASSADOR CEROX:
To peace.

CREIGHTON:
To peace.

FADE TO:

SCENE 13. EXT. OUTSIDE THE PATH'S ALMSHOUSE—NEXT MORNING

ANNOUNCER:
Time until the battle begins: fifty-four hours.

ATMOS: The city is coming awake. A soft wind soughs through the streets. People are going about their business. Birds chirp loudly.

FX: Someone is filling a bucket of water from an outside tap. We follow them as they carry it inside, into:

SCENE 14. INT. PATH'S ALMSHOUSE—CONTINUOUS

ATMOS: People are preparing breakfast. Chopping vegetables, boiling water. The clanging of pans.

FX: The person carrying the bucket of water places it down on a wooden bench. It's Marda.

MARDA:
Here, Phinea. More water.

PHINEA:
(KINDLY CHIDING)

Marda—fetching water is my job.

MARDA:
Yes, but I was out there anyway, getting some morning air. I thought I'd save you another trip. I know your back has been troubling you these last few days.

PHINEA:
(CHUCKLES)

These last few *years* if truth be told.

(MORE SERIOUS)

But you're right. The cold here on Jedha—it seeps into your bones. Do you feel it, too?

MARDA:

I feel it. You'd be wise to wrap up for the protest march this morning. There's a chill wind blowing in off the desert.

FX: In the background, people begin serving food into bowls. Under the rest of the scene, we hear people eating—spoons scraping against bowls, et cetera.

PHINEA:

I wonder how much longer I'll be able to take part in the marches. I'm not getting any younger.

MARDA:

I know it's hard adjusting, Phinea. Jedha isn't like Dalna. But the Path can make a real difference here.

(FORCEFULLY, AS IF REPEATING A MANTRA)

Our voices *will* be heard.

PHINEA:
(AMUSED, IMPRESSED)

To have the energy and zeal of youth! You'll take us far, young Marda. I know it.

MARDA:
The Mother has already taken us to the stars.

PHINEA:
And now she is guided by you. We all are. You show us the way. Because of you, the Force will be free.

MARDA:
Because of *all* of us. Because of the Path.

Soon, the Herald will go before the Convocation to petition our cause. A rightful place on their council. Think of the good we'll be able to do.

PHINEA:

With you at his side, this so-called Convocation is certain to agree.

MARDA:
(DOWNBEAT)

I'm not going, Phinea.

PHINEA:
(CONFUSED)

No?

MARDA:
(HOLDING HER EMOTION IN CHECK)

The Evereni are not trusted in the wider galaxy. Those beyond the Path see us as monsters. As warmongers and liars. I think the Mother worries that my attendance might have a negative impact on the Convocation's decision. That the prejudice of those who would see me as somehow *lesser* might serve as a distraction from the truth of the Herald's words.

FX: Someone at one of the breakfast tables places their spoon back in their bowl and stops eating.

THE MOTHER:
No, Marda. That's not why I forbade you from going, although there is, as ever, wisdom in your words.

MARDA:
(SURPRISED)

Mother. I didn't see you there.

THE MOTHER:
It's just as Phinea says. You are our Guide, now. Your advice and counsel steer the very future of the Path. I need you by my side, if I am to hear it.

MARDA:
But Mother—if I were to attend the petition—

THE MOTHER:
(CUTTING HER OFF, BUT KINDLY)

—the outcome would be the same. We must trust in the Herald to do what is best. Unless you doubt him?

MARDA:
Of course not.

FX: A chair scrapes back as the Mother gets up, slowly.

THE MOTHER:
You, Marda Ro—you must guide from *within.* Your counsel is too valuable. Soon our work on Jedha will be done, and we must conceive of our next journey upon the *Gaze Electric,* to carry our word amongst the stars themselves. As it was foretold in my vision.

MARDA:
(RESIGNED)

Yes, Mother.

THE MOTHER:
Now I shall retire to my chambers to prepare for a momentous day.

MARDA:
The Force will be free.

THE MOTHER:
The Force will be free.

FX: The Mother leaves. Her walk is not as sprightly as you might expect.

PHINEA:
Now, Marda—have you broken your fast?

MARDA:
Not yet, Phinea.

FX: Phinea pulls out a chair.

PHINEA:
Then take a seat and allow me to fetch you something. As the Mother says—today is going to be a long and fruitful day. You can't face it on an empty stomach, now, can you?

CUT TO:

SCENE 15. EXT. JEDHA STREET—CLOSE TO THE DOME OF DELIVERANCE—SOON AFTER

ATMOS: We can hear distant bells ringing. The birds are still singing. Speeders zip by, and there's a general hubbub as the people of the city begin to emerge from their homes.

FX: The trudging of two pairs of feet.

CREIGHTON:
Silandra?

(Beat, then LOUDER)

Silandra?

FX: The trudging feet stop.

SILANDRA:
Creighton! Is that you?

CREIGHTON:
(DELIGHTED)

It's me.

SILANDRA:
(HAPPY)

It's been ages!

FX: Silandra hurries over and embraces Creighton, who emits a grunt at the sudden, unexpected embrace.

CREIGHTON:
(GRUNTS)

It's been *years.*

You look good. The frontier suits you well.

SILANDRA:
And Coruscant continues to *spoil* you. Those are some fine robes you're wearing.

CREIGHTON:
(LAUGHS)

These? Just something I threw together.

SILANDRA:
(LAUGHS)

CREIGHTON:
Truth is, I'm here for the treaty signing.

SILANDRA:
Mesook told me! You always were a diplomat at heart.

CREIGHTON:
I don't know whether to take that as a compliment or not.

SILANDRA:
(TEASING)

I suppose that depends on your perspective.

CREIGHTON:
Hmmm.

How is life out on the frontier?

SILANDRA:
Illuminating.

CREIGHTON:
And Rooper?

SILANDRA:
Enjoying some contemplation time on Batuu. But she's doing well. Growing into a fine Padawan.

CREIGHTON:
I heard about what happened on Aubadas. I'm sorry we couldn't get there sooner.

SILANDRA:
The war between Eiram and E'ronoh has had more of an impact than any of us know. It's hard out there, Creighton.

CREIGHTON:
It's hard *everywhere,* even with a cease-fire in place.

SILANDRA:
I'm just glad to hear the conflict's over. The signing of that treaty can't come soon enough.

CREIGHTON:
(CAUTIOUS)

Assuming everything goes according to plan.

SILANDRA:
You sound worried. Is the situation really that precarious?

CREIGHTON:
Not at all. It's just that . . . we've already had to deal with several assassination attempts and a near-breakdown in the peace process. There has been tremendous resolve on both sides, but . . . if anything were to go wrong now . . .

SILANDRA:
It *won't.* Have faith. In yourself. In the people. And in the Force.

CREIGHTON:
(SIGHS)

You're right, of course. I just—

SILANDRA:
—can't help worrying. I get it. It's a heavy burden.

CREIGHTON:
It's not about the burden.

Well, I suppose it is. But more, it's about the consequences of failure. Not for me or the Order, but for the people of Eiram and E'ronoh who have lost so much. And all those others you mentioned, caught up in the shock waves of a conflict that has nothing to do with them.

There's a real will to see this finished now. At least, from the heirs and those sections of the populace who support their union. But I worry there are other factions that are finding it more difficult to see their former enemies as friends. Factions on both sides that would prefer to see the war continue. Citizens who have suffered so much because of the war that they've forgotten how to imagine peace. The populations on both worlds are divided between those who hunger for peace and those who no longer understand how to stop fighting.

SILANDRA:
Walk with me?

FX: Silandra and Creighton start walking together.

SILANDRA:
You're right. The repercussions of a failure here would be catastrophic.

But you've done everything you can. You've helped to shepherd the ambassadors to this point. You, Gella, and the others have offered them every opportunity for peace.

There's nothing more you can do, Creighton. You cannot sign the treaty *for* them.

CREIGHTON:
I know. I just wish that people were more willing to talk to one another. To *listen.*

SILANDRA:
They usually are. Once everything else has been stripped away. Once they see what's really at stake and understand that the people they're trying to hurt are exactly that—*people.* Just like them.

CREIGHTON:
Now you're starting to sound like Aida.

SILANDRA:
Maybe that's because we're both talking sense.

CREIGHTON:
You might have a point there, you know. She told me to take the morning off to visit the Kyber Mirrors beneath the Dome of Deliverance.

SILANDRA:
Another good idea. I'm on my way there now, too. We can go together.

CREIGHTON:
I'm sorry—I just realized—I haven't even asked why you're here? For the Season of Light, presumably?

SILANDRA:
(BRIGHTLY)

You mean the Festival of Balance.

CREIGHTON:
Ah, yes. The Convocation's big idea to bring everyone together.

SILANDRA:
It does make sense. A broad celebration of the Force. Something that appeals to the many factions here on Jedha. It's a pleasing idea. Have you seen the preparations going on in the city?

CREIGHTON:
No—I've been stuck in the Second Spire since I arrived . . . until now.

SILANDRA:
It'll be fun. Stalls selling trinkets and foodstuffs, animals on show from all corners of the galaxy, performers and preachers standing shoulder-to-shoulder . . .

CREIGHTON:
I think I might give it a wide berth.

SILANDRA:
(LAUGHING)

My, you are becoming an old cynic . . .

FX: They trudge on for a moment in silence. We hear another speeder pass by and a droid making a squealing sound.

CREIGHTON:
Have you been before? To the mirrors, I mean.

SILANDRA:
I have. A long time ago, soon after I'd lost my Padawan braid.

CREIGHTON:
Soon after we'd *both* lost our Padawan braids.

So, how do they work, exactly?

SILANDRA:
The mirrors?

CREIGHTON:
Yes.

SILANDRA:
It's just like their name implies. An opportunity for quiet reflection. Sometimes, the mirrors show you nothing but your own face staring back at you. Other times, I'm told, they reveal inner truths, glimpses of the past or future, of possibilities still being written within the Force.

CREIGHTON:
I'm not certain I *want* to know what the future has to hold.

SILANDRA:
The point of the mirrors is to show you what you *need* to see, not what you *want* to see. What you do with that is, of course, up to you.

CREIGHTON:
And people find this *relaxing*?

SILANDRA:
(LAUGHS)

FX: Their footsteps come to a stop.

SILANDRA:
The Dome of Deliverance.

CREIGHTON:
It's . . .

SILANDRA:
Breathtaking, isn't it? You could fit half the city's population inside, and there'd still be room to spare.

Come on, I'll show you where to go.

FX: They enter the building.

CUT TO:

SCENE 16. INT. JEDHA—KETH'S APARTMENT— SOON AFTER

ATMOS: All is silent, until:

FX: A comlink trills.

KETH:
What? What! Wha—

FX: Keth bats at the comlink like it's an alarm.

KETH:
(GROANS TIREDLY)

Stupid alarm. Doesn't it know I was working all night?

MORTON SAN TEKKA:
(VIA COMM)

(CLEARS THROAT)

KETH:
What was that, Pee-Three?

MORTON SAN TEKKA:
(VIA COMM)

(AMUSED)

I think you'll find that wasn't your droid, Mr. Cerapath.

KETH:
Wasn't my . . .

Oh. *Oh!*

FX: Keth scrambles up from his bunk, overturning something that smashes.

KETH:
No no no no no . . .

Pee-Three? Where are you?

MORTON SAN TEKKA:
(VIA COMM)

(CLEARS THROAT AGAIN)

KETH:
Mr. San Tekka. Sir. I'm so sorry. I . . . umm . . .

MORTON SAN TEKKA:
(VIA COMM)

(STILL AMUSED)

You were working all night, I think was the excuse, was it not?

KETH:
(SHEEPISH)

Well . . . I . . .

Am I *very* late?

MORTON SAN TEKKA:
(VIA COMM)

You still have ample time to attend to your duties, Mr. Cera-path. The signing ceremony doesn't start for . . . let me see . . . two and a half hours.

KETH:
(TO SELF)

Oh, no. I'm *so* late.

MORTON SAN TEKKA:
(VIA COMM)

Do you think you could see to it that you join me in the Second Spire within the next half hour to assist me in making the final preparations for the ceremony?

KETH:
I . . .

Of course. I shall be there before you know it, sir.

MORTON SAN TEKKA:
(VIA COMM)

And Keth?

KETH:
Yes, sir?

MORTON SAN TEKKA:
(VIA COMM)

Try not to get waylaid.

KETH:
Yes, sir.

FX: The comlink shuts off. Keth breathes a heavy sigh.

KETH:
(GRUMPY)

Pee-Three!

FX: The whir of P3-7A's thrusters enters the room as the droid hovers in.

P3-7A:

The Force is a lake, spoke the prophet, and our movements naught but ripples. Thus, we should tread gently, lest the ripples become waves that unbalance those around us.

KETH:

What is *that* supposed to mean?

Why didn't you *wake* me?

P3-7A:

We are each of us children of the Force. To deny one is to deny us all.

KETH:

(WITH DISBELIEF)

So, this is about leaving you outside Enlightenment yesterday, is it?

Well, that's very mature of you, Pee-Three. Very mature.

You know, it's things like this that make it impossible to take you places with me in the first place.

P3-7A:

Only those who truly know the ways of the Force understand when not to use it.

KETH:

Bah!

FX: Keth starts stomping around his room, opening drawers and cupboards as he pulls out clothes.

KETH:

You really do expect me to give in, don't you?

How can I take you to the peace conference, Pee-Three? There are no droids allowed inside the ceremonial chamber. For security.

P3-7A:

The Force is not seen, and yet it remains ever-present.

KETH:

Fine! Fine! I'll open a viewport when no one's looking. But if you get blasted to oblivion by one of the Guardians of the Whills, it's on you.

All right?

P3-7A:

The Force is benevolent. It is the way to peace.

KETH:

Good. Now hurry up and help me get ready, before I find myself on the San Tekkas' "most wanted" list . . .

CUT TO:

SCENE 17. EXT. JEDHA—OUTSIDE THE DOME OF DELIVERANCE—LATER

ATMOS: The general hubbub of the Jedha streets. It's busier now than before.

FX: We follow Creighton's footsteps as he exits the Dome of Deliverance and approaches Silandra, who is sitting outside on a wall.

SILANDRA:
It's quite something, isn't it?

CREIGHTON:
It's . . . not what I was expecting. And yet . . .

SILANDRA:
You can feel it, can't you? The Force is strong down there, amongst the mirrors.

CREIGHTON:
Yes.

It was . . . *comforting.*

(Beat, then UNSURE)

I saw . . .

FX: Creighton hesitates. He takes a seat beside Silandra on the wall.

SILANDRA:
(KINDLY)

It's all right. It's personal. Whatever you saw is for *you*.

You don't have to say anything at all.

CREIGHTON:
Thank you.

I shall meditate on it.

SILANDRA:
Thank Aida. It was her idea.

CREIGHTON:
Yes. I will.

How about you? Did you find what you were searching for?

SILANDRA:
I saw Peleth.

FX: There's a moment of silence.

CREIGHTON:
I'm sorry. Losing a Padawan. It can't be easy. No matter how much time has passed.

SILANDRA:
That's just it. It was . . . *beautiful*. She's one with the Force now. It took me too long to see it. To stop blaming myself.

But I'm at peace with it now.

CREIGHTON:
And you have Rooper.

SILANDRA:
(LAUGHING)

Yes. I do.

Never still for a moment, that one. Bursting with questions. Always craving adventure.

CREIGHTON:
(LAUGHING)

Now, who does that remind me of? I wonder.

SILANDRA:
(GROANING)

Oh, no. Not this again.

CREIGHTON:
(TEASING)

You're saying you don't remember that time on Taltos, when we were barely Padawans ourselves, and you decided to crawl into a saphantine's burrow.

SILANDRA:
(WITH MOCK PROTEST)

I thought there might be relics down there!

CREIGHTON:
That's what you told old Master Ick'rik, anyway . . .

SILANDRA:
(LAUGHING)

I can't believe you're bringing this up. *Again.*

CREIGHTON:
All I'm saying is, I still have the scars.

SILANDRA:
You don't!

FX: Creighton rolls up the bottom of his robes.

CREIGHTON:
There! Look! I'll have you know that hurt. A lot! I've never been able to go near a saphantine again.

SILANDRA:
Why would you want to?

CREIGHTON:
Precisely my point! Who would ever even consider getting stuck headfirst inside one of their burrows, and needing some-one to pull them out—and get bitten in the process?

SILANDRA:
I wasn't stuck!

CREIGHTON:
You were, and you know it.

Sounds as if Rooper's more like you than you'd care to admit.

SILANDRA:
You're right.

And you always were ready to roll your sleeves up and dive in, weren't you? Whenever someone needed help. You haven't changed.

CREIGHTON:
Not even a little?

SILANDRA:
Not even a bit. You're still getting stuck in where no one else is willing. Trying to make the galaxy a better place, one good deed at a time.

CREIGHTON:
I don't think any of us could stand by and watch people in need. It's what makes us Jedi.

SILANDRA:
It's what makes you one of the best of us.

You've got this, you know. This whole peace treaty. The end of the war. I know you have a habit of doubting yourself. But you've already won. The war's over. You can relax. Find some peace.

CREIGHTON:

And as Aida keeps reminding me: There's no better place than the Holy City to find peace.

SILANDRA:

Just know that I'm here if you need a friend.

(Beat, then TEASING)

But I should warn you—hang around with me long enough and there's every chance you might get bitten again.

CREIGHTON:

(TEASING)

Perhaps it's time I was getting back to the spire . . .

SILANDRA:

Yes. Go. Get back to Aida and the ambassadors. Make sure that treaty gets signed this afternoon.

CREIGHTON:

Let's speak again. *Tomorrow,* when it's all over.

SILANDRA:

Very well. I'll seek you out at the Second Spire. We can celebrate.

CREIGHTON:

Good.

FX: Creighton gets up off the wall.

CREIGHTON:

It's good to see you, Silandra.

SILANDRA:

May the Force be with you, Creighton.

CUT TO:

SCENE 18. INT. THE SECOND SPIRE—GRAND CHAMBER—SOON AFTER

ANNOUNCER:
Time until the battle begins: forty-eight hours.

ATMOS: The Grand Chamber has been prepared for the signing of the treaty. The atmosphere is like a courtroom before session—reverent, with people speaking in hushed tones. We can hear the bells of Jedha ringing very faintly in the distance, and droids moving about.

FX: Footsteps come hurrying toward us.

MORTON SAN TEKKA:
Ah, Keth.

(Beat, then TEASING)

Good, um . . . *afternoon.*

KETH:
(BREATHLESS)

Please accept my apologies, Your Honor. I would have been here sooner, but the security arrangements were—

MORTON SAN TEKKA:
(FINISHING KETH'S SENTENCE)

—comprehensive. I know.

KETH:
Two Guardians of the Whills dragged me off into a side chamber for questioning. I tried to tell them I'd already been cleared, but they insisted on turning out all my pockets.

MORTON SAN TEKKA:
(AMUSED)

And did they find anything?

KETH:
Only the last of my dignity.

MORTON SAN TEKKA:
(LAUGHS)

Ah, well. Some of us lost that a long time ago.

KETH:
(LAUGHS)

How are the preparations?

MORTON SAN TEKKA:
Finished. In a few moments the Republic observers will begin filing in through that door, and the rest of the invited audience will take their seats over there in the stalls.

Once everyone else is in place, the delegates from Eiram and E'ronoh will be escorted into the chamber by our Jedi friends, I shall give a mercifully short speech, and then the signing of the treaty shall commence. It'll all be over within half an hour.

KETH:
And then?

MORTON SAN TEKKA:
And then you'll be pleased to hear there's another party. And this time the celebrations will likely go on long into the night.

This is, after all, something of a momentous occasion.

KETH:
Oh. Right.

MORTON SAN TEKKA:
(CHUCKLES)

Do not fear, Mr. Cerapath. You shall be relieved of your duties once the celebrations have begun. I have no desire to see you suffer as I circulate amongst the gathered dignitaries to offer platitudes and compliments.

(Beat, then WHISPERED)

In truth, I have no desire to suffer such embarrassments myself. I fully intend to show my face for a short time before making my excuses and retreating to my chambers to hide. But don't you dare tell anyone.

KETH:
(RELIEVED)

My lips are sealed. Thank you.

MORTON SAN TEKKA:
Don't thank me yet. There are errands still to be run.

Speaking of which, would you be so kind as to fetch me a glass of water from one of the service droids?

KETH:
It'd be my pleasure.

CUT TO:

SCENE 19. INT. THE SECOND SPIRE—GRAND CHAMBER—GALLERY—MOMENTS LATER

ATMOS: As before. Footsteps approach.

AIDA:
There you are. I was starting to worry. I know I was the one who suggested you take some time to visit the reflection mirrors this morning, but I was beginning to think something had happened.

CREIGHTON:
I met an old friend. Master Sho. She's here on a pilgrimage.

AIDA:
Silandra? The last I heard she was out on the frontier with a Pathfinder team.

CREIGHTON:
She was.

AIDA:
It'd be good to see her again. I hope there's time before we have to leave for Coruscant.

CREIGHTON:
There will be. She's going to seek us out tomorrow, here at the spire.

AIDA:
I shall look forward to it.

And the mirrors? Did you find some time to reflect?

CREIGHTON:
(UPBEAT)

I did. And I thank you for the suggestion.

FX: In the background, people begin to file into the room below, taking their seats in the stalls.

CREIGHTON:
Now, though, we have somewhere to be.

AIDA:
Yes! Think what Ambassador Cerox would say if her favorite Jedi wasn't there to walk her to the signing.

CREIGHTON:
You're incorrigible.

AIDA:
And you're too easy to tease.

Come on. Let's finish this.

CUT TO:

SCENE 20. INT. THE SECOND SPIRE—UPPER FLOOR—CONTINUOUS

ATMOS: We can hear the people milling about in the Grand Chamber, but it's muffled as we're on the empty floor above.

FX: Keth opens a viewport with a whoosh of powering-down force field.

KETH:
(HISSING WHISPER)

Pee-Three? You there?

FX: There's a beat of silence.

KETH:
(MORE URGENT)

Pee-Three?

FX: We hear P3-7A's thrusters as he powers up to the viewport.

KETH:
Hurry up! I was only supposed to be fetching a glass of water. I'm already in enough trouble.

FX: P3-7A flies in through the viewport. Keth closes it behind him.

P3-7A:

If one remains calm, they will always find peace in the Force.

KETH:

That's enough of your sarcasm. And I'm not *calm* because I've had to rush up here to let you in.

Now I'm heading back down. You can watch—discreetly—from here. Close the viewport behind you. And remember, if you get caught, I'm having nothing to do with it.

P3-7A:

Learn to love the Force and you shall be rewarded.

FX: Keth is already walking away.

KETH:
(WALKING AWAY)

Yeah, yeah. Whatever, Pee-Three.

CUT TO:

SCENE 21. INT. THE SECOND SPIRE—GRAND CHAMBER—MOMENTS LATER

ATMOS: As before, but we're now backstage with Creighton and Ambassador Cerox. The crowd murmurs in the background.

CREIGHTON:
(LOW VOICE)

This way, Ambassador Cerox.

FX: Three raps with a wooden staff. The murmur of the audience dies away to silence. In the background, we hear Morton San Tekka begin his speech.

MORTON SAN TEKKA:
(IN BACKGROUND)

Welcome, all, on this most momentous occasion.

I, Morton San Tekka, thank you all for gathering in this holiest of places, to witness what will surely become known as one of the most important triumphs of peace of our generation.

Today we stand on the precipice of something bigger than us all.

Today, two worlds will set aside their profound differences—differences that have led to years of terrible conflict—to instead focus on their commonalities, to reach out hands and embrace across the vast gulf of space. To welcome a new age of peace.

FX: *When Ambassador Cerox and Creighton speak, it's in the foreground, their voices low.*

AMBASSADOR CEROX:
(LOW VOICE)

My, this mediator fellow does go on a bit, doesn't he?

CREIGHTON:
(LOW VOICE)

I believe he's attempting to capture the sheer gravity of today's undertaking.

MORTON SAN TEKKA:
(IN BACKGROUND)

Gathered witnesses—I give to you, the chosen representatives of Eiram and E'ronoh, Ambassadors Cerox and Tintak.

FX: *A round of applause from the audience. In the background, we can hear Ambassador Tintak calling to the audience.*

AMBASSADOR TINTAK:
(IN BACKGROUND)

Thank you! Thank you! There's really no need! Thank you!

AMBASSADOR CEROX:
(LOW VOICE)

Just look at him, posturing for the audience. Silly fool.

CREIGHTON:
(LOW VOICE)

It'll all be over in a few minutes.

Are you ready?

AMBASSADOR CEROX:
Yes, yes. Of course. Let's get it over with.

FX: Creighton and Ambassador Cerox begin to walk out. Creighton catches Ambassador Cerox's arm.

CREIGHTON:
Wait!

AMBASSADOR CEROX:
What's the meaning of this? I really must pro—

CREIGHTON:
(CUTTING HER OFF)

Something's wrong.

(Beat, then FIRM)

Wait here.

FX: Creighton's lightsaber activates. He runs out into the ballroom proper. We follow him out. We hear a droid's thrusters.

AMBASSADOR CEROX:
Really!

MORTON SAN TEKKA:
(SURPRISED)

What's that droid doing in here? There aren't supposed to *be* any droids!

CREIGHTON:
(CALLING)

Stop! Everyone—please. That droid! Sto—

FX: But he's too late. There's a massive, deafening explosion. It fills the soundscape, rumbling through the whole spire.

END OF PART ONE

Part Two
FALLOUT

SCENE 22. INT. THE SECOND SPIRE—GRAND CHAMBER

ATMOS: The room is on fire. Rubble is collapsing. People are screaming and running.

CREIGHTON:
(STRAINING)

Unnghhh!

AIDA:
Creighton!

CREIGHTON:
(STRAINING)

Can't . . . keep . . . it . . . from . . .

AIDA:
Let me help!

FX: A splintering as stone and broken wooden beams come under stress.

AIDA:
(STRAINING)

We won't be able to . . . maintain it . . . for long.

AMBASSADOR TINTAK:
(ASTOUNDED)

By the Light! They're holding up the wall!

FX: Several Guardians of the Whills come running over.

CREIGHTON:
(STRAINING)

Mesook. Selik.

Get . . . them . . . clear . . .

MESOOK:
Ambassadors.

AMBASSADOR CEROX:
Thank goodness. Please—the exits are blocked.

SELIK:
Everyone who can walk—follow the Guardians, now! We'll lead you to safety.

AMBASSADOR TINTAK:
But—

CREIGHTON:
(SHOUTING)

Go!

FX: The ambassadors and their people hurry off, following the Guardians of the Whills.

CREIGHTON:
(GRUNTS WITH EFFORT)

Ready?

AIDA:
Ready.

BOTH:
Arrghhhh!

FX: There's an almighty crash as they allow a section of the wall to collapse to the ground.

CREIGHTON:
(BREATHING RAGGEDLY)

Check for any survivors who might be trapped in the wreckage. We don't have long before the fire takes hold.

FX: Creighton and Aida begin lifting aside broken beams as they search for survivors.

AIDA:
(CALLING)

Hello? Is anyone under there?

Hello?

CREIGHTON:
(CALLING)

Can anyone hear me?

FX: There's no reply. They continue to shift rubble and fallen beams for a few moments, until:

CREIGHTON:
(LEVEL)

Aida. Over here. It's the mediator, Morton San Tekka.

FX: Aida hurries over.

AIDA:
Oh, no.

CREIGHTON:
Stand back.

FX: Creighton's lightsaber ignites with a hum. He uses it to cut a fallen girder in two. The pieces fall away with a clang. He extinguishes his lightsaber.

CREIGHTON:
Help me with this.

FX: The two of them shift one of the bits of severed girder. It thuds to the ground.

CREIGHTON:
Morton? Can you hear me? Morton?

FX: Footsteps come running at pace.

MESOOK:
(SHOUTING IN THE BACKGROUND)

Stop! You! You can't go back in there!

KETH:
(SHOUTING)

Mr. San Tekka? Are you there?

Mr. San Tekka?

CREIGHTON:
(CALLING TO KETH)

Over here.

FX: Keth skids to a halt by the Jedi.

KETH:
Mr. . . .

Oh.

Oh, no.

Is he . . . ?

AIDA:
His light has gone out. He is one with the Force.

I'm sorry.

KETH:
What happened?

CREIGHTON:
(COUGHS, then CALMLY)

Keth, isn't it?

KETH:
Yes. That's right. But . . . I don't understand. I was . . . I went to fetch a glass of water . . . I should have been . . .

CREIGHTON:
There was an explosion. There was nothing you could have done.

KETH:
But *how*?

AIDA:
That's what we need to figure out. But I can only think . . .

CREIGHTON:
Sabotage. Someone wanted to stop the peace treaty being signed.

And they were prepared to kill all of us to do it.

There was a droid. It was carrying a bomb.

KETH:
A *droid*?

FX: A beam collapses. The fire flares. Mesook approaches.

MESOOK:
(COUGHING)

All of you. It's time to leave. All the other survivors are out of immediate danger.

CREIGHTON:
All right.

(TO AIDA)

Come on. Help me with the body. We can't leave him to the flames. Not like this.

AIDA:
Of course.

FX: Aida and Creighton heft Morton San Tekka's body between them.

KETH:
I can't believe it. He was such a generous man. He . . . he was so *nice.*

I'll have to inform the wardens at the church. And they'll need to speak with the San Tekka family. And . . .

CREIGHTON:
Come on. There'll be time for all that later. First, we have to get you out of here.

KETH:
Wait! Pee-Three!

AIDA:
Pee-Three?

KETH:
My droid. He was here.

CREIGHTON:
(SUSPICIOUS)

Your *droid*? It's missing?

KETH:
Yes! He was here. Upstairs.

CREIGHTON:
(URGENT)

What sort of droid?

KETH:
A heap of annoying junk. An old ceremonial model with a bunch of additions I salvaged or bought from the Bonbraks.

CREIGHTON:
(PRESSING HIM)

A ceremonial model? From the church?

KETH:
Yes, but . . .

(Beat, then HORRIFIED)

You're not thinking . . .

CREIGHTON:
At the minute I don't know *what* to think.

FX: Another section of the wall collapses, causing them to choke and splutter.

AIDA:
We *need* to leave.

KETH:
But . . .

CREIGHTON:
Now!

FX: Coughing, they all exit the room as the fire roars and spits in their wake.

CUT TO:

SCENE 23. INT. PATH'S ALMSHOUSE—SOON AFTER

ATMOS: As previous. Domestic sounds. Ailing people being tended to by members of the Path.

FX: A child is crying.

MARDA:
(SOOTHING TONE)

There, there, little one.

Don't worry. You'll feel better soon. Your fever will break, and all will be well.

You're welcome here, among the Path. That's what this alms-house is for. It is a house of healing, for those who are sick or in need of shelter. That's why we've come to Jedha. To *help* those who cannot help themselves.

FX: The child's crying slows to a whimper.

MARDA:
There, that's right. Now, why don't you let Phinea fetch you something to eat.

FX: Someone comes charging into the almshouse.

PELA:
(URGENT)

Marda? Marda?

MARDA:
Pela? What's wrong?

PELA:
Marda. Thank the Force.

There's been an explosion.

MARDA:
What? Where?

PELA:
In the Second Spire. Where they're holding the peace conference.

MARDA:
Show me.

FX: They hurry outside.

PELA:
Look. You can see the smoke.

MARDA:
The Jedi were involved.

PELA:
In the explosion?

MARDA:
In the peace talks. The Force has found balance.

PELA:
What do we do?

MARDA:
Gather as many of our people as you can. We must help the injured. You can bring them here.

PELA:
Yes, Marda. Will you come, too?

MARDA:
No. I'll remain here and speak with the Mother. She must be told of what's happened.

And what it means for the Path.

Now, go! Go! Show the people of Jedha the good that the Path can do!

CUT TO:

SCENE 24. EXT. OUTSIDE THE SECOND SPIRE— LATER

ANNOUNCER:
Time until the battle begins: forty-five hours.

ATMOS: People are picking through the wreckage. Water is still being sprayed upon the smoldering building, causing steam to hiss.

FX: A shuttle door closes, and the shuttle lifts off, roaring away into orbit.

AIDA:
Is that the last of them?

CREIGHTON:
Yes. The local sects have all rallied to help anyone who was injured, and both ambassadors have retreated to their orbital transports until we give them the all-clear.

AIDA:
Ambassador Tintak was badly shaken.

CREIGHTON:
And Ambassador Cerox was furious. She's already insisting that E'ronoh is to blame.

AIDA:
(SIGHS)

This could set us back weeks.

CREIGHTON:
(SERIOUS)

It could jeopardize the entire peace process. *Again.* This had to be a calculated attempt by someone to derail the treaty.

AIDA:
Or to commit a murder under the guise of a terrorist attack. Morton San Tekka is the *only* person whose death has been confirmed. Others were badly injured, but by all accounts are stable.

CREIGHTON:
(INCREDULOUS)

Murder?

AIDA:
We can't rule it out. Not after the previous assassination attempts you told me about. The San Tekkas are high-profile targets.

CREIGHTON:
(SIGHS)

We can't rule *anything* out. Not yet.

We're on unstable ground here, Aida. If we get this wrong, if we implicate the wrong people or as much as say something out of place . . .

AIDA:
It could light the kindling to restart the war. I know.

This is a difficult line to walk. We—and the Republic—need to be seen to be impartial, and yet we must protect the ambassadors, too.

CREIGHTON:

But we need answers. We must prove that neither Eiram nor E'ronoh were responsible for the bombing.

AIDA:

Assuming, of course, that they *weren't*.

CREIGHTON:

I'm choosing to believe that—after everything—the delegates of both Eiram and E'ronoh are still committed to peace.

This *has* to be an outside party, just like it was before. Just like Axel Greylark.

AIDA:

But who? Axel Greylark is in prison several systems away.

CREIGHTON:

Gella *said* that she was still unsure about his motives. Or who else he might have been working with, for that matter.

(Beat, then FRUSTRATED)

The truth is, we don't know anything.

AIDA:

What do you make of that young adjunct, Keth?

CREIGHTON:

He seemed genuine enough. But it's suspicious that his droid went missing around the exact time a droid was used to effect the attack.

AIDA:

Hmmm.

Where is he now?

CREIGHTON:

I let him go. He searched out here for the droid for a while, but you've seen the mess.

He's not going anywhere. He lives at the Temple of the Kyber. He'll be easy enough to find.

AIDA:
You think he could be to blame?

CREIGHTON:
He could be. Or someone might have gotten to his droid.

AIDA:
(SIGHS)

The whole thing's a *mess,* Creighton.

CREIGHTON:
I know. And there was me thinking this was going to be easy.

I'll try to get a message to the Council. And to Phan-tu, Xiri, and Chancellor Mollo. Although I don't hold out much hope of reaching Eiram and E'ronoh, given the current communication situation. Still, we should at least try to make them aware of what's happening.

And *Silandra, too . . .*

I need to speak with her. I have an idea.

AIDA:
You do?

CREIGHTON:
Whether it's a good one remains to be seen . . .

AIDA:
Did she tell you where she was staying?

CREIGHTON:
This is Silandra we're talking about. She's not going to be any-where *near* her quarters . . .

AIDA:
. . . she's going to be helping the wounded.

CREIGHTON:
Of course she is.

I'll start with the temporary med station the disciples of the Whills have set up in the old refectory.

AIDA:
And I'll keep an eye on things here.

But Creighton—watch your step. For all we know, *the Jedi* could have been the intended targets of that bomb.

CUT TO:

SCENE 25. INT. PATH'S ALMSHOUSE—MOTHER'S CHAMBERS

ATMOS: A fire crackles in the grate. The Mother sits by the fire. Juk-kyuk and Qwerb stand at the back of the chamber. The Herald has recently entered.

HERALD:
Mother?

(The Mother makes him wait an uncomfortable moment too long, BEFORE)

THE MOTHER:
You have news, Herald?

HERALD:
In a manner of speaking. I have talked with our contacts and made a preliminary search of the city.

THE MOTHER:
(WITH FALSE JOLLITY)

Then we are to celebrate?

You have it?

HERALD:
(WITH RELUCTANCE)

Not yet.

It is proving . . . *difficult* to glean any useful information from the locals. The object will take time to locate. And perhaps even longer to secure.

This is no easy task you have placed upon my shoulders, Mother.

THE MOTHER:
(CLIPPED)

I see.

HERALD:
Perhaps it is best to call off the search for a short while. To focus on the forthcoming meeting with the Convocation, and the other important work we are doing here on Jedha.

THE MOTHER:
You think it for the best? That you have *failed* me.

HERALD:
(RISING ANGER)

Failed you?

FX: From across the room, Jukkyuk issues a low growl of warning.

JUKKYUK:
(GROWLS)

THE MOTHER:
(TO JUKKYUK)

It's all right, Jukkyuk. The Herald didn't mean to raise his voice. He's merely frustrated by his own inability to do what is necessary.

Isn't that right, Herald?

HERALD:
(BARELY RESTRAINED)

As you say.

THE MOTHER:
(IMPERIOUS)

We shall continue with the search.

HERALD:
(DOUBTFUL)

I do not think—

THE MOTHER:
(CUTTING HIM OFF)

It does not matter what you *think*.

It is our duty to stop all such Force-related artifacts from falling into the wrong hands. Especially *Jedi* hands. The object must be found. At all costs. Only the Path can keep it safe.

HERALD:
As you wish.

THE MOTHER:
Leave us now, Herald. You have given me much to consider.

HERALD:
(TIGHT, CONTAINED)

The Force will be free.

THE MOTHER:
(DISTRACTED, ALREADY MOVING ON TO OTHER THINGS)

Yes. The Force will be free.

FX: The Herald exits the room.

CUT TO:

SCENE 26. INT. THE SECOND SPIRE—MEDICAL STATION—OLD REFECTORY

ATMOS: This is where the most severely wounded are being treated after the explosion—those who couldn't go home or be taken to one of the local sects, such as the Path's almshouse. People are moaning in pain, droids and medical staff are treating patients, monitors are bleeping.

FX: Silandra is mopping someone's brow. She wrings out the cloth and continues.

SILANDRA:
There.

WOUNDED DUROS:
(WHIMPERS)

SILANDRA:
It's all right. The droids will be with you soon. I know it hurts, but you're going to be okay.

WOUNDED DUROS:
(CLEARLY PAINED)

Thank you.

FX: Footsteps approach.

CREIGHTON:
I had a feeling I'd find you here.

SILANDRA:
(SURPRISED)

Creighton.

(THEN CONCERNED)

Are you hurt?

CREIGHTON:
No, no. Thank the Light. I'm okay. Aida and I—we're both okay.

SILANDRA:
And the ambassadors?

CREIGHTON:
Safe.

SILANDRA:
(RELIEVED)

That's good to hear.

What *happened*?

CREIGHTON:
Walk with me?

SILANDRA:
Yes, all right.

(TO WOUNDED DUROS)

I'll be right back.

WOUNDED DUROS:
(STILL PAINED)

I'll be fine. There are others who need you more.

SILANDRA:
You're very brave. May the Force be with you.

FX: Silandra and Creighton walk out of the temporary medical station to:

SCENE 27. EXT. JEDHA—OUTSIDE THE MEDICAL STATION—CONTINUOUS

ATMOS: It's a still night, now. Just the distant roar of speeders and night creatures chirping.

SILANDRA:
Creighton—you, Aida, Mesook. You're all okay?

CREIGHTON:
We're fine.

But time is against us, and someone clearly wants to disrupt the peace process here on Jedha. Force only knows what faces us if we don't get this situation under control.

SILANDRA:
Then you believe it was a purposeful attack?

CREIGHTON:
I saw it with my own eyes.

(BERATING HIMSELF)

I *felt* it. Too late.

A droid, packed with explosives. It flew right into the chamber. We didn't stand a chance.

Morton San Tekka is dead. He took the full brunt of the explosion.

SILANDRA:
You think he was the target?

CREIGHTON:
That was Aida's conclusion. But I can't believe this was a simple assassination attempt. They took out the entire floor of the spire. If it hadn't been . . .

SILANDRA:
If it hadn't been for you and Aida, the ambassadors would be dead, too. I understand.

CREIGHTON:
It just doesn't feel right. If they were aiming for a single target, they could have killed him at any point before the signing event. Instead, they chose the highest-profile, highest-security opportunity they could find.

SILANDRA:
A statement of intent?

CREIGHTON:
Precisely. After we foiled all the attempts to prevent Eiram and E'ronoh's heirs from uniting, this feels like an escalation. Someone doesn't want the war to end.

SILANDRA:
How can I help?

CREIGHTON:
That's just it. I know you're here on a pilgrimage. I shouldn't even ask, but . . .

SILANDRA:
Go on.

CREIGHTON:

Aida and I—we need to remain impartial if we're to hold the peace process together. We can't be seen to be taking sides or implicating anyone in sabotage and murder. Not while the treaty is hanging in the balance.

Plus, we don't know if the bomb was successful—the people behind it might try again to make a move against the ambassadors. We need to remain by their sides.

SILANDRA:

So, you want *me* to investigate the bombing.

CREIGHTON:

I do. I'm sorry to ask. It's just . . .

SILANDRA:

I'm *here.*

CREIGHTON:

And I *trust* you. Implicitly. And you know what's at stake. You've seen what might happen here if we fail.

SILANDRA:

Well, it's not as if I was planning to stand by regardless, is it now?

CREIGHTON:
(RELIEVED)

Thank you. I knew we could count on you.

Look, you'll have to keep a low profile.

SILANDRA:
Undercover?

CREIGHTON:

No. Not exactly. It's just—you're here on a pilgrimage. I see no reason for us to let the ambassadors know any different.

SILANDRA:
I understand.

Any thoughts on where to start?

CREIGHTON:
With the people who were there. Someone *must* have seen who was with that droid.

You can leave the ambassadors and their people to me and Aida. But you should start with the young adjunct from the Church of the Force. Keth Cerapath. He had ties to Morton San Tekka. And his droid went missing during the attack.

SILANDRA:
That must be more than a coincidence.

CREIGHTON:
My thoughts exactly.

SILANDRA:
All right. I'll start immediately, before the trail goes too cold. Lots of the potential witnesses bearing minor wounds were taken away by followers of the local sects, keen to help. I'll speak to anyone here who might remember anything, and then make a start farther afield.

And you?

CREIGHTON:
As soon as the spire is secured, we'll be bringing the ambassadors back to finish their work. The Guardians of the Whills are doubling security. We can't be seen to run. So, we stand our ground.

SILANDRA:
Good. I'll work as fast as I can, but don't let anyone lose sight of signing that treaty.

CREIGHTON:
I won't.

Short-range comms are patchy because of the storms. Don't rely on reaching me that way. Probably best we speak in person, anyway, given the sensitivity of what you're doing.

SILANDRA:
I understand.

CREIGHTON:
And Silandra?

SILANDRA:
Yes?

CREIGHTON:
Thank you. I know this isn't what you came here for.

SILANDRA:
But it *is* what's needed. How could I do anything else?

CREIGHTON:
May the Force be with you.

SILANDRA:
And fortune on your side.

CUT TO:

SCENE 28. INT. PATH'S ALMSHOUSE—MOTHER'S CHAMBERS

ATMOS: We're back in the Mother's private chambers in the almshouse. A fire crackles in a pit. It's quiet.

FX: There's a rap at the door.

JUKKYUK:
Rrraaaghhh!

THE MOTHER:
Yes, it's all right, Jukkyuk. She's expected.

(Beat, then CALLING)

Come in.

FX: The door creaks open and Marda enters. Jukkyuk leaves, closing the door behind him.

MARDA:
Mother.

THE MOTHER:
Marda. You're cold. Come, warm yourself by the fire.

MARDA:
Thank you.

FX: Marda stands for a moment, rubbing her hands before the crackling flames.

MARDA:
For a holy place, Jedha can seem a little . . . unwelcoming.

THE MOTHER:
(CHUCKLES)

It is not the place, Marda, but the *people.* It was ever thus, when those who would speak the truth try to make their voices heard.

MARDA:
That's why I wanted to speak with you.

You've heard about the explosion during the peace conference?

THE MOTHER:
Yes. A shocking, if perhaps not surprising, development.

MARDA:
The Jedi were involved. I can't help thinking . . .

THE MOTHER:
. . . that the Force once again sought to balance itself. To find a *level.* Yes. The thought had occurred to me, too. The Jedi's continued manipulation of the Force proves a threat to us all.

But what can we do? Without a seat on the Convocation . . .

FX: The Mother leaves this hanging for a beat.

MARDA:
When will the Herald make his petition?

THE MOTHER:
Soon.

MARDA:
(ZEALOUS)

They will embrace us openly. I am sure of it. They will see what the Path could do for Jedha. How we can help to ensure balance and steer the future of the Force.

THE MOTHER:
(LESS CERTAIN)

Perhaps.

People see only what they wish to, Marda.

And yet, I remain hopeful for change here on Jedha.

MARDA:
I have another idea that might help.

THE MOTHER:
I'd like to hear it.

MARDA:
The Republic officials overseeing the peace conference had installed an impartial mediator to oversee proceedings. A man named Morton San Tekka.

THE MOTHER:
Had?

MARDA:
He's dead. Killed in the explosion.

THE MOTHER:
Interesting.

Surely, given the union between the heirs of Eiram and E'ronoh, this mediator role was ornamental at best, designed to look good for the Republic, to show their chancellors understand the people of the frontier. As if they expected a San Tekka to *do* anything!

Now they must appoint a new, impartial mediator to save face, before the signing of the treaty can continue.

MARDA:
Precisely. And with long-range communications down, they will be unable to reach their chancellors. The decision on the replacement will be taken locally, by the small contingent of Republic officials here on Jedha. And they will no doubt be mindful of their chancellor's earlier instructions and insist upon an impartial figure, rather than step in themselves and risk upsetting the delicate political balance.

THE MOTHER:
You would volunteer a disciple of the Path?

MARDA:
It would seem only prudent, would it not?

THE MOTHER:
(THOUGHTFUL)

Prudent, yes. To ensure the Republic select the person of our choosing for this most ornamental of roles . . .

MARDA:
Then we should propose Elder Delwin? He seems the obvious choice.

THE MOTHER:
I do believe you're right. Elder Delwin it is.

Once again, Marda, your guidance has proved most illuminating. You shall stand by my side as we make our benevolent offer to the Republic.

After all: Peace must be assured, and the Path will do all it can to assist.

CUT TO:

SCENE 29. INT. ENLIGHTENMENT TAPBAR

ATMOS: Despite the traumatic events of the day, things haven't changed in Enlightenment. The harp still plays melodically in the background, and the general atmosphere is the same as before.

FX: An empty glass hits the counter.

KETH:
(SWALLOWING)

He was just lying there. His eyes were open and staring up at me, as if he was about to ask me where his drink of water had got to.

FX: Liquid sloshes into the empty glass.

KRADON:
Here, my boy. Have another drink.

KETH:
On the house?

KRADON:
On the tab.

KETH:
Such is life.

FX: Keth knocks back the other drink and slams the glass back on the bar.

KETH:
(COUGHS BACK THE LIQUOR)

MOONA:
It'll help you sleep. It's hard to rest easy when you've come face-to-face with the dead.

Trust me.

PIRALLI:
What would you know about it, Moona?

MOONA:
You forget, Piralli—I had a life before Jedha. Out amongst the stars.

PIRALLI:
(TEASING)

Oh, yeah. That's right. A pirate queen or something?

MOONA:
(HISSES)

You jest all you want, but I've seen more death than Kradon's served shots of Retsa. I know what Keth's going through.

FX: Moona unsheathes a large blade from a scabbard at her waist.

MOONA:
And remember—I might be a little out of practice with my blade, but there's such a thing as muscle memory . . .

PIRALLI:
(LAUGHS)

I've told you before—I don't *have* any treasure for you to plunder.

MOONA:
It's not your treasure I'm after.

KRADON:
(COUGHS POLITELY)

Kradon suggests that if you two are finished flirting, perhaps you could put the blade away, mmm?

Kradon doesn't want to upset the Twinkle sisters, does he?

MOONA:
Just trying to help a friend in need, Kradon. That's all.

FX: Moona sheathes her blade.

MOONA:
The poor kid's been bereaved.

PIRALLI:
He'd only just met the guy!

MOONA:
What difference does that make?

KETH:
(MOROSELY)

It wasn't just the mediator I lost.

PIRALLI:
It wasn't?

KETH:
Pee-Three, too. He's gone.

PIRALLI:
(INCREDULOUS)

Hang on a minute—you took your droid, *that* droid—to the signing of a peace treaty? Are you mad?

KETH:
He wanted to watch.

PIRALLI:
He wanted to . . .

(TO THE OTHERS)

Are you hearing this?

MOONA:
Who's ever heard of a droid that was interested in politics?

KETH:
I told you before. Pee-Three is my—

(CATCHES HIMSELF)

—*was* my friend. He wanted a record of such a momentous occasion.

And now he's gone.

KRADON:
I'm sorry, kid.

MOONA:
(PUTTING TWO AND TWO TOGETHER)

Hold on. Didn't you say that the explosion was *caused* by a droid?

KETH:
Yes, but—

MOONA:
And Pee-Three was there to *watch*?

KETH:
Yes, I suppose—

MOONA:
And now Pee-Three is missing, too, even though everyone else has been accounted for . . .

KETH:
We don't know that for sure—

MOONA:

Have you considered that your so-called friend might have had something to do with the attack?

KETH:

Of course he didn't! How could he? I'd have known!

PIRALLI:

You must admit, Keth—it does look suspicious.

KETH:

But . . .

FX: There's a commotion by the door.

CAMILLE:

(IN BACKGROUND)

No!

DELPHINE:

(IN BACKGROUND)

Droids!

FX: There's a metallic clang. And then:

KETH:

Wait!

KRADON:

What's this?

CAMILLE:

(IN BACKGROUND)

No.

DELPHINE:

(IN BACKGROUND)

Droids.

FX: The sound of a droid's thrusters.

MOONA:
Is that . . . ?

PIRALLI:
Looks like you were wrong, Moona.

KETH:
(OVERJOYED)

Pee-Three!

P3-7A:
The Force abides.

KETH:
You made it!

P3-7A:
He who walks in fire is tempered by the flame.

KETH:
I *told* you he didn't have anything to do with the explosion!

MOONA:
I'm not so sure, myself. It's still mighty suspicious. It had the opportunity.

KETH:
(INCREDULOUS)

But . . . he didn't blow himself up. He's *right* here.

MOONA:
I'm just saying . . .

P3-7A:
Those who are lost to the beauty of the Force see only that same loss in others.

Only the pious can truly comprehend the truth.

MOONA:
I don't think it likes me.

PIRALLI:
You *did* just accuse it of murder.

MOONA:
Well, I was just looking at the *facts...*

KETH:
(EXASPERATED)

What facts?

Come on, Pee-Three. Let's get you cleaned up at home.

Kradon—put those drinks on my tab.

KRADON:
Kradon already has, my boy. Kradon already has.

FX: Keth and P3-7A leave. Moona empties her glass and puts it back on the bar.

MOONA:
I still don't trust that droid.

FX: Piralli swallows down his drink, too.

PIRALLI:
I know what you mean.

'Nother round?

MOONA:
Don't mind if I do.

CUT TO:

SCENE 30. INT. THE SECOND SPIRE—LOWER FLOOR—THE NEXT DAY

ANNOUNCER:
Time until the battle begins: twenty-nine hours.

ATMOS: The sounds of industry, as Ambassador Tintak is moved into new chambers in the spire. Crates are being moved in by droids, and there are lots of guards milling about.

AMBASSADOR TINTAK:
Are you *certain* it's safe?

AIDA:
Quite certain, Ambassador Tintak. The building has been thoroughly checked and remains structurally sound, despite the . . . um . . . *unfortunate* episode yesterday.

AMBASSADOR TINTAK:
(CHIDING)

That's not what I meant, and you know it.

AIDA:
Nevertheless, you have my assurances. I shall remain by your side until the ceremony has been reconvened and the treaty is signed. And besides, you have . . .

. . . *plenty* of guards.

AMBASSADOR TINTAK:
Well, we can't be too careful, can we?

We still don't know who was responsible for that bomb. Although I certainly have my suspicions.

AIDA:
You do?

AMBASSADOR TINTAK:
Well, I can't prove anything of course—not yet—but one of my people claims to have seen a woman dressed in Eiram military colors speaking with a ceremonial droid before the signing ceremony.

AIDA:
(SURPRISED)

They did? And they'd swear to that?

AMBASSADOR TINTAK:
They would if I ordered them to.

AIDA:
That's not quite the same.

AMBASSADOR TINTAK:
Well, yes—but all the same, it's an eyewitness report. I expect something to be done about it. I'll be speaking to the Republic representatives later today, and recommending we postpone the signing until the matter is resolved.

AIDA:
(THOUGHTFUL)

Of course. Although—don't you think it's a *little* strange?

AMBASSADOR TINTAK:
Strange? What do you mean, strange?

AIDA:

That the bomber would so blatantly wear the uniform of your previously sworn enemy? And allow themselves to be seen in the open.

Why expose themselves like that? Surely, they'd have been better served wearing a disguise, or at least a heavy cloak. It sounds just a little too convenient to me.

AMBASSADOR TINTAK:

Perhaps they didn't expect any of us to survive to tell the tale.

AIDA:

But then they'd be killing their own people in the blast. Don't forget, there were plenty of representatives from Eiram in that room, too. High-ranking officials, at that.

AMBASSADOR TINTAK:

(FLUSTERED)

Collateral damage?

AIDA:

Perhaps. But more likely there's something else going on. Some ploy intended to ensure the treaty falls through, regardless of the bomb's success.

AMBASSADOR TINTAK:

(DUBIOUS)

Hmmm.

AIDA:

Will you trust me?

AMBASSADOR TINTAK:

With what?

AIDA:

Time.

We both know the best thing for both E'ronoh and Eiram—for *all of your people*—is for that treaty to be signed. Hold off doing anything hasty. The ceremony is being rescheduled for tomorrow. Leave it in place.

AMBASSADOR TINTAK:
(UNSURE)

Perhaps . . .

But how can we be assured of our safety? More than anything, I want this thing over with. The treaty signed, and the war ended—for good.

But I can't do it if I'm dead, can I?

AIDA:
As you said—we don't even know who's responsible for the bombing yet. But I know that, even now, there are people out there doing their very best to find out.

Please—let them do their work before we inadvertently unravel all the efforts you've already made toward a peaceful resolution to this war.

AMBASSADOR TINTAK:
(SIGHS)

Very well, Jedi Forte. We shall see it through as planned. For all our sakes.

Just . . . make sure we don't die in the process, won't you?

AIDA:
Thank you, Ambassador. I can assure you—the Jedi and the Guardians of the Whills will do everything in our power to protect you and the other delegates from any harm.

And I promise you—the people responsible for this horror will be brought to justice. But neither will we give them what they want. The peace process will continue.

It *must.*

CUT TO:

SCENE 31. INT. THE SECOND SPIRE—LOWER FLOOR—ELSEWHERE

ATMOS: We're outside Ambassador Cerox's quarters in the Second Spire. The sounds of industry here are more distant, but we can still hear repair work going on.

FX: Footsteps tap loudly as Ambassador Cerox walks along the passageway, accompanied by two guards.

NERVOUS AIDE:
(CALLING OUT)

Ah! Ambassador Cerox. Are you returning to your quarters?

AMBASSADOR CEROX:
(IMPATIENT, SNAPS)

What do *you* think? Would I be here if I wasn't?

(Beat, then MUTTERED)

Honestly . . .

FX: The footsteps come to a halt.

NERVOUS AIDE:
(NERVOUS)

Only that you . . . umm . . . you have a visitor.

AMBASSADOR CEROX:
A visitor? *Now?*

Is it the Jedi?

NERVOUS AIDE:
No. It's . . .

AMBASSADOR CEROX:
(IMPATIENT)

Oh, out of the way!

FX: She taps a code into the control panel, and the door slides open.

NERVOUS AIDE:
. . . Mr. Tilson Graf.

TILSON GRAF:
(AMUSED)

Hello, Ambassador.

AMBASSADOR CEROX:
(SURPRISED)

What are *you* doing here?

TILSON GRAF:
(WITH MOCK HURT)

Now, is that any way to welcome an old friend?

FX: There's a moment of awkward silence.

NERVOUS AIDE:
Um, will you be needing anything else, Ambassador?

AMBASSADOR CEROX:
(SNAPS)

What?

No. Leave us.

NERVOUS AIDE:
(RELIEVED)

Gladly, Your Honor.

FX: The door slides shut.

AMBASSADOR CEROX:
You shouldn't be here.

TILSON GRAF:
On Jedha?

AMBASSADOR CEROX:
Anywhere *near* me.

TILSON GRAF:
Ah, but circumstances have changed somewhat, haven't they? The small issue of a bomb and a dead mediator.

FX: Ambassador Cerox crosses the room. Ice drops into a glass, followed by a glug of liquid as she pours herself a drink from a bottle on a side table.

AMBASSADOR CEROX:
I don't see how that changes anything.

TILSON GRAF:
You don't? Then you're thinking too small, Lian.

It changes *everything*.

And yes, thank you, I will take a drink.

AMBASSADOR CEROX:
I'll ask you again, Tilson: What are you doing here?

TILSON GRAF:
I'm merely a concerned citizen with an interest in the peace process. I wish to play my part.

AMBASSADOR CEROX:
(SIGHS)

FX: Ambassador Cerox pours a second drink. She walks over and hands it to Tilson Graf.

TILSON GRAF:
My thanks.

FX: Ambassador Cerox sits down.

AMBASSADOR CEROX:
All right, Tilson. Tell me what you want . . .

CUT TO:

SCENE 32. INT. JEDHA—TEMPLE OF THE KYBER—CHURCH SECTOR—ENTRANCE HALL

ATMOS: We're inside the massive Temple of the Kyber, in the area assigned to the Church of the Force. The entrance hall is a cavernous space, with polished stone floors, so everyone's footsteps ring out and echo. There's soft singing in the background, coming from elsewhere in the temple structure. It continues throughout the scene.

FX: Silandra's footsteps echo out as she walks into the hall and stops.

PREFECT SAOUS:
Master Jedi!

(Beat, then WARMLY)

Welcome, *welcome*! The Church of the Force is indeed honored to receive such an illustrious visitor.

I am Prefect Resamond Saous. And you are . . . ?

SILANDRA:
Silandra Sho.

PREFECT SAOUS:
Most welcome. Although I fear your visit may prove a little untimely. An incident yesterday has given rise to a great deal of concern among our followers.

SILANDRA:

Yes. That's why I'm here. The Jedi Order wishes to establish the truth of what happened yesterday. We're anxious to protect the peace process and identify the people behind the attack.

PREFECT SAOUS:

Indeed. The San Tekka family are great supporters of our church. Morton's loss is keenly felt by us all.

SILANDRA:

I understand he'd been assigned an aide? An adjunct named Keth Cerapath.

PREFECT SAOUS:

Ah, yes. Poor Keth. I know he blames himself for not being at Morton's side, but the truth is, there was little he could have done. We're just thankful that the Force deemed he should escape harm.

SILANDRA:

May I speak with him?

PREFECT SAOUS:

Of course. Please, wait here and I'll send him along.

And rest assured—the church will do everything in their power to assist with your investigation. I have already promised the San Tekka family that we shall keep them apprised of any developments.

FX: Saous leaves, his footsteps clicking on the stone floor. For a moment, we're accompanied by just the low, melodic song of the distant chanting—and then Keth comes hurrying over.

KETH:

(NERVOUS AND A BIT HUNGOVER)

Um . . . hello. I'm Keth. Keth Cerapath. I understand that you wanted to see me.

SILANDRA:
Hello, Keth.

How are you holding up?

KETH:
What? Oh. I'm fine. Thank you. Yes. Just . . . yesterday was a bit of a shock, and I . . . well . . . I'm not feeling quite myself this morning, is all.

SILANDRA:
(AMUSED AND KNOWING)

I see. I won't keep you. I'm trying to get to the bottom of what happened yesterday at the ceremony. I hoped you might be able to talk me through what you saw.

KETH:
Well, that's just it. I didn't see anything. At least, not until it was too late.

SILANDRA:
What do you mean?

KETH:
(LOWERS VOICE)

The truth is, I overslept. I was late arriving at the spire. Mr. San Tekka had already set up at the podium, ready to give his speech, and he sent me off to fetch a glass of water.

SILANDRA:
And?

KETH:
And the place was crawling with Guardians of the Whills and officials from Eiram and E'ronoh. I went to fetch the water but got waylaid, and I was on my way back down when . . .

SILANDRA:
You heard the explosion.

KETH:

I felt it first. The whole building seemed to slide sideways. I dropped the drink and ran to find Morton, but when I got to the main chamber he was already dead, and two Jedi were lifting the wreckage off him. Everything was on fire.

SILANDRA:

So, you didn't see anything suspicious? No sign of the mysterious droid that was carrying the explosives?

KETH:

(A LITTLE CAGEY)

No. No. Nothing. Nothing like that at all. No unexpected droids.

SILANDRA:

Only, Master Creighton mentioned that your own droid had gone missing during the attack . . .

KETH:

(ANXIOUS)

He did! But he's back now! He turned up last night. Found his way back from the spire.

SILANDRA:

He did?

KETH:

Yes! You can meet him if you like.

Whatever Master Creighton thought, I promise you, neither me or Pee-Three had *anything* to do with it. We wouldn't want to hurt anyone.

SILANDRA:

All right. And you don't remember anything else?

FX: Footsteps as Saous approaches the pair of them.

PREFECT SAOUS:
Keth? Is everything all right?

KETH:
Yes. Just a little shaken. It's all a bit of a blur.

PREFECT SAOUS:
No doubt.

KETH:
I'm sorry. I wish I could do more to help. Morton was a kind man. I feel as though I let him down.

PREFECT SAOUS:
You didn't let anyone down, Keth. The Force willed that you were spared. Take comfort in that.

SILANDRA:
Indeed. Although . . . there *is* something you could do if you're up to it?

KETH:
Well, I . . .

PREFECT SAOUS:
Of course. How can we help, Master Sho?

SILANDRA:
Many of the injured were escorted away by the local sects for treatment. I'd like to speak with them, see if anyone witnessed anything suspicious. But I'm unfamiliar with Jedha.

I could use a guide who knows the streets and the sensitivities of the locals—and who might be able to offer insight into the different religious orders here. If my brief experience in the markets is anything to go by, the Jedi aren't always welcomed with open arms.

Plus, of course, I'd like to meet this droid of yours . . .

FX: Saous claps Keth on the shoulder.

PREFECT SAOUS:
Then Keth is just your man.

KETH:
But my duties here . . .

PREFECT SAOUS:
Have already been waived. You must assist Master Sho in any
way she requires, for the duration of her investigation.

KETH:
Of course.

(Beat, then MORE EMPHATICALLY)

Of course.

SILANDRA:
My thanks. Then we'll start with the Path of the Open Hand.
I saw some of their members at the medical station yesterday.
Do you know where they're based?

KETH:
In the old healing house on the far side of the market.

SILANDRA:
Excellent. Then we'll be on our way.

KETH:
What, now?

SILANDRA:
There's no time like the present.

Thank you, Prefect Saous.

PREFECT SAOUS:
May the Force be with you, Master Sho.

And you, Keth.

CUT TO:

SCENE 33. INT. THE SECOND SPIRE—LOWER AUDIENCE CHAMBER

ATMOS: It's quiet in this chamber in the lower spire, aside from the ever-present ringing of distant bells and some banging from above, where repair work is being carried out on the spire.

CHAIRPERSON MELDAN:
The chair of the Republic committee on Jedha now recognizes representatives of the Path of the Open Hand.

THE MOTHER:
Thank you, Chairperson Meldan.

CHAIRPERSON MELDAN:
And you are ...?

THE MOTHER:
The Mother will suffice.

MARDA:
And I am Marda Ro.

CHAIRPERSON MELDAN:
(WARILY)

Yes. The Path of the Open Hand. We're *aware* of your activities here on Jedha.

THE MOTHER:
Then you know of our house of healing, and the work we are doing to support the poor and infirm.

CHAIRPERSON MELDAN:
Well, yes . . .

THE MOTHER:
And just yesterday, in the aftermath of that terrible accident, our disciples were among the first on the scene to administer aid. Even now, several of the injured remain in our care.

CHAIRPERSON MELDAN:
Quite so, but I was . . .

THE MOTHER:
. . . referring to our peaceful processions, yes. I understand. But please be clear, the emphasis is steadfastly on *peaceful.*

MARDA:
We believe that the living Force should be free. That there is danger in its continued manipulation.

CHAIRPERSON MELDAN:
Quite a challenging belief to bring to Jedha.

THE MOTHER:
Where better to test our faith and make the greatest difference to those who might heed our word?

MARDA:
We are here to petition the Convocation for a seat at their table. To help steer the future of the Force.

CHAIRPERSON MELDAN:
And now you come to petition the Republic, too.

THE MOTHER:
We come to graciously offer our services.

CHAIRPERSON MELDAN:
In what capacity?

THE MOTHER:
There is one among us by the name of Elder Delwin. We propose that he be considered for the role of mediator to help oversee the restoration of the peace process between Eiram and E'ronoh.

CHAIRPERSON MELDAN:
I see. But we—

MARDA:
(INTERRUPTING)

We understand that the Republic must remain impartial in this process, lest they be accused of interfering to promote their own interests in the region.

CHAIRPERSON MELDAN:
Well . . .

MARDA:
And that the Jedi who have so far assisted in the negotiations also wish to remain outside of the process, so as not to be seen to take sides.

CHAIRPERSON MELDAN:
That *is* true.

MARDA:
Then you require a truly impartial mediator. Someone whose perspective is not colored by the wants and desires of their people. Whose only goal is to help find peace and establish balance. To help everything find its *level.*

We can offer you that perspective. That person.

THE MOTHER:
We seek no gain. We wish only to help, in our humble way. Consider this a gift given freely.

FX: A murmur ripples through the panel. It doesn't sound positive.

CHAIRPERSON MELDAN:
We thank you for your kind offer.

(Beat, then FIRM)

But I'm afraid we cannot support your proposal for a member of the Path of the Open Hand to be instated as the new mediator at this time.

MARDA:
(CONFUSED)

But—

THE MOTHER:
(CUTTING HER OFF)

Of course. We understand, and we thank you for your time.

CUT TO:

SCENE 34. INT. FORMAL GARDENS CLOSE TO THE SECOND SPIRE—SOON AFTER

ATMOS: Birds twitter happily. A breeze ruffles the leaves of a tree. Droids move about, tending plants. Water bubbles.

FX: Ambassador Cerox and Creighton walk as they talk, their feet crunching lightly on a gravel path.

AMBASSADOR CEROX:
Who'd have thought?

CREIGHTON:
Ambassador Cerox?

AMBASSADOR CEROX:
A garden like this could exist on a cold, dry world like Jedha.

CREIGHTON:
It's remarkable, isn't it? I believe it's maintained by the Church of the Force—a place of quiet contemplation, away from the bustle and clamor of the Holy City. A haven of solitude and peace.

AMBASSADOR CEROX:
The perfect spot for a walk.

CREIGHTON:
How are you? I imagine the events of yesterday were something of a shock.

AMBASSADOR CEROX:
You forget, Master Sun—my home has been a place of war for five long years. Sadly, I've grown used to the rhythms of battle and bombs. Of always looking over one shoulder in case someone is waiting in the shadows to make an attempt on my life.

CREIGHTON:
I'm sorry. No one should have to live like that. It's why it's so important that the peace treaty still goes ahead.

AMBASSADOR CEROX:
(LAUGHS KNOWINGLY)

And here I was thinking this was a social call.

CREIGHTON:
I *am* concerned for your well-being, Ambassador. But surely you see the need to push forward with the signing? Now more than ever.

AMBASSADOR CEROX:
You think I'd back down because someone tried to kill me? No, Master Sun. That only makes me more determined.

CREIGHTON:
I'm pleased to hear it.

FX: They walk for a moment.

AMBASSADOR CEROX:
I take it you've heard the murmurings amongst my people.

CREIGHTON:
They're blaming E'ronoh for the attack.

AMBASSADOR CEROX:

To be expected. Two of them even claim to have seen a woman in E'ronoh military attire speaking with a droid before the explosion.

CREIGHTON:

Do you believe the accusations carry any weight?

AMBASSADOR CEROX:

I believe there are a lot of very tense, angry, sorrowful people on both sides of this war, Creighton.

If it was E'ronoh trying to stop us from signing, then surely our best counter is to make certain the treaty *does* get signed.

CREIGHTON:

An admirable sentiment. I couldn't agree more.

AMBASSADOR CEROX:

Then you think E'ronoh *were* responsible for the attack?

CREIGHTON:

I don't know what to think. Not yet. But something tells me there's more to what's going on here than seems obvious at first glance.

Tell me, have you been able to reach the heirs, to apprise them of the situation? I tried to contact them, but the communication problems have made it impossible.

AMBASSADOR CEROX:

We're encountering the same problems. I'm afraid, for the time being, we're on our own.

CREIGHTON:

Then we have no choice but to press ahead.

AMBASSADOR CEROX:

Indeed. The sooner we get things over and done with the better. Not everyone feels the way the heirs do. We all of us lost loved ones in this war. Not everyone is so willing to forgive and forget. If someone gives them an excuse to pull the trigger . . .

CREIGHTON:
You think we're at risk of seeing the conflict break out again?

AMBASSADOR CEROX:
I think the sooner we can all get back to the reason we're here, the better . . .

CUT TO:

SCENE 35. EXT. JEDHA MARKETS

ATMOS: As previous, but busier. The place is bustling with people. Vendors are shouting to sell their wares, and preparations are continuing for the Festival of Balance, with stalls being erected, crates being transported, et cetera.

FX: The thud of a huge beast of burden plowing through the busy street. People cursing as they hustle out of its way. The whir of P3-7A's thrusters.

SILANDRA:
Mind your step, Keth.

KETH:
What? I . . .

FX: The thud of a massive footstep close by.

KETH:
Whoa!

FX: Silandra grabs him and pulls him back out of the way as the creature stomps past.

P3-7A:
The path of the Force is clear and unobstructed. Those who stray from its course will often find themselves lost.

KETH:
Be quiet, Pee-Three.

And, umm, thanks, Master Sho.

SILANDRA:
You're welcome.

What *was* that thing?

KETH:
I have *no* idea.

It's busier than usual down here. People are preparing for the coming celebrations.

SILANDRA:
(CONFUSED AND THEN REALIZING)

The celebra—ah! I almost forgot, what with the bombing yesterday.

The Festival of Balance.

KETH:
I know the Convocation are promoting it as a celebration to help bring everyone together from all the different sects and religions, but to me it just looks like an excuse for a massive party.

SILANDRA:
(LAUGHS)

And what else is a party but a chance to bring people together?

KETH:
It doesn't bother you that it's taking place during the Season of Light? I know there were elders amongst the disciples of the Whills who were unhappy with the decision.

SILANDRA:
The Season of Light is a time of spiritual reflection. A time to look inward to consider one's place within the galaxy. The Fes-

tival of Balance, as I understand it, is an opportunity to recognize others and *their* place in the Force.

I see no reason why the two things are mutually exclusive.

KETH:
That's a remarkably clear perspective. I hadn't thought of it like that.

P3-7A:
Those who seek fulfillment in the Force must first seek fulfillment in themselves.

KETH:
Yes, thank you, Pee-Three.

SILANDRA:
(AMUSED)

You were right about Pee-Three. He is a little ... *unusual* for a church droid, isn't he?

FX: P3-7A makes a disconcerted bleep.

KETH:
He's not a church droid. Not really. I saved him from scrap and paid some Bonbraks to install some manipulator arms and the head and vocoder from an old processional droid that the church had decommissioned.

SILANDRA:
Ahhh. So now—

KETH:
—he can only speak in epithets derived from the processional droid's limited vocabulator, yeah.

SILANDRA:
(SNIGGERING)

That must be ... frustrating for him.

KETH:

For *him?* Try living with him.

P3-7A:

The Force knows all. The Force hears all. Be mindful, for there can be no secrets from the Force.

SILANDRA:

(LAUGHS)

I think he has the measure of you, Keth.

KETH:

And *I* think he needs to remember the Bonbraks would be only too pleased to take him back . . .

FX: They walk on for a moment.

SILANDRA:

Does the church have much to do with the other sects here on Jedha?

KETH:

Of course. We have a representative on the Convocation. We believe in bringing all Force rel—

FX: Keth is cut off by a huge bang, originating elsewhere in the market.

KETH:

What?

SILANDRA:

Another bomb.

FX: Silandra's shield flares to life, rippling with energy. People around them are screaming and running for cover.

KETH:

That's a . . .

SILANDRA:
A shield, yes. Now, come on!

FX: Silandra runs. Keth starts after her.

KETH:
(CALLING BACK AS HE RUNS)

Come on, Pee-Three!

P3-7A:
Haste is the precursor to error in all things.

CUT TO:

SCENE 36. EXT. JEDHA STREET—MOMENTS LATER

ATMOS: People are running scared. It's chaos. Screaming echoes through the streets.

FX: Silandra and Keth come hurtling through the mass of fleeing people.

SILANDRA:
Where? Where is it?

KETH:
Over there! There's a thin column of smoke.

SILANDRA:
(CALLING)

Move back, please. Get to safety.

FX: There's another massive boom.

SILANDRA:
(SHOUTING)

Down!

FX: People drop to the ground. More screaming. And then:

CANTANKEROUS CIVILIAN:
(SHOUTING)

It's all right! It's all right!

SILANDRA:
Here.

FX: Silandra helps Keth up.

KETH:
Thanks. What's going on?

SILANDRA:
Let's find out.

FX: They push farther through the crowd.

KETH:
I don't believe it. It's just—

SILANDRA:
(RELIEVED)

—a backfiring speeder.

FX: Silandra powers off her shield.

KETH:
I guess the bomb yesterday has everyone on edge.

SILANDRA:
Hmmm. Something's not right.

Who are those people with the speeder? Do you recognize them?

KETH:
Yes. Members of a sect known as the Brothers of the Ninth Door. You can tell by the bone masks they wear. It's said they fashion them from the skulls of their own dead.

SILANDRA:
Pleasant. They have a following on Jedha?

KETH:
Yes. A small one. They must have a temple or lodge somewhere, but I don't know, exactly. You see them around the markets sometimes.

SILANDRA:
Preaching, like the Path of the Open Hand?

KETH:
No. They're nothing like the Path of the Open Hand. They generally keep to themselves. Or at least, no one seems to want to talk to *them.*

They have a bit of a . . . *dubious* reputation. I've heard it said that they have a tendency toward the dark side of the Force.

SILANDRA:
That doesn't make them villains. Misguided, perhaps . . . and driven by their emotions and fears.

KETH:
All I know is that it's best to give them a wide berth.

SILANDRA:
Hmmm. Were they present at the peace conference yesterday?

KETH:
No. I'd have noticed.

SILANDRA:
Very well. Stay behind me.

KETH:
Oh . . .

Oh, okay.

FX: Silandra walks over to where three members of the sect are tinkering with the speeder.

SILANDRA:
(PLEASANTLY)

Do you three need some help with that?

FX: The brothers continue to hammer and tinker with the speeder, ignoring Silandra.

SILANDRA:
(STILL PLEASANT AND CALM)

Your engine misfire scared people just now. Do you require any assistance getting it fixed?

FX: When Mytion and the other brothers speak, it is with a strange, unnerving triple-layered voice.

MYTION:
We require nothing from a Jedi.

SILANDRA:
Ah. That's a shame. I'm rather handy when it comes to misaligned intake regulators.

INOKE:
Misaligned . . .

FX: A metal-on-metal bang as he knocks the regulator back into place.

INOKE:
Try it.

FX: The speeder fires up normally.

SILANDRA:
There, now.

MYTION:
You're always so damn smug, you Jedi. It doesn't mean anything, you know, just because you guessed what was wrong with our speeder.

SILANDRA:

It means no more people will be scared by a misfiring engine today.

MYTION:

I suppose it does.

FX: The speeder engine revs, and the brothers speed off into the streets.

KETH:

I think they liked you.

SILANDRA:

Yes. I seem to be having that effect wherever I go on Jedha.

P3-7A:

Blessed and loved are those who acknowledge their own insignificance against the immensity of the Force.

KETH:

Oh, caught up finally, did you, Pee-Three?

TILSON GRAF:
(CALLING AS HE APPROACHES)

Silandra?

FX: Tilson Graf comes hurrying over.

SILANDRA:

Mr. Graf.

Tilson.

TILSON GRAF:
(CONCERNED)

I was in the markets when I heard the explosions and headed this way. Is everything okay? Not another terrorist attack, surely?

SILANDRA:

No. Thankfully. Just a misfiring speeder.

TILSON GRAF:
(RELIEVED)

Ah. That's a relief.

I was in the galleries at the ceremony yesterday when the bomb detonated. My ears are still ringing.

SILANDRA:
I'm glad you're okay.

TILSON GRAF:
I must admit, I've never been so terrified in my life.

Puts a different complexion on the trip, certainly.

(TO SILANDRA)

I daresay your time on Jedha so far has been a little more eventful than you'd planned, no?

SILANDRA:
You might say that.

TILSON GRAF:
Well, my offer for dinner stands . . .

SILANDRA:
Thank you, but I should be going. Come along, Keth.

Tilson, try to stay out of trouble, won't you?

TILSON GRAF:
Alas, trouble seems to be my middle name.

CUT TO:

SCENE 37. EXT. APPROACHING THE PATH'S ALMSHOUSE—SOON AFTER

ATMOS: The streets here are quieter, but we can hear someone rinsing and scrubbing clothes in a barrel.

KETH:
(WRYLY)

Well, it seems not *everyone* on Jedha has taken against you. That Graf fellow seemed more than happy to see you.

SILANDRA:
Hmmm.

You're sure we're in the right place?

KETH:
Yeah. The Path of the Open Hand purchased this almshouse recently. They've opened the doors to anyone who's in need of food and shelter.

SILANDRA:
A worthy cause. Then this must be where they brought the injured people they were helping yesterday.

FX: Silandra walks up to the person doing washing.

SILANDRA:
(TO PATH DISCIPLE)

Hello. My name is Silandra Sho. I'm here to speak with the people who were injured in yesterday's attack at the peace conference. I understand some of them were brought here to be looked after.

PELA:
(WITH DISTASTE)

Those who abuse the Force are not welcome here.

SILANDRA:
(SIGHS)

Please. I only wish to speak with the witnesses. I'm investigating what happened and—

FX: Footsteps sound as another person—the Herald—walks over.

PELA:
(CUTTING HER OFF)

I said you weren't welcome, *Jedi.*

HERALD:
Now, now, Pela. We must be mindful of our tempers. The Jedi and her friend do not mean us any harm, no matter how misguided their beliefs might be.

SILANDRA:
And you are?

HERALD:
I speak for the people of the Path. They call me their Herald.

SILANDRA:
I am—

HERALD:
I heard.

SILANDRA:

And this is Keth Cerapath, an adjunct with the Church of the Force.

HERALD:

(MAKES DISSMISSIVE SOUND)

SILANDRA:

I understood your doors were open to all in need.

HERALD:

And you're in need?

SILANDRA:

In need of answers. I've come to speak to the people in your care.

HERALD:

Of course. They're inside. We have nothing to hide.

Come—this way.

CUT TO:

SCENE 38. INT. PATH'S ALMSHOUSE—CONTINUOUS

ATMOS: As before.

FX: The Herald leads them through a series of rooms, past where the food is being prepared and into another chamber with a crackling fire. He stops.

HERALD:
Here. Our three guests. As you can see, they've been treated well.

SILANDRA:
I didn't doubt it.

(TO INJURED PEOPLE)

Hello. How are you?

WOUNDED FEMALE TWI'LEK:
As the Herald said, we've been well looked after. The people here—the disciples of the Path—they were the first on the scene after the explosion.

WOUNDED MALE HUMAN:
They brought us here, tended our wounds, provided food and water. We're very grateful.

KETH:

We're glad to hear it. We should be able to reunite you with your people very soon. The Guardians of the Whills are working hard to ensure everyone's safety.

WOUNDED EIRAM COUNCILOR:

What *happened*? One minute we were in the stalls, listening to the mediator give his welcome speech—the next everything was on fire.

SILANDRA:

Someone deliberately sabotaged the signing of the peace treaty. There was a droid, packed with explosives . . .

WOUNDED FEMALE TWI'LEK:

Yes! I saw a droid. A ceremonial droid. It was hovering just below Morton San Tekka's pedestal. But . . .

SILANDRA:

Go on . . .

WOUNDED FEMALE TWI'LEK:

But I saw the same droid with a *Jedi* earlier, in the lobby . . .

KETH:

A *Jedi*?

WOUNDED MALE HUMAN:

No. You're wrong. That wasn't a Jedi. It was a *Lew'elan*.

WOUNDED FEMALE TWI'LEK:

No, it was a Jedi. I'm certain of it.

KETH:

Every person seems to have a different report. Someone from Eiram, someone from E'ronoh, a Jedi, a Lew'elan . . .

HERALD:
(AMUSED)

It seems your saboteur wears many faces.

But none of them are to be found here. Now, if you're quite finished?

SILANDRA:
We're finished.

(TO INJURED PEOPLE)

Thank you. You've been most helpful. May the Force be with you.

HERALD:
The Force *will* be free.

SILANDRA:
We'll see ourselves out.

HERALD:
No, no. I'll show you the way.

I *insist.*

SILANDRA:
Very well.

FX: They leave.

SCENE 39. INT. THE SECOND SPIRE—LOWER AUDIENCE CHAMBER

ATMOS: As previously. It's quiet, with just the low background ringing of bells and the distant sounds of repairs.

FX: In the distance, walking past outside, we hear the Path of the Open Hand carrying out another procession, with shouting:

PATH DISCIPLES:
(IN BACKGROUND)

The Force will be free! The Force will be free!

FX: There's a ripple of murmuring amongst the gathered members of the Republic panel that sits in session in this room.

TILSON GRAF:
(CLEARS THROAT)

If I may begin . . . ?

FX: The murmuring stops.

CHAIRPERSON MELDAN:
(A LITTLE HAUGHTY)

The chair of the Republic committee on Jedha now recognizes Tilson Graf.

Please, state your business, Mr. Graf. The only reason this panel has agreed to grant you audience at all is because of your family's . . . *connections.*

We *are* in the midst of crisis here.

TILSON GRAF:
It is the crisis I am here to speak with you about.

CHAIRPERSON MELDAN:
Well?

TILSON GRAF:
Given the sad loss of Mediator San Tekka in the accident yesterday, I thought it only proper to volunteer myself to stand in his stead.

I understand the peace conference cannot continue without a replacement. I hereby formally offer my services.

(Beat, then GREGARIOUSLY)

Free of charge, of course.

FX: Another ripple of low-level murmuring passes through the panel of Republic representatives. Nothing clear enough to discern.

CHAIRPERSON MELDAN:
And what makes you, Mr. Graf, believe yourself suitable for such a position?

TILSON GRAF:
You said it yourself, Chairperson Meldan—my family is well connected and well respected. Our prospecting business is equal to that of only the San Tekkas, and we remain impartial regarding the outcome of this terrible war.

CHAIRPERSON MELDAN:
I said no such thing. I said your family had *connections.*

TILSON GRAF:
Indeed. There you are, then.

CHAIRPERSON MELDAN:
(LEVELLY)

And yet there is also your family's *reputation* to consider. Is it not true that your cousins were recently sanctioned by the Senate for failing to declare newly discovered hyperspace routes that, if disclosed, might have prevented an emergency from killing thousands on the moon of Grast?

TILSON GRAF:
You wound me, Chairperson, and you wound the good name of the Grafs.

While it is true that some outlying members of my clan have demonstrated the occasional propensity for . . . *poor judgment,* surely it is unfair to tar us *all* with the same brush?

The Grafs have done a great deal of *good* for the galaxy, too. Surely that far outweighs the misdemeanors of a couple of rogues?

What other options do you have? The treaty must be signed tomorrow before relations between the two hostile parties break down for good. There is no time to send for another San Tekka, who will all be in mourning for their lost kin. Surely, you cannot be considering deputizing one of the small sects or partisan religious orders on Jedha to oversee such a delicate situation.

I am here, I am capable, and I am ready.

CHAIRPERSON MELDAN:
Hmmm.

Your willingness to assist us in this time of need *does* reflect well. And, as you so ably point out, we do find ourselves in desperate need.

What do you hope to gain from this, Mr. Graf?

TILSON GRAF:
(SENSING TRIUMPH)

Peace, Chairperson Meldan. An end to the war that's been a thorn in the side of the Outer Rim ever since it began. The cessation of hostilities and needless death.

Is that not enough?

FX: There's more muttering from amongst the gathered panel, with only the distant chanting of the Path of the Open Hand audible in the background.

PATH DISCIPLES:
(IN BACKGROUND)

The Force will be free! The Force will be free!

TILSON GRAF:
If it were to aid you in your decision, I do have the following endorsement, from Ambassador Cerox of Eiram, no less.

FX: Tilson places a small holoprojector on the desk before the Republic panel.

TILSON GRAF:
She sends her apologies that she could not be here in person, but then she is rather busy . . .

FX: Tilson presses a button. The holo begins to play.

AMBASSADOR CEROX:
(VIA HOLORECORDING)

I have no hesitation in recommending Mr. Tilson Graf be appointed as interim mediator to oversee the final signing of the Eiram-E'ronoh peace treaty, following the appalling death of Morton San Tekka.

I have every reason to believe Mr. Graf to be of sound mind and reputation, and while we of Eiram have, in the past, had some small business dealings with Mr. Graf, he has more than demonstrated his wholehearted impartiality to our current situation.

Indeed, I have conferenced with my learned and honorable colleague Ambassador Tintak from E'ronoh, and he, too, is pleased to lend his unequivocal support to Mr. Graf's most generous proposal. I speak for us both in this matter.

Knowing Chancellor Mollo as I do, and aware of the communication issues currently plaguing the Eiram-E'ronoh sector and preventing the ready transmission of messages, I feel confident that the chancellor would champion the appointment of Mr. Graf in Mr. San Tekka's stead, to serve as an impartial mediator representing another of the great families of the frontier.

I therefore conclude Mr. Graf would be a most fitting mediator, and urge you to consider his appointment promptly, so that the signing may continue, and the treaty be finalized forthwith.

FX: The holorecording ends.

CHAIRPERSON MELDAN:
Thank you, Mr. Graf, for that most surprising testimony.

If you would give us a moment.

FX: The panel returns to murmuring in inaudible whispers. After a few moments, they stop.

TILSON GRAF:
You've come to a decision?

CHAIRPERSON MELDAN:
We have.

Given the pressing situation and the communication issues preventing us from conferring with Chancellor Mollo, I am forced to act in his stead. I am pleased to say that the Republic gratefully accepts your offer, Mr. Graf.

The role of mediator is yours.

TILSON GRAF:
(WITH SATISFACTION)

A wise decision. I thank you all. The Grafs shall not let you down.

CUT TO:

SCENE 40. INT. PATH'S ALMSHOUSE—MOTHER'S CHAMBERS

ATMOS: The fire still crackles, but the Mother is alone, except for...

FX: The Leveler, close by, makes a lizardlike purring sound.

THE MOTHER:
(WITH FONDNESS, BUT WEARY)
There, there.

Yes. The time approaches.

FX: The Leveler makes another contented sound.

THE MOTHER:
I know. I understand. You're unsettled. But rest assured, I have everything under control, my love.

Everything.

FX: The Leveler screeches, like a carrion bird.

THE MOTHER:
Yes, yes. The Herald grows discontented with his lot. I can see the ambition in his eyes, the tightness around his mouth when he speaks. He tries to hide his hatred, but it is like a fire that burns deep within, fueling his every word.

He thinks not of the Path, but of himself. He dreams of usurpation.

He is a fool.

But his time, too, will come.

FX: The Leveler issues a chirp, almost as if agreeing with her.

THE MOTHER:
Not yet, though. Not yet.

Time is on our side. The Force guides our hand.

The Herald still has a part to play.

FX: The Leveler gives a final, lizardlike growl and pads off, leaving the Mother alone by the fire.

THE MOTHER:
And he shall play it well.

CUT TO:

SCENE 41. INT. THE SECOND SPIRE—PASSAGE TO PRIVATE CHAMBERS

ATMOS: We can hear the distant banging of the repair work still going on.

FX: Creighton and Ambassador Cerox are walking down the passage side by side. They stop.

AMBASSADOR CEROX:
Well, Master Jedi. Your company has been, once again, enlightening. I now intend to retire for a long, relaxing soak. Thank the Force there's no parties or receptions to worry about this evening.

CREIGHTON:
(WITH FEELING)

I hear you there, Ambassador Cerox.

AMBASSADOR CEROX:
(A LITTLE SHEEPISH)

Unless you'd like to come in for a drink . . . ?

CREIGHTON:
(AWKWARD)

No . . . I . . . Thank you all the same. I have duties to see to.

AMBASSADOR CEROX:
(KNOWING)

Duties. Yes. Of course.

Well, I shan't keep you any longer.

FX: There's a series of beeps as Ambassador Cerox begins to key in a code to the lock.

CREIGHTON:
(SUDDEN, STARTLED)

No. Wait! Don't open that!

AMBASSADOR CEROX:
Wha—

FX: The door slides open and . . . there's a tremendous boom!

END OF PART TWO

Part Three
UNBALANCED

SCENE 42. INT. THE SECOND SPIRE—PASSAGE TO PRIVATE CHAMBERS

FX: We recap the boom from the end of the previous episode.

AMBASSADOR CEROX:
(UNGH)

FX: Ambassador Cerox is thrown back along the passageway, colliding with the wall. There's the sickening crunch of a bone breaking, and a gasp of pain.

AMBASSADOR CEROX:
(GASPS IN PAIN)

ATMOS: The aftereffects of the explosion in the doorway can be heard in the background—fire, collapsing bits of masonry, and a dull alarm, bleeping urgently.

FX: Footsteps run closer.

CREIGHTON:
(ALL BUSINESS NOW)

Ambassador Cerox?

AMBASSADOR CEROX:
(SHAKEN)

I'll live. Thanks to you.

CREIGHTON:
I'm sorry. I had no choice. If I hadn't thrown you out of the way of the blast . . .

AMBASSADOR CEROX:
(WINCING)

. . . I'd be dead now. I know. As it is, I just have a mangled arm and a badly torn dress.

CREIGHTON:
Let me see.

FX: There's a beat while Creighton examines her arm.

CREIGHTON:
We need to get you help right away.

AMBASSADOR CEROX:
(WOOZILY)

The refectory . . . Medical station . . . still . . .

FX: Creighton stoops down and picks her up.

CREIGHTON:
(GRUNTS)

Stay with me, Lian.

FX: Multiple sets of footsteps come running.

SELIK:
Master Sun!

CREIGHTON:
Selik. Thank the Light. There's been another attack.

SELIK:
The ambassador?

CREIGHTON:
She's hurt, but she'll live. I need to get her to the medical station.

SELIK:
We'll secure the scene. Barruk, Jance—go with him. Watch his back.

CREIGHTON:
Thank you. And Selik—inform her people. Immediately. From this point on, she goes *nowhere* without a full escort. Even with me.

SELIK:
Understood. Force be with you.

FX: Creighton hurries off with Ambassador Cerox.

CUT TO:

SCENE 43. EXT. JEDHA MARKETS—ELSEWHERE—CONTINUOUS

ANNOUNCER:
Time until the battle begins: eighteen hours.

ATMOS: The markets are bustling as the festival preparations continue to take over the city. Music plays. People cheer. Meat roasts on spits. Animals chirp and squeal. There's the constant murmur of crowds.

FX: People are unloading crates from a vehicle. The crates contain quiet creatures. These are wargarans—large wolflike creatures that appear friendly and harmless.

MYLAS:
Aww! Look at the animals!

FX: The wargarans make docile, whimpering noises. They sound cute.

MARDA:
Mylas! Don't get too close!

MYLAS:
But they look so *cute!*

MARDA:
And *huge* . . .

NADDIE:
Can I look, too, Marda?

MARDA:
Yes, go on then, Naddie. But remember what I said to Mylas. They may look friendly, but they might bite.

MYLAS:
(TO ONE OF THE MEN UNLOADING CRATES)

What are they?

WARGARAN KEEPER:
They're wargarans.

And you should listen to your friend there. They may seem sleepy and friendly when they're in their crates, but wargarans are hunters.

FX: The wargarans whimper again. They don't sound like hunters at all.

NADDIE:
(UNCONVINCED)

Hunters!

WARGARAN KEEPER:
Predators. And clever ones, too. They hunt in packs—never more than three—feeling out their prey through the murmurations they leave in the Force.

MYLAS:
(SCANDALIZED)

They hunt with the *Force.* You mean . . . are they like *Jedi*?

MARDA:
No, Mylas. It's different. These creatures don't manipulate the Force for their own ends. What they do is perfectly natural. They're just attuned to the ripples that all of us leave in the Force. They can feel it.

WARGARAN KEEPER:
That's right.

MYLAS:
Do they *eat* the Force?

WARGARAN KEEPER:
(LAUGHS)

Eat the Force! No, they eat *meat,* like most other animals. They just use the Force to help them catch it.

NADDIE:
But why bring them here?

WARGARAN KEEPER:
For the festival, of course! People love to see animals, don't they? And the wargarans are rarer than most.

NADDIE:
And you're locking them up in that . . . *warehouse*? It looks dark and miserable.

WARGARAN KEEPER:
Only until the festival is up and running.

And listen—don't you go worrying about the wargarans, kid. They can look after themselves.

They're kept under lock and key. But they'll be well rewarded after the festival.

MARDA:
All right, both of you. I think you've seen enough. Let's get back to the others.

(TO WARGARAN KEEPER)

Thank you.

WARGARAN KEEPER:
Enjoy the festival now, won't you?

MARDA:
The Force will be free.

FX: Marda, Mylas, and Naddie leave, walking away into the bustling market. It's busier than ever as preparations are finalized for the coming festival.

NADDIE:
Oh, Marda! Marda! I've left my flowers.

MARDA:
Where?

NADDIE:
Back there, by the warehouse. I put them down while we were looking at the animals.

MARDA:
(SIGHS)

All right. We'll wait here while you run back and fetch them. But be *quick*!

NADDIE:
I will!

FX: Naddie hurries off. We stay with her as she darts through the bustling crowds.

EXUBERANT TIP-YIP TRADER:
(DISTANT)

Roasted tip-yip! Roasted tip-yip!

FX: Naddie approaches the warehouse again but hangs back. We can hear the wargarans whimpering pathetically as before.

WARGARAN KEEPER:
(MEAN)

Quiet! You mangy runts. I'm starting to wish I'd never brought you here. You'd better earn your keep tomorrow.

EXUBERANT TIP-YIP TRADER:
(DISTANT)

Roasted tip-yip! Roasted tip-yip!

FX: The wargaran keeper closes the door to the warehouse.

WARGARAN KEEPER:
(WALKING AWAY)

Here! I'll take some roasted tip-yip.

FX: He walks away, footsteps fading into the background hubbub of the crowd. After a moment, Naddie's smaller footsteps creep closer. She slowly opens the warehouse door with a creak. The wargarans whimper again.

NADDIE:
(WARMLY)

Shhh! Quiet now. Quiet. It's all right.

FX: More whimpering.

NADDIE:
You're so cute! You don't like being in those crates, do you?

No, you don't. Now, just give me a moment to find a rock . . .

There. That should do it. Stand back while I try to smash this lock, okay?

FX: Naddie starts to smash a lock on the crate. After a few attempts, it breaks and drops to the floor.

NADDIE:
There!

Marda said you're part of the Force, like everyone else. That you weren't like the Jedi.

And if the Force will be free, I think you should be, too.

Now, one more to go . . .

FX: Naddie smashes another lock. It falls free and the crate door swings open. The wargarans come charging out. They start to howl.

NADDIE:
Go! Go! Shoo! Get away while you can!

FX: More howling as the wargarans charge off into the crowds. People start screaming. One of the wargaran growls viciously.

NADDIE:
No. No! I'm your friend, remember. Don't growl like that.

FX: The wargaran growls again, threateningly.

NADDIE:
But . . . but . . .

FX: Naddie runs.

NADDIE:
(DESPERATE, TERRIFIED)

Marda!

Marda!

FX: The wargaran howls as it thunders after Naddie. People scream.

NADDIE:
(SCREAMING)

Marda!

MARDA:
(ANXIOUS, CALLING)

Naddie! What is it? What's—

FX: Naddie comes running, feet pounding. The wargaran roars.

MYLAS:
(TERRIFIED)

Naddie! It's right behind you!

FX: Naddie throws herself down. The wargaran leaps.

SCARED NUT SELLER:
(TERRIFIED)

Take cover! Take cover!

MYLAS:
(TERRIFIED)

Arrghhhh!

MARDA:
(URGENT)

Mylas! *Run!* Head for the almshouse!

MYLAS:
But . . .

MARDA:
Just go!

FX: Mylas runs off into the crowd. The wargaran issues a low, ominous growl of warning.

NADDIE:
(SCARED)

No!

Get back!

MARDA:
(ANXIOUS)

Naddie!

FX: The wargaran howls as it pounces for Naddie.

NADDIE:
(SCREAMS)

FX: There's a thud as the wargaran knocks Naddie to the ground.

MARDA:
(DETERMINED)

No!

Here! Give me that!

SCARED NUT SELLER:
(TERRIFIED)

But . . . but . . .

MARDA:
(HURRIED)

Just give me the electroprod!

SCARED NUT SELLER:
Here! *Here!*

FX: The wargaran growls savagely.

NADDIE:
Marda!

FX: The wargaran savages Naddie.

NADDIE:
(PAINED SCREAM)

FX: Marda's electroprod sparks noisily.

MARDA:
(ANGRY, DEFIANT YELL)

Leave her be!

FX: Marda rushes over and thrusts the electroprod into the side of the wargaran's neck. The wargaran howls in pain, then snorts and pads away from Naddie, following Marda as she edges back. Close by, Naddie whimpers.

NADDIE:
(WHIMPERS)

MARDA:
(DEFIANT)

That's right! Follow me.

FX: The wargaran matches her slow steps, growling.

MARDA:
Yes. Over here. That's right . . .

FX: The wargaran leaps. Marda grunts as she lurches, pulling the nut seller's stall down on top of the wargaran. There's an almighty clatter, the sizzle of spilled hot coals, and a thud as the wargaran is struck by the stall's beams and knocked to the ground. It mewls pitifully.

MARDA:
(GRUNTS)

SCARED NUT SELLER:
My stall!

MARDA:
Naddie!

FX: Marda runs to Naddie's side. Naddie groans.

NADDIE:
(GROANS)

MARDA:
Force be with me. The *blood.*

NADDIE:
(FAINT)

Marda?

FX: Marda scoops Naddie up into her arms.

MARDA:
(THROUGH TEARS)

Oh, your poor face . . .

It's all right, Naddie. You're going to be all right. I'll get you back to the almshouse. They'll know what to do.

FX: They hurry off.

SCARED NUT SELLER:
(CALLING AFTER THEM)

What about my stall!

CUT TO:

SCENE 44. EXT. JEDHA MARKETS—EVENING

ATMOS: As per the previous scene.

BORED MEAT TRADER:
Spit roast tip-yip! Seared Spiridian lizards! Crunchy Batuuan spider-roach!

FX: Someone screams.

THEELIN PILGRIM:
(HORRIFIED)

What *is* that thing?

FX: There's a low, animal growl. Menacing. It's a wargaran, loose now and a lot less friendly.

TERRIFIED PANTORAN CIVILIAN:
Get back! Get back!

FX: More growling, now coming from multiple directions at once.

THEELIN PILGRIM:
By the Light! There's more of them.

HUMAN FEMALE CIVILIAN:
Run! *Run!*

FX: People scatter. We follow the pilgrims as they run, panting.

THEELIN PILGRIM:
Out of the way! *Move!*

FX: They barge past people in the crowds, who exclaim in annoyance. We can hear laughter trilling from people who don't know what's happening.

THEELIN PILGRIM:
(GASPING)

Can't you see them?

MOVE! RUN!

FX: Civilian 1 hurtles down a quiet alleyway. They skid to a stop. There's a low, menacing growl.

THEELIN PILGRIM:
Oh, no. No no no no no . . .

FX: They back up a few steps. The growling grows louder. And now comes from behind, too. There are three of the wargarans, hunting as a pack.

THEELIN PILGRIM:
(SOBBING)

Just . . . leave me alone . . . leave . . .

FX: The pack is closing in.

THEELIN PILGRIM:
(SHOUTING/SCREAMING)

Help me! Please! *Help!*

FX: The pack leap, roaring.

CUT TO:

SCENE 45. INT. PATH'S ALMSHOUSE

ATMOS: It's late. Most of the Path's disciples have retired, so it's quiet, too.

FX: The wooden door bursts open on its ill-kept hinges and Marda hurries in, carrying an unconscious Naddie.

MARDA:
Pela! Clear that table. Quickly, now.

PELA:
What in the na—Oh!

MARDA:
(NOTE OF WARNING)

Now, Pela!

FX: Pela hurries over and clears a space on the table with her arm, sweeping stuff onto the floor with a clatter.

MARDA:
Good.

FX: Marda lays Naddie gently down on the table.

MARDA:
(RELIEVED)

Good. Now fetch clean water and towels. There's been . . . Naddie has been hurt.

PELA:
(SHOCKED)

Of . . . of course.

FX: Pela sets about fetching the water and towels.

MARDA:
(GENTLY)

Naddie? Naddie?

FX: Naddie doesn't reply. Pela hurries over with the water and towels.

PELA:
(WORRIED)

Is she . . . ?

MARDA:
She's passed out. She's going to be okay. She'll have some nasty scars, but she'll be all right.

PELA:
Thank the Force. What happened?

FX: Marda starts cleaning up Naddie.

MARDA:
Wargarans. At the markets. A trader had brought them in for the festival, and Naddie . . .

I think she set them free. They attacked her . . .

PELA:
(STIFLING A SOB)

Oh, no. That poor, sweet child. Look at her face!

Why? Why did she do it?

MARDA:
The stall holder. He told her they hunt through the Force. I think she thought . . .

(Beat, then VOICE CATCHING IN THROAT)

. . . she thought they should be free, just like the Force.

PELA:
Oh, no. What have we done, Marda?

MARDA:
It'll be all right, Pela.

PELA:
How can it be?

FX: Marda places the dirty towel in the bowl of water and steps back from Naddie.

MARDA:
There. Why don't you apply some salve to her wounds, and make sure she gets some rest?

I'd better speak to the Mother about this.

PELA:
But Marda—

MARDA:
Just do as I say, Pela. I'll see to it.

CUT TO:

SCENE 46. INT. THE SECOND SPIRE—ANTEROOM

ATMOS: As per the opening scene of part 1. Quiet, save for the sound of transports coming in to land in the distance.

FX: Aida enters the room.

CREIGHTON:
Aida. Thank the Light.

There's been another attack.

AIDA:
(SERIOUS)

I know.

CREIGHTON:
You do?

AIDA:
I was with him. It was awful. As soon as the shuttle door started to open . . . I was too slow. I was able to save him, but he's lost his left hand. And the pilot's dead.

CREIGHTON:
(SURPRISED)

Ambassador Tintak?

AIDA:
(CONFUSED)

Who else?

CREIGHTON:
Aida—this is much worse than we thought. There was a bomb for Cerox, too. Planted to trigger when she opened the door to her chambers, right here in the spire.

Whoever's behind this seems able to operate right under our noses.

AIDA:
Perhaps we should evacuate the delegations back to their ships. Tintak was right—they'll be safer there.

CREIGHTON:
How can we be sure?

AIDA:
We can't. But it has to be better than remaining here on Jedha like sitting ducks.

CREIGHTON:
(FRUSTRATED)

Whoever it is doing this, Aida—I admit it. They've got me rattled. Why didn't I sense anything until the last moment?

AIDA:
Why didn't either of us?

CREIGHTON:
Where's Tintak now?

AIDA:
With his people. They're seeing to his medical needs themselves.

And Cerox?

CREIGHTON:

At the medical station the Guardians threw up yesterday. With a *lot* of guards.

AIDA:

Have you heard from Silandra? Is she any closer to figuring out who's behind this?

CREIGHTON:

Not yet. But she needs to know about what's happened tonight. I'll reach out.

AIDA:

Good. We need to contact the Council. They must know what's happening here. And Gella, too. Perhaps she can shed some light on this.

CREIGHTON:

Good idea. I'll ask Bee-Nine to try to establish a connection.

CUT TO:

SCENE 47. INT. PATH'S ALMSHOUSE—MOTHER'S CHAMBERS

ATMOS: The fire has burned low. It's quiet, late.

THE MOTHER:
So, the child, Naddie—she let these beasts run amok on purpose?

MARDA:
She wanted to set them free, like the Force. She felt sorry for them trapped in their crates.

THE MOTHER:
Interesting . . .

And now they're causing an uproar?

MARDA:
More than that, Mother. It seems that they're *hunting*.

THE MOTHER:
Hunting what?

MARDA:
People.

Naddie was hurt. Her face scarred. She'll live, but never look the same again.

THE MOTHER:
The poor child.

MARDA:
The beasts are savage, Mother. More people will die if they're not contained.

And it is our fault.

THE MOTHER:
Then I see another opportunity for the Path to help provide balance and calm.

Round up as many of the disciples as we can spare. Take Juk-kyuk and Qwerb, too.

MARDA:
To do what?

THE MOTHER:
To find the creatures and stop them from hurting anyone else, of course. To return them to their master.

MARDA:
But . . . surely that's a job for the security forces here on Jedha?

THE MOTHER:
Who are otherwise engaged with the goings-on at the peace conference. No, Marda—this is our chance to prove that the Path really are here to help the people of Jedha.

MARDA:
Yes, Mother. I see. But . . .

THE MOTHER:
What is it?

MARDA:
Only that Yana is our best fighter. If she could be allowed to come with us, we could deal with the beasts more swiftly.

THE MOTHER:
Your cousin is busy with another matter, Marda. One that is crucial to the future of the Path. You must trust me on this.

MARDA:
I do trust you.

THE MOTHER:
Then go. See it done. Prove to the people of Jedha that the Path can be their saviors.

MARDA:
Yes, Mother. Of course.

CUT TO:

SCENE 48. INT. ENLIGHTENMENT TAPBAR

ATMOS: As per usual. Enlightenment doesn't change. The harpist plays on. The drinks flow. The chatterers chat.

PIRALLI:
So, what's she like, then, this Jedi?

FX: Kradon finishes cleaning a glass and places it down on the counter.

KRADON:
Ah, yes. Kradon would hear more of the Jedi woman.

KETH:
(HESITANT)

I don't know. She's . . . ummm . . .

She has this amazing *shield*.

MOONA:
A shield? Who's ever heard of a Jedi with a *shield*?

KETH:
Well, she has one. And a lightsaber, but I've not seen her use that yet.

KRADON:
Kradon's advice is to hope you never do, boy. If a Jedi is using their lightsaber, then you is losing your life.

KETH:
(A LITTLE DEFENSIVE)

Jedi use their lightsabers to protect others. They're not just weapons.

KRADON:
Hmmmm.

FX: Piralli glugs from his drink, then wipes his mouth.

PIRALLI:
Hey. Where's that droid of yours? You left it outside again?

(MUTTERED)

Just as well, if you ask me. I don't trust it, not after what went down at the peace conference.

KETH:
You've *never* trusted Pee-Three. He had nothing to do with what happened at the peace conference. And if you must know, he's with Silandra.

I think he's taken a bit of a liking to her.

MOONA:
(LAUGHS)

Oh, that's precious. Now Keth's competing with his own droid for the Jedi's affections.

KETH:
(EMBARRASSED)

I don't *want* her affections! Just her respect.

MOONA:
Chance would be a fine thing. Jedi respect no one but each other.

KETH:

I don't think that's true. Not for a minute.

MOONA:

Well, I think you deserve better, kid. That's all I've got to say on the subject.

KETH:

(GRUMPILY)

That's plenty enough.

PIRALLI:

So, you going to bring her down here to meet us?

KETH:

A Jedi, in *here*?

KRADON:

Kradon has welcomed *many* Jedi into Enlightenment. All are welcome here. Look around, see for yourself. Many peoples, from many worlds. Your friend would enjoy herself.

KETH:

I'm not sure she's the type to enjoy herself.

KRADON:

Nonsense! Everyone enjoys Enlightenment!

PIRALLI:

(SLYLY, TEASING)

Or maybe *you're* the one who doesn't want to bring her in here.

KETH:

Look, we have a job to do. An *important* job.

PIRALLI:

(LAUGHING)

He's living the life he's always wanted, and he hasn't even realized it himself! You're the one who wanted excitement, Keth!

MOONA:
(GENUINE)

Leave him alone. We should be proud of him. He's in the big leagues now.

KETH:
Thanks, Moona.

MOONA:
Just—you look after yourself, all right? Like Kradon said, hanging around with Jedi can get you killed, and I . . .

Well, I need you sticking around to help me keep Piralli in line, don't I?

FX: There's a long beat as they all take in this rare moment of actual, dyed-in-the-wool emotional display.

KRADON:
(GREGARIOUSLY)

Kradon thinks it's time for another round of drinks!

KETH:
Yeah. I'll drink to that.

CUT TO:

SCENE 49. INT. THE SECOND SPIRE—BRIEFING CHAMBER

ATMOS: As per the scene in part 1. The hum of machinery and computers. The crackle of static.

FX: The holo is very choppy and tinged with static and dropouts.

GELLA NATTAI:
(VIA HOLO)

Aida? Is that you?

By the Light, the connection's even worse than last time.

AIDA:
We're here, Gella.

CREIGHTON:
We're sorry to tear you away from your rest.

GELLA NATTAI:
(VIA HOLO)

It was time to get up for training anyway.

How are things there? I take it from the fact you're calling again so soon that they're not going to plan . . .

AIDA:
Not at all. There was a bomb. At the signing ceremony.

GELLA NATTAI:
(VIA HOLO, SHOCKED)

A *bomb*! Someone *really* doesn't want that treaty to be signed.

CREIGHTON:
Bomb*s*. Plural. There's been another two attacks since, both targeting the ambassadors.

GELLA NATTAI:
(VIA HOLO)

Light. And there we were thinking neutral ground was going to make things easier.

Dare I ask if there have been any casualties?

AIDA:
The mediator selected by Chancellor Mollo, Morton San Tekka. And a shuttle pilot.

Ambassador Tintak is seriously wounded, too.

CREIGHTON:
It seems Republic security was right to worry. If the chancellor had been here . . .

GELLA NATTAI:
(VIA HOLO)

I dread to think.

Did they finalize signing the treaty?

CREIGHTON:
Everything is balanced on the head of a pin. As things stand, both parties wish to carry on and complete the signing ceremony tomorrow. But we're taking precautions. It'll be just us, the delegates, and the new mediator.

AIDA:
And a *lot* of guards.

GELLA NATTAI:
(VIA HOLO)

I wish you the best of luck. That's not an easy assignment. I should know.

But how can *I* help?

AIDA:
We're not having much luck getting to the bottom of who's behind the attacks. We thought perhaps you could help narrow the field.

GELLA NATTAI:
(VIA HOLO)

Ah. I see.

CREIGHTON:
Has there been any more word from Axel or Chancellor Greylark?

GELLA NATTAI:
(VIA HOLO)

No, I'm afraid not. I've heard nothing more since we last spoke.

CREIGHTON:
I feared as much.

I know we established Viceroy Ferrol and Axel were behind two of the attacks on E'ronoh, but are you still convinced Axel was working with another party? And do you have any suspicions *at all* who they might be?

GELLA NATTAI:
(VIA HOLO)

I have plenty of thoughts, but no evidence. That's the problem.

AIDA:
Go on.

GELLA NATTAI:
(VIA HOLO)

I don't know to what end, but Axel had something to do with a religious sect known as the Path of the Open Hand.

CREIGHTON:
(SURPRISED)

The Path of the Open Hand?

AIDA:
They're here on Jedha. In numbers. They're protesting in the streets, and they've set up an almshouse to tend to the poor and needy.

GELLA NATTAI:
(VIA HOLO)

They were present on Eiram and E'ronoh, too, giving speeches and spreading the word of their faith. There's nothing to connect them to any wrongdoing, though. For all I know, they're simply another religious sect like the thousands of others out here on the frontier.

CREIGHTON:
Anything else?

GELLA NATTAI:
(VIA HOLO)

Only that Axel had been in communication with *someone* during that plot, but he remained tight-lipped on exactly who. The only thing he let slip was "They are free—from the Jedi."

AIDA:
Do you think it could be the Path of the Open Hand?

GELLA NATTAI:
(VIA HOLO, SIGHS)

I don't know. There's no evidence either way. It might simply be that something about their teachings spoke to Axel on a spiritual level.

He always did seem cynical about the Jedi and the Force. He might have found faith with the Path. But if he did, he never spoke of it to me.

(UNSURE)

There's nothing to say they're anything more than they seem.

CREIGHTON:
But your instinct—you don't trust them?

GELLA NATTAI:
(VIA HOLO)

Let's just say that I think they're worth a closer look.

AIDA:
Thank you, Gella. We'll look into it.

GELLA NATTAI:
(VIA HOLO)

Good luck. And be careful. This could all be over tomorrow.

CREIGHTON:
(BROODING)

Yeah. One way or another.

CUT TO:

SCENE 50. EXT. JEDHA MARKETS—NIGHT

ATMOS: In the markets, people are still screaming and running.

FX: The low growl of one of the wargarans.

QWERB:
Over here!

JUKKYUK:
Rwwaaaarrraahh!

QWERB:
No! We're not supposed to kill them!

JUKKYUK:
Arrrwoooo?

QWERB:
(EXASPERATED)

Just—give me the rope.

FX: The wargaran growls again. Then snaps its jaws.

QWERB:
Stay there . . . stay . . .

FX: The hissing of an uncoiling rope as Qwerb throws a lasso. The wargaran growls again, then whimpers.

QWERB:
Ha! Got you!

(TO JUKKYUK)

How many did Marda say there were?

JUKKYUK:
Wraarwooo rah.

QWERB:
(SIGHS)

We're going to be here all night.

CUT TO:

SCENE 51. EXT. JEDHA MARKETS—ELSEWHERE—CONTINUOUS

ATMOS: The crowd is more distant here, and the revelries have started up again.

FX: Three of the wargarans are growling and snapping and running. And Marda's running, too.

MARDA:
(HUFFING)

That's it! Come on! Hunt!

FX: Marda keeps on running, feet pounding the stone streets.

MARDA:
Draw you away from the crowds. Get you to . . .

FX: Marda skids to a halt.

MARDA:
. . . stay on my . . .

Oh. *Clever.*

FX: Three more wargarans appear, circling Marda, growling, ready to pounce.

MARDA:

When I say . . .

FX: The wargarans gnash their teeth viciously . . .

MARDA:

Now! The nets!

FX: Weighted nets fall from rooftops above, ensnaring the wargarans. They gnash and howl for a few moments more, and then start whimpering, thrashing uselessly against the nets.

MARDA:

Got you!

That's another six.

PELA:

I think that's the lot of them. Assuming Qwerb and Jukkyuk rounded up that other one.

MARDA:

Well done, everyone. Come on, let's get them back to where they're supposed to be.

And be *careful*—we've managed to get this far without being bitten.

FX: Path disciples gather up the nets to lead the wargarans back through the market. One of the wargarans snarls and snaps.

PELA:

Easy now. Easy. Come on. Let's get you home.

FX: As they lead the captured wargarans through the market, people notice them.

IMPRESSED AZUMEL CIVILIAN:

Look! They did it!

FX: People begin to clap and cheer, slowly at first, but then growing as the Path disciples lead the wargarans on through the parting crowds.

WATER MERCHANT:
The Path of the Open Hand!

CROWD:
(CHEERS)

FX: More clapping and hooting.

PELA:
They've never treated us like this before, Marda.

MARDA:
Just smile and wave, Pela. Tomorrow, these people will cheer our parade in the same way. We've made a difference tonight. We've saved people's lives. They'll remember it.

(SHOUTING, TO CROWD)

The Force will be free!

PATH DISCIPLES:
The Force will be free!

CROWD:
(CHEERS)

The Force will be free!

CUT TO:

SCENE 52. EXT. OUTSIDE A STREET VENDOR'S STALL—THE NEXT MORNING

ANNOUNCER:
Time until the battle begins: five hours.

ATMOS: The atmosphere is a bit lower-key out in the city this morning. Just the hiss of boiling water, the clatter of pots, and the soft braying of working animals being led through the streets, their hooves clopping on stone.

FX: Creighton sips from a hot drink.

CREIGHTON:
(DUBIOUS)

What do they call this again?

SILANDRA:
(AMUSED)

Supata. It's a Twi'lek drink from Aaloth.

CREIGHTON:
It's . . . umm . . .

SILANDRA:
An acquired taste. Stick with it.

CREIGHTON:
(DUBIOUS)

If you say so.

FX: Creighton takes another sip.

SILANDRA:
How are you, Creighton?

CREIGHTON:
It's not me you should be worried about.

SILANDRA:
But I am. The pressure . . . all these attacks, jeopardizing your hard work. It takes a toll.

CREIGHTON:
(SIGHS)

It does. But what else is there but to forge ahead? We can't let them win, can we? Those who'd see everything we're trying to do torn down.

SILANDRA:
It doesn't make it any easier though, does it?

CREIGHTON:
No. I'll admit that much. I'm tired, Silandra.

(Beat, then BRIGHTER)

But the treaty will be signed today. And I can go back to drinking coolers on Coruscant.

SILANDRA:
(LAUGHS)

I'll never get you city people. There's a whole frontier out there to be explored.

CREIGHTON:

And there's people like you keen to explore it. Thank the Light.

FX: A procession trundles past, jangling small bells and beating skins. Creighton and Silandra wait until they've passed before continuing.

CREIGHTON:

How goes the investigation?

SILANDRA:

We're making slow progress.

CREIGHTON:

We?

SILANDRA:

The adjunct from the Church of the Force.

CREIGHTON:

Keth? The one whose droid was missing?

SILANDRA:

Yes. His droid turned up a few hours after the bombing. It wasn't the one you saw explode. I've met it. It's . . . strange, to say the least. But harmless.

CREIGHTON:

I'm pleased to hear Keth is innocent. But it does mean we're back to square one in our search for culprits.

So, you've enlisted the adjunct to help?

SILANDRA:

He's assisting, helping me navigate the different sects and factions here on Jedha.

CREIGHTON:

Good. But are you any closer to identifying the bombers?

SILANDRA:

Not yet. Frustratingly, everyone I talk to who was there at the ceremony claims to have seen a different person talking to the droid. A soldier from Eiram, or E'ronoh. A Guardian of the Whills. A Lew'elan. A Jedi.

CREIGHTON:

But no one from the Path of the Open Hand?

SILANDRA:

No. Why? What do you know?

CREIGHTON:

We spoke to Gella. She suspects them to have been involved somehow in the attacks on Eiram and E'ronoh's royals, but had no significant evidence. Chancellor Greylark's son, Axel, told her that his co-conspirators were "free of the Jedi," whatever that means.

SILANDRA:

Interesting. It certainly *sounds* like the Path. You know they were here in the markets last night, making waves?

CREIGHTON:

No. I was a bit tied up . . .

SILANDRA:

Of course. Well, apparently some of the animals brought in for the festival escaped from their cages. They wounded a small child from the Path, and some civilians, including their keeper. They were hunting people in the crowds. The Path stepped in and rounded them all up. They're being hailed as heroes.

CREIGHTON:

And they were on hand to help with the injured after the first bombing, too.

SILANDRA:

I know they're a bit intense, and distrustful of Jedi, but do you really think they could be behind the attacks? Or are we just singling them out because they've spoken out against the Order?

CREIGHTON:
Honestly, I don't know. But we should trust in Gella's instincts. We can't rule *anything* out. Things are so volatile here. They could be trying to capitalize on that for their own gain.

SILANDRA:
I met their "Herald" yesterday. A Nautolan who didn't seem particularly welcoming, but neither did he seem to have an agenda beyond wanting to help people and preach his beliefs.

Still, perhaps I can find a way to speak with their leader, the Mother. Leave it with me. I'll head over there next.

CREIGHTON:
Thank you, Silandra.

FX: Creighton gets up and places his drink on the wall where they were sitting.

CREIGHTON:
I'd best find Aida. There's a lot to be done before the signing later.

And . . . There's more supata here if you want it.

SILANDRA:
(AMUSED)

To think I had you down as a man of taste and distinction.

CREIGHTON:
(CHUCKLING)

Whatever gave you *that* idea?

CUT TO:

SCENE 53. INT. PATH'S ALMSHOUSE—MOTHER'S CHAMBERS

ATMOS: As before.

HERALD:
The hour of our petition to the Convocation nears.

Although I have grave doubts about their willingness to listen. The more I hear about them, the more I believe they are a force for ill here on Jedha, just like all the others.

MOTHER:
Indeed. Even if they were to accept us, I no longer think it will be enough.

We must show the people of Jedha that our faith is strong. That the Force *will* be free.

HERALD:
And how do you propose we do that?

MOTHER:
Ah . . . The child Naddie has provided the spark of an idea . . .

FX: A creature pads into the room and issues a low growl—this is the Nameless, the Leveler.

HERALD:
(SHOCKED)

You're not suggesting . . . ?

MOTHER:
I am. The moment of the Leveler has arrived.

CUT TO:

SCENE 54. EXT. OUTSIDE THE PATH'S ALMSHOUSE—LATER

ATMOS: There's a jubilant atmosphere here this morning. Upbeat chatter and the sounds of industry as the Path disciples prepare to go out into the city for their daily procession.

FX: Keth, P3-7A, and Silandra are approaching.

KETH:
Are you sure about this? I mean, they didn't make us particularly welcome yesterday.

SILANDRA:
Sometimes, Keth, the places we're least welcome are the places where we most need to be.

KETH:
Now you're starting to sound like Pee-Three.

SILANDRA:
(TEASING)

Ha! In that case, maybe you should listen to him a little more?

P3-7A:
Truth can be found in the mouths of those who truly give themselves to the Force.

KETH:
Yes, well—be that as it may, Pee-Three, you're still waiting out here while we talk to the Path.

P3-7A:
The ignorant ever lead the ignorant toward catastrophe.

SILANDRA:
(LAUGHS)

FX: Pela is gathering the Littles outside as Keth and Silandra come to a stop.

TROMAK:
Will the people cheer us again today, Pela?

PELA:
Yes, I think that they will, Tromak.

SILANDRA:
I hear you did a good thing for the people of Jedha last night. Thank you.

PELA:
Oh. *You.*

NADDIE:
(PANICKED)

It's the Jedi from the market! *Here!*

SILANDRA:
(PATIENT)

Please, don't worry. I'm only here to speak with your Mother.

PELA:
(HOSTILE DISBELIEF)

The Mother! As if she'd want to talk to *you.*

FX: Footsteps approach.

HERALD:
I can only concur with Pela.

You've seen our operation here. How we're trying to help people. We have no more time for your *interference*.

KETH:
Is your faith really so fragile that you're scared of a few simple questions?

SILANDRA:
(NOTE OF WARNING)

Keth . . .

KETH:
How can we possibly do any harm? We'd just like to talk with your Mother. That's all.

THE MOTHER:
(ALL CHARM)

And talk you shall.

HERALD:
I really *must* protest. This is outrageous. You surely cannot even begin to entertain the idea of answering the questions of these Force-abusers?

THE MOTHER:
(CALM)

As the young man says, what harm can it do?

(TO SILANDRA AND KETH)

Come. Step inside. We can speak in my chambers. But please, leave your droid out here.

KETH:
Pee-Three—we'll be back shortly.

HERALD:
Mother, I really don't think—

THE MOTHER:
(CUTTING HIM OFF)

Qwerb and Jukkyuk will be on hand if I have need of them. Please, continue your preparations for the festival.

Pela—take the Littles. Marda will meet you in the markets.

PELA:
Yes, Mother.

THE MOTHER:
It is an important day. For everyone. We shall not be long.

SILANDRA:
Thank you.

THE MOTHER:
Herald. You may leave us.

FX: They go inside.

HERALD:
(MUTTERED, TO SELF, SPITEFUL)

That's right, "Mother." You just do what you think is best . . . for *yourself.* Like you always do.

You're nothing without that damn Leveler. *Nothing.*

But at least now *I* can put it to good use . . .

CUT TO:

SCENE 55. INT. PATH'S ALMSHOUSE—MOTHER'S CHAMBERS—CONTINUOUS

ATMOS: As before. The fire crackles and spits as always. The Mother lowers herself into a chair.

THE MOTHER:
Sit, please. There are cushions.

SILANDRA:
(UNEASY)

I'll stand, thank you.

THE MOTHER:
Now, how can I help? As you saw, today is to be a busy day for the Path of the Open Hand. We will give our gifts, freely, in the markets, and I will personally lead a procession through the markets.

SILANDRA:
Yes. I'm sorry to disrupt your plans. Only—I'm investigating the bombings at the peace conference and . . .

(BOTHERED BY SOMETHING)

. . . and, well, I hoped you might . . .

THE MOTHER:
Are you quite all right, Master Jedi? You seem a little . . . un-well.

SILANDRA:
(SHAKY)

Yes. Yes, I'm fine. Thank you. It's just . . . it's rather hot in here.

THE MOTHER:
Ah. I do so feel the cold. The fire is a constant companion. There is fresh water in the jug over there.

FX: Keth pours a glass and passes it to Silandra.

KETH:
Here.

FX: Silandra drinks.

SILANDRA:
Thank you. As I was saying—

THE MOTHER:
(INTERRUPTING)

You've heard rumors about the Path of the Open Hand and wondered if we have anything to do with the bombings.

SILANDRA:
Well . . . yes.

THE MOTHER:
(AMUSED)

The answer is no. We are a peaceful sect who seek only harmony and freedom for the Force. How could that possibly be served by the bombing of a peace conference?

SILANDRA:
That's what I wished to ask you.

THE MOTHER:
Well, it cannot. It is not.

If you seek evidence, I cannot show you proof of what I haven't done. But perhaps I can point you to what the Path has already done on Jedha.

This almshouse, for instance. It was abandoned. Close to ruin. We purchased it and fixed it up and returned it to its original purpose—to help the needy. Hundreds of people have already passed beneath this very roof, seeking shelter, food, and warmth. And they have received it, freely.

We were there in the aftermath of the bombing to help treat the injured, and I believe when you spoke to them yesterday, you received no complaint.

SILANDRA:
(STILL A LITTLE SHAKY)

No. I did not.

THE MOTHER:
We even offered our services as mediators to help restore the peace process but were summarily rejected. Just as, it seems, our membership in the Convocation is unwelcome.

And then yesterday, after a dreadful incident in which a pack of wargarans were accidentally set loose in the streets, the Path stepped in to deal with the matter, rounding up the errant beasts so that no more people were hurt.

SILANDRA:
So I heard.

THE MOTHER:
And where were the Jedi when all of this was going on, hmmm?

SILANDRA:
There were further bomb attacks.

THE MOTHER:
There were?

Well, some might make the argument that the Jedi were present at the scene of all the attacks so far. And yet the Path were nowhere to be seen.

In fact, we seem to be the ones picking up the pieces.

SILANDRA:
(INCREDULOUS)

You believe the *Jedi* were responsible for the bombings?

THE MOTHER:
It's as believable as implicating the Path of the Open Hand. More so, in fact.

SILANDRA:
(STRAINED)

There were Jedi *there.* Within the blast radius. They could have been killed.

THE MOTHER:
Ah, but Jedi are Force-abusers, are they not? They could easily protect themselves from something as trivial as a *bomb.*

SILANDRA:
(STRAINED)

The Jedi *had nothing to do with it.* In fact, if we hadn't been there, more people would have died.

FX: There's a beat, a moment while things hang in the air between them, before the Mother breaks the tension again.

THE MOTHER:
What do I know? I wasn't there. And to answer your question— my people stand to gain nothing from the bombings, or the war between Eiram and E'ronoh, or the death of any of the people involved in your political games.

(Beat, then WITH A WARNING NOTE)

So, I will ask you, Master Jedi, more respectfully than you deserve—leave my people *alone.*

SILANDRA:
If you and your people hold true to what you claim, then there will be no reason our paths should ever cross.

But if I find—

THE MOTHER:
(CUTTING HER OFF)

Get out. I'm tired of your threats. You fear what we are, what we represent. And you seek to diminish us. I will not allow it. *Go!*

KETH:
Master Sho?

SILANDRA:
Come on. Time we were leaving.

CUT TO:

SCENE 56. EXT. JEDHA STREET—A SHORT DISTANCE FROM THE PATH'S ALMSHOUSE—SOON AFTER

ATMOS: The streets sound busy, if distant here. Jedha is coming alive as the day goes on, with processions, pilgrims, stalls, and the like. P3-7A has rejoined them.

KETH:
Are you okay?

SILANDRA:
(STILL NOT QUITE WITH IT)

Just . . . give me a moment.

KETH:
Here, sit.

FX: They sit down on a bench.

KETH:
Can I get you anything?

SILANDRA:
No. No. I'll be fine in a minute. I just need to let it pass.

KETH:

Let what pass? You said the heat in there was getting to you? But it's cool out here. Are you sure you're okay? You weren't like this when we visited the almshouse yesterday. Has something changed?

SILANDRA:

It wasn't the heat. Something about being in there, with her . . .

KETH:

The Mother?

SILANDRA:

I . . . I think so. I don't know. Something felt wrong.

Did you feel anything?

KETH:

No. Not a thing.

SILANDRA:

Whereas my head was swimming.

KETH:

And you think *she* was doing that?

SILANDRA:

I don't know. I don't understand how she could.

KETH:

I have to say, she sounded pretty reasonable to me. Annoyed, but she did have a point.

SILANDRA:

I know.

But . . . something isn't right. I've never felt anything like that before.

KETH:

Maybe we should take you somewhere to rest for a while.

There's a place in the next street. A tapbar called Enlighten-ment. We can go there.

SILANDRA:

All right.

Lead the way.

CUT TO:

SCENE 57. INT. ENLIGHTENMENT TAPBAR—SOON AFTER

ATMOS: Same as it ever was.

KRADON:
Keth! You're early today, boy! And Kradon sees you've brought a guest. Allow Kradon to introduce himself.

FX: Kradon slithers out from behind the bar, his multiple legs chittering against the floor.

KETH:
Ah—look, she's not feeling very well, Kradon. I thought we'd have some grassroot stew and some water.

KRADON:
Yes, yes! Stew for the Jedi. Bring it.

FX: Kradon snaps his fingers. Someone scurries off.

KRADON:
And oil for the droid, perhaps?

FX: P3-7A gives an encouraging beep.

KETH:

No, he's fine. He's under strict instructions to keep a low pro-file, aren't you, Pee-Three?

P3-7A:

To silence a great orator is to abandon the pursuit of all knowl-edge, for only from those with wisdom can we better learn how to live.

KETH:

(NOTE OF WARNING)

Thank you, Pee-Three . . .

FX: They approach the bar.

MOONA:

What's this? *Keth?*

You actually went and *did* it. You brought the Jedi woman *here.*

KETH:

(SHEEPISH)

I did.

MOONA:

I'm impressed. Wait till Piralli hears about this. And the fact that he missed her. We'll never hear the end of it.

KETH:

(LOWERS VOICE)

Look, I don't want to make a fuss, okay?

MOONA:

Fuss? *Me?* You *know* how I feel about Jedi.

KETH:

Exactly.

MOONA:

Pfft. She'll hear nothing from me. Unless she's buying rounds, of course.

KETH:

I think it's a bit early for that.

MOONA:
(PERPLEXED)

It is?

KRADON:

Kradon will just say hello, no? A quick word of greeting, to welcome the lady to Enlightenment.

KETH:
(GIVING IN)

Please yourself, Kradon.

FX: Kradon moves over to the booth where Silandra is sitting, legs clattering. Keth follows.

KRADON:

Master Jedi! Most welcome. Most welcome indeed, to Enlightenment, our little haven in the Holy City. Any friend of Keth is a friend of the house. You pay only the rate of friends, yes?

KETH:

Hang on. What *friends'* rate?

SILANDRA:
(AMUSED)

You know Keth?

KRADON:

Know him? The boy is practically one of Kradon's family!

SILANDRA:

Ahh. That explains it.

KRADON:
Explains what?

SILANDRA:
Why Keth was so . . . *eager* to come here.

KRADON:
Of course! Of course! Keth knows that Enlightenment is nourishment for the soul, yes?

Ah, and here comes your stew. Only the best for a Jedi.

FX: A waiter comes running over with the bowl and places it on the table.

SILANDRA:
Well, thank you. It smells delicious.

KRADON:
Yes, yes! Eat up! Enjoy!

FX: Kradon scuttles off. Keth sits down in the booth.

KETH:
(LOWERS VOICE)

I'm sorry about that.

SILANDRA:
No need.

This place is . . . quite something.

KETH:
Yeah. Kradon likes to say it's the only place on Jedha where *everyone* is welcome, no matter what sect or creed or planet they're from.

SILANDRA:
Neutral ground.

KETH:
Exactly. Light side and dark side, Outer or Inner Rim. They all come through Enlightenment at some point.

SILANDRA:

If only the rest of the galaxy got along as easily.

KETH:

I know. What time's the signing ceremony today?

SILANDRA:

Soon. Creighton and Aida will be finalizing preparations as we speak.

I only hope things go a little more smoothly this time around . . .

CUT TO:

SCENE 58. INT. THE SECOND SPIRE—MEETING CHAMBER

ATMOS: We can hear the distant sounds of the busy city outside.

CREIGHTON:
A *Graf*! Serving as official mediator?

AIDA:
It does make sense if you think about it. Chancellor Mollo wanted someone from one of the established frontier families to stand in his place. After the San Tekkas, the Grafs are an obvious choice.

Besides, the role is largely ceremonial. It's not as if he's going to have to do anything beyond giving a speech and shaking some hands.

CREIGHTON:
(SIGHS)

You're right.

It's just ... they have a certain *reputation*. Last year they were sanctioned for dealing in illegal weapons on Carburo and fined for selling exclusive access to hyperspace routes to multiple bidders.

Hardly the sort of people you'd choose to oversee a treaty signing.

AIDA:
Well, he'll have to do. With no way to reach Chancellor Mollo, Chairperson Meldan's decision is final.

Besides, it'll all be over soon.

CREIGHTON:
Let's hope you're right.

Have you checked the security arrangements with Mesook and the other Guardians?

AIDA:
Only five times.

CREIGHTON:
Then let's make sure we're ready to welcome the ambassadors back from their transports. They'll be here shortly.

AIDA:
Yes. All right. And Creighton?

CREIGHTON:
Yes?

AIDA:
It's going to be *fine.*

CUT TO:

SCENE 59. EXT. OUTSIDE ENLIGHTENMENT—SOON AFTER

ATMOS: The streets are busy here now, too—full of people. Keth and Silandra walk through them, accompanied by the whir of P3-7A's thrusters as he hovers along beside them.

SILANDRA:
Well, Kradon was right.

KETH:
He was?

SILANDRA:
Yes. The stew was excellent.

KETH:
You're feeling better, then?

SILANDRA:
Much.

FX: The sound of a speeder comes roaring up behind them. It's loud, and getting louder as it comes straight for Silandra and Keth.

SILANDRA:
Down!

FX: Keth is thrown to the ground.

KETH:
(OOMPH)

FX: Silandra's shield flares to life. People shout as the speeder turns.

KETH:
They're coming back around!

FX: A blaster fires several shots as the speeder roars again. The shots are deflected by Silandra's shield.

SILANDRA:
Stay down! Get to safety!

FX: Silandra's lightsaber ignites, shining blue. The blaster fires another burst. This time the shots are deflected by the lightsaber.

KETH:
Silandra!

SILANDRA:
I'll lead them away from these people.

KETH:
But—

FX: But Silandra is already running. The speeder is giving chase, unrelenting. P3-7A's thrusters flare.

P3-7A:
(FADING OUT AS HE MOVES AWAY)

The enemy of faith is doubt. The enemy of reason is fear.

KETH:
Pee-Three, where are you going?

FX: Silandra grunts as she leaps over some barrels. A blaster shot causes one of them to explode, spraying water.

SILANDRA:
(GRUNTS)

Coming too, are you, Pee-Three?

P3-7A:
To abandon one's faith is to lose sight of all meaning.

SILANDRA:
Thanks.

FX: The speeder slews closer.

SILANDRA:
Now, if you don't mind . . .

(UNGH)

FX: Silandra does a running jump, aided by the Force, and, using P3-7A as a stepping-stone, leaps up onto the roof of a nearby building. It's a big leap, and she lands running. P3-7A continues to soar along close to her, using his thrusters.

P3-7A:
There is no dignity in holding onto misplaced beliefs.

SILANDRA:
(BREATHLESS, SHOUTING TO P3-7A)

Sorry, Pee-Three! I needed the step up to the roof.

FX: More blasterfire, which is deflected by a mix of shield and light-saber. The speeder is still roaring along the street below, while Silandra runs along the rooftops.

SILANDRA:
Now let's find out who you are . . .

If I can just time this right . . .

FX: Silandra leaps with another grunt.

SILANDRA:
(GRUNTS)

FX: She lands atop the speeder (engines getting louder, loud clang as she lands).

FX: When we hear the attacker speak, their voice has a strange, layered effect to it, as if two or three different people are all saying the words at the same time.

ATTACKER:
No!

FX: Silandra's lightsaber bisects the speeder. It flips. Silandra lands softly.

SILANDRA:
(UNGH)

FX: The attacker shouts as he's thrown clear. People are shouting in the nearby crowd.

YOUNG MAN:
(FROM BACKGROUND)

Look out!

ATTACKER:
(ARGHHH)

FX: The sparking halves of the speeder crash into a wall and explode. Silandra spins her lightsaber in her hand.

SILANDRA:
Who are you?

FX: The ruined halves of the speeder burn on the ground close by. The attacker slowly gets up. And then pulls a blaster and starts shooting. Silandra deflects the blows with her lightsaber.

SILANDRA:
There are innocent people here.

Lower your weapon.

ATTACKER:
Innocent?

(SLYLY)

Yes.

FX: More blaster shots.

SILANDRA:
No!

(SHOUTING, TO PEOPLE IN THE CROWD)

Get down!

FX: Silandra sends her shield out with a push, aided by the Force, making a whooshing sound, to deflect the blows. Her lightsaber deactivates.

YOUNG MAN:
(AMAZED)

Look at her shield!

YOUNG GIRL:
(CONFUSED)

How's she moving it around like that? She's not even *holding* it!

FX: The attacker makes a run for it into the crowd.

ATTACKER:
Out of my way!

SILANDRA:
Get back here!

FX: Silandra gives chase. The crowd parts for her, but ...

SILANDRA:
(HUFFS)

Lost him.

FX: She recalls her shield using the Force, and powers it down. The crowd claps and cheers. P3-7A comes hovering over.

P3-7A:
Blessed are those who walk the path of Light.

SILANDRA:
Hmmm.

Come on, we'd better find Keth.

CUT TO:

SCENE 60. EXT. CENTRAL SQUARE—MOMENTS LATER

ANNOUNCER:
Time until the battle begins: one hour.

ATMOS: We're thick in the midst of the busy city now. All the colorful sounds we were hearing before are now amplified, along with the hubbub of people enjoying themselves. The festival hasn't started yet, but the city is heaving with people. They're gathering in the central square.

SILANDRA:
He's got to be around here, somewhere, Pee-Three.

Unless he's gone back to Enlightenment. Perhaps we should try there bef—

What's this?

FX: Fade up on the Herald's speech as Silandra moves through the bustling crowd. There are a lot of people here, listening to the Herald give a speech from outside the Convocation building.

HERALD:
(GIVING SPEECH, RILING UP THE CROWD)

Faithful of Jedha.

It is time you know the truth. About this *city*. About the organization that sits behind those doors. This so-called Convocation.

I have just been thrown from their chambers for daring to question their authority. For *daring* to hold a belief contrary to their own.

I have been told that my views are *preposterous,* my concerns without merit, but let me ask you this, is it wrong to question those who *lie* to us, each and every day?

Is it wrong to demand the *truth*?

FX: The crowd roars its support.

CROWD:
(IN UNISON)

No!

SILANDRA:
I don't like the sound of this, Pee-Three.

P3-7A:
And so the false prophet cried to the stars, and the people did swear their allegiance.

SILANDRA:
Exactly what I'm worried about.

HERALD:
I have it on good authority that the venerable Yacombe were recently *insulted* and *attacked* when they petitioned to join the Convocation.

They barely escaped with their lives.

Are we surprised? No, because the Convocation exists only to further their own *agenda,* to maintain a conspiracy that places the entire galaxy in danger.

Why, even as I approached the chamber this very hour, I over-heard a plot to deceive *you,* the people of Jedha, a city that has already been rocked by violence at the so-called peace confer-ence between Eiram and E'ronoh.

FX: The crowd roars again. They're angry and getting more riled as the speech goes on.

HERALD:
Earlier today, there was an explosion at the Temple of the Kyber, a disaster that left a senior disciple of the Whills killed and many others injured.

SILANDRA:
(SHOCKED)

Another explosion? That's the first I've heard of another attack.

HERALD:
You have been told it was an *accident,* but that is not the case. It was a *deliberate attack* upon the city, the blast caused by an *explo-sive device* planted by unknown forces.

FX: The crowd goes ballistic. Someone tries to step in front of the Herald.

TARNA MIAK:
(SHOUTING)

That. Is. *Enough!*

HERALD:
(ENCOURAGING THE CROWD)

And here we have a member of the Convocation come to its defense, Tarna Miak, a *Sorcerer of Tund* no less, a coven whose crimes against the Force know no end.

TARNA MIAK:
I must ask you to stop this. It isn't helping anyone.

HERALD:
And there you have it. I am to be *silenced,* the Herald of the truth.

FX: The crowd is bellowing.

ANGRY KESSURIAN:
Let him be heard!

FX: The crowd takes up the chant.

CROWD:
(IN UNISON)

Let him be heard! Let him be heard! Let him be heard!

TARNA MIAK:
(SHOUTING)

Guardians!

FX: The chanting stops as the Herald speaks again.

HERALD:
Ask yourself this, my friends . . . *why* would the Convocation lie to you? Why would they cover up an act of *terrorism*? To protect their precious Festival of Balance?

Or is the truth more *sinister*? Is it because one of their own was behind the attack? The sorcerers? The Matukai?

Or maybe even the *Jedi*?

RILED HUMAN DOCKWORKER:
Yeah. Why would they *lie*?

ANGRY KUDON TRADER:
We want to know. We *demand* to know!

FX: Fighting begins to break out in the crowds. Guardians tackle the Herald.

HERALD:
(SHOUTING WHILE STRUGGLING)

Defilers of the Force!

Liars and deviants!

ANGRY KESSURIAN:
Let him go! Let him speak!

SILANDRA:
Come on, Pee-Three. We need to find Keth, and then warn Creighton and Aida before this gets out of ha—

FX: Silandra is cut off by a shrill, terrifying scream. It pierces the air, rising above the clamor of people. There's a ripple of hush, followed by more screaming. The screams belong to a man.

SILANDRA:
Pee-Three, with me.

FX: Silandra hurries through the crowd toward the screaming. People are fleeing all around her. They're shouting angrily, too.

HUMAN RIOTER:
(AGGRESSIVE)

Out of my way!

WEEQUAY RIOTER:
(AGGRESSIVE)

Move, you fool!

FX: People are starting to fight amongst themselves. We hear punches being thrown. A blaster goes off. More screaming. More blasters. A full riot is breaking out.

SILANDRA:
No! Stop! What are you *doing*?

What are you running from?

FX: Silandra skids to a halt.

SILANDRA:
Oh, no.

P3-7A:
In death, our true face is revealed.

FX: Silandra stoops and reaches out to the body of a dead male. It crumbles to dust at her touch. The riot is gaining momentum in the background as people scrabble to get away.

SILANDRA:
(UNCERTAIN)

A Brother of the Ninth Door. He's . . . dead, but when I touched him . . .

Something turned him to *dust*. Like an empty *husk*.

(Beat, then TO TERRIFIED HUMAN MALE)

You. What happened here?

TERRIFIED HUMAN MALE:
(TERRIFIED)

It . . . It just came out of nowhere. That man—he started screaming, and then . . . it . . . he . . . it just . . . it *drained* the life out of him before our eyes. And now . . .

SILANDRA:
Dust.

What was it?

TERRIFIED HUMAN MALE:
I don't know. It was *monstrous.* It . . . it went *that* way.

SILANDRA:
Get to safety.

TERRIFIED HUMAN MALE:
(HORRIFIED)

You're going *after* it?

SILANDRA:
Someone has to.

FX: Silandra hurries in the direction indicated by the terrified civilian. Around her, the riot is spilling out like a wave, and she's at the epicenter. She powers on her shield.

SILANDRA:
Pee-Three—see if you can get any higher. I need to know what's going on, and I can't see anything in this chaos.

P3-7A:
As the Force wills it.

FX: P3-7A's thrusters fire. Silandra runs on for a moment. Close by, a woman is weeping.

DEVASTATED WOMAN:
(WEEPING)

FX: Silandra stops.

SILANDRA:
(BREATHLESS)

Are you hurt?

FX: The woman shifts position.

DEVASTATED WOMAN:
No. My wife. She's . . . she's *dead.* That *creature,* it just lashed out as it passed. It's out of control!

SILANDRA:
I'm so sorry. I don't understand what's doing this.

(Beat, then FIRMLY)

But I intend to find out.

FX: There's another scream up ahead. This time we hear the distant shriek of the Nameless, too. This is the Leveler, set loose by the Herald—the Mother's pet Nameless, brought with her from Dalna.

SILANDRA:
I'll be right back. Just . . . I'm sorry.

FX: Now Silandra's lightsaber flares to life again, too. She runs on.

SILANDRA:
(SHOUTING TO P3-7A)

Pee-Three—any luck?

FX: There's no answer. The Nameless shrieks again. It's a little closer.

SILANDRA:
What . . . what *is* that . . . ?

FX: Silandra's footsteps begin to falter.

SILANDRA:
(WOOZILY)

Same . . . feeling . . . as . . . the almshouse.

FX: The soundscape goes wonky here, to imitate the Nameless effect that we've seen elsewhere in art—the world starts to warp for Silandra as she finds herself in relative proximity to the creature.

FX: The Nameless shrieks again, loudly.

SILANDRA:
What . . . *what* . . . (SCREAMS)

CUT TO:

SCENE 61. INT. THE SECOND SPIRE—MEETING CHAMBER

NOTE: *This is a direct reprisal of the opening scene at the beginning of part 1.*

ANNOUNCER:
Time until the battle begins: zero hours.

ATMOS: We're in the Second Spire on Jedha, an old, previously abandoned temple that has been recently refitted for the peace conference. We're in a large meeting chamber on the lower level of the spire. A small group of people has gathered, but the mood is subdued as everyone waits for proceedings to begin.

From outside, we can hear the general murmur of distant crowds. As the scene progresses, however, the sounds of angry people grow louder in the background, as a riot is heading this way...

FX: Tilson Graf, the serving mediator, is rapping his fingertips nervously on the pedestal before him.

TILSON GRAF:
(NERVOUS)

Right, then.

It's almost time to begin.

AMBASSADOR TINTAK:
Indeed. Let's get it over with. I'm eager to return to E'ronoh to help with the reconstruction efforts, just as, I'm sure, Ambassador Cerox wishes to return to her people on Eiram.

TILSON GRAF:
(HESITANT)

Yes, Ambassador Tintak. If you could just give me a moment . . .

CREIGHTON:
Is everything all right, Mediator Graf?

TILSON GRAF:
(DISTRACTED)

What? Yes, yes. Of course, Master Sun.

(PULLING HIMSELF TOGETHER)

Everything's fine. I just need a minute to compose myself. This is, after all, a momentous affair. The signing of this peace treaty is a key moment in galactic history. Eiram and E'ronoh have been at war for over *five years*. And now, following the marriage of their heirs, the worlds have finally come together in peace. We're gathered here in the Second Spire on historic Jedha to—

AMBASSADOR CEROX:
(INTERRUPTING)

Mediator Graf?

TILSON GRAF:
(PUT OUT)

Yes, Ambassador Cerox?

AMBASSADOR CEROX:
(IMPATIENT)

With the greatest respect, we are all aware of the reasons why we're here. Please, get on with it before—

FX: Ambassador Cerox is drowned out by the sudden, surging sounds of the riot just outside the building.

AMBASSADOR TINTAK:
(ANGRY, BARKING FRUSTRATION)

Oh, what *now*?

TILSON GRAF:
Umm . . .

CREIGHTON:
Aida. What's going on outside?

AIDA:
There's a crowd of people approaching the spire, Creighton. They're . . .

FX: A thrown rock puts out a window. The bellowing from outside grows louder. The crowd is angry.

AIDA:
(SHOCKED)

It's a *riot*!

CREIGHTON:
(WORRIED)

Get back, everyone. Away from the windows.

FX: A lightbow fires, somewhere else in the building.

MUFFLED SHOUT:
(FROM "OFF-SCREEN")

Stay back! All of you!

FX: More banging and clanging. The riot is spilling into the building close by. A door bursts open into the meeting chamber. It's Mesook, a Guardian of the Whills.

MESOOK:
(DESPERATE)

It's the civilians. They're rioting. They're swarming the building. We can't hold them back without a massacre.

FX: There are sounds of brutal close-quarter fighting from behind him. The Guardians aren't firing on the civilians unless they must.

TILSON GRAF:
(QUIETLY, AS HE RETREATS)

I . . . ummm . . . I think we'd better make for safety.

CREIGHTON:
(COMMANDING)

Ambassadors, to me.

AMBASSADOR TINTAK:
(FURIOUS)

Oh, no! I've had just about enough of this. Neutral ground? A peaceful place to sign the treaty. Pah!

There's been *three* bombings! And now you Jedi can't even keep the locals under control! This was all a terrible mistake.

AMBASSADOR CEROX:
Ambassador Tintak, please . . .

AMBASSADOR TINTAK:
No, Ambassador Cerox. No more! I'm leaving before anyone else gets hurt. Before *I* get hurt.

Guards—take me to my shuttle. *Now!*

E'RONOH GUARD:
Yes, sir!

FX: Tintak's guards muster.

AMBASSADOR CEROX:
(DESPERATE)

But what about the treaty?

AMBASSADOR TINTAK:
Damn the treaty, Cerox. What about our *lives*?

FX: Tintak starts to leave with his guards, but:

AIDA:
Ambassador, wait, don't—!

FX: There's a massive crash as a speeder bike bursts through the plate-glass window, splintering shards everywhere.

CREIGHTON:
Get down!

AIDA:
A speeder!

Ambassador Tintak!

FX: A blaster fires three times.

AMBASSADOR TINTAK:
(CRIES OUT IN PAIN)

AIDA:
(HORRIFIED)

Ambassador Tintak!

FX: Tintak slumps heavily to the floor, dead. The speeder slews around.

E'RONOH GUARD:
The ambassador! He's dead!

FX: Creighton's and Aida's lightsabers ignite. The speeder driver guns the throttle. The engine revs.

CREIGHTON:
Stop that speeder!

AMBASSADOR CEROX:
Light protect us!

FX: Blasters fire at the speeder and its driver.

E'RONOH GUARD:
(SHOUTING)

He's from Eiram! Look! He's wearing a uniform. The assassin is from Eiram!

AMBASSADOR CEROX:
No! That's not true!

FX: The speeder rushes off, roaring away, splintering more glass. All the while we can hear the riot spilling into the spire as angry people mass outside.

E'RONOH GUARD:
Soldiers of E'ronoh! The cease-fire is broken! Ambassador Tintak is dead! Deploy! Deploy!

FX: Blasters start firing.

CREIGHTON:
No! *Stop!*

EIRAM GUARD:
Return fire! Protect Ambassador Cerox! For Eiram!

FX: More blasters fire, from both sides. People cry out in pain as shots hit their marks. Furniture splinters. It's carnage. And it's loud.

AIDA:
(DISTRAUGHT)

What are you doing? *Stop! Think!* This isn't what any of you want!

FX: Aida's lightsaber whirls, deflecting blaster shots.

CREIGHTON:

There's nothing we can do, Aida. There are too many of them, and the rioters will be in here soon. We must get Ambassador Cerox to safety.

AMBASSADOR CEROX:
(BROKEN-SPIRITED)

It couldn't have been one of Eiram's. Not like that.

CREIGHTON:

No time to dwell on that now, Ambassador Cerox. Get behind me.

FX: Creighton's lightsaber whirls as they retreat.

AIDA:

Creighton, follow me! Through here. Quickly. There's a passage to the outside.

FX: They hurry through a small passage.

AMBASSADOR CEROX:

But the treaty. The *war* . . .

FX: They emerge outside. The sounds of the riot are all-consuming, and the battle rages between the guards inside, blasters firing indiscriminately.

CREIGHTON:
(LEVELLY)

I fear it's too late for that now.

AIDA:
(WITH DAWNING HORROR)

Look. The orbital transports.

AMBASSADOR CEROX:
(SHOCKED)

Forces from E'ronoh are deploying.

AIDA:
They're dropping war machines to the surface. Of the *Holy City.*

Deploying troops and skirmish ships . . .

FX: There's an appalled silence among the three of them for a moment as they weigh up what's happening.

AMBASSADOR CEROX:
(APPALLED)

We've failed.

The war is coming.

Here. On *Jedha.*

END OF PART THREE

Part Four
OUTBREAK

SCENE 62. EXT. JEDHA MARKETS

ATMOS: We're opening only a few moments after the end of the previous chapter. The riot is still in full swing, with people shouting, fighting, running, and the occasional discharging of a weapon.

FX: The Nameless shrieks loudly.

SILANDRA:
(WOOZY, PAINED)

No . . . I . . . where . . .

FX: Silandra staggers and falls to her knees. Her lightsaber powers off as it rolls from her fingers.

SILANDRA:
(PAINED)

So . . . arghhhhhh . . .

FX: The sound of the Nameless padding closer, but it's still some way off. We hear another person scream:

DYING FORCE-USER:
(DEATH SCREAM)

FX: And then slowly turn into a husk. Like a dry, crackling noise, followed by the sound of dust sifting into a heap.

SILANDRA:
No . . . no no no.

FX: The sound of P3-7A's thrusters as he powers in from above.

P3-7A:
The Force provides. Always.

FX: P3-7A grabs Silandra and begins to drag her away from the scene, back toward the crowds.

SILANDRA:
What . . . (UNGH) . . . Pee . . . Pee-Three?

P3-7A:
Sometimes the search for clarity requires perspective; to reach understanding, one must first put themselves at a distance from the problem they seek to resolve.

FX: P3-7A stops dragging Silandra.

SILANDRA:
(SIGHS WITH RELIEF)

I—thank you, Pee-Three, for pulling me out of there.

(Beat, then A LITTLE TREMULOUS)

I don't understand. I'm not sure what happened. It was like . . . like I couldn't *see*. As if I'd been shut off from the Force, and the world was closing in around me. Just this overwhelming sense of *pain*.

Just being near that thing was *terrifying*. I don't even know what it *was* . . .

P3-7A:
It takes time to understand one's place in the Force. And in the galaxy. Let patience be your guide.

FX: Silandra gets to her feet and staggers unsteadily.

SILANDRA:

And time to find one's balance, too, it seems.

I have to go back. To find that thing before it hurts anyone else.

P3-7A:

Sometimes, we come to someone too late to make a difference, and all we can do is mourn their loss and celebrate their union with the Force. The time for action has passed.

SILANDRA:

You mean it's gone.

P3-7A:

Hunger can be sated. Faith cannot.

SILANDRA:

All right. But I need to find my . . .

FX: P3-7A extends a mechanical arm, holding out her lightsaber.

P3-7A:

In faith, that which was lost might easily be found again.

SILANDRA:

My lightsaber! Ah. Thank you. I think I might be needing that.

(Beat, then MORE LIKE HERSELF)

Then we find Keth. Make sure he's safe. And then we warn the others of what's happened here.

P3-7A:

All travelers in the Force seek enlightenment.

SILANDRA:

Yes. That's exactly what I was thinking, too.

CUT TO:

SCENE 63. INT. INSIDE THE SECOND SPIRE

ATMOS: The battle continues to rage inside the building, with blaster-fire shrieking, people crying out, barked commands. On top of that, the rioting locals are now tearing the building apart as they rampage.

CREIGHTON:
Ambassador Cerox. *Lian.*

We *must* get you to safety.

FX: Aida and Creighton use their lightsabers to deflect errant blaster shots.

AIDA:
Is there somewhere we can take you? To your people?

AMBASSADOR CEROX:
Yes. My shuttle. It's in a private dock around the other side of the spire.

CREIGHTON:
All right. Come with us. And stay close.

AMBASSADOR CEROX:
I assure you, I'm not going anywhere.

FX: They begin to hurry around the other side of the spire. As they do, the sound of rioters grows louder.

ANGRY HUMAN RIOTER:

There! Look! Jedi! You heard the Herald! It's all their fault!

FX: There's a roar from the crowd. Thrown items start to clatter around the Jedi and Cerox.

AIDA:

We're going the other way around then, I guess.

FX: They retreat, circling back around the spire as the rioters give chase, still throwing things.

AIDA:

What could have driven people to *this*?

CREIGHTON:

They mentioned "the Herald." It has to be something to do with the Path of the Open Hand. But I don't think they're going to listen to reason. Not at the moment.

AMBASSADOR CEROX:

Can't you just . . . use the Force to stop them?

CREIGHTON:

The Force should *never* be used as a tool to manipulate others. Imposing our will on these civilians, no matter how angry or upset they are, could never be justified.

AMBASSADOR CEROX:

They might be civilians. But those ships up there—they're military vessels. Soon this place is going to be swarming with E'roni soldiers.

CREIGHTON:

Even more reason to get to your shuttle.

Come on, we're almost there.

FX: They run for a moment, feet crunching on gravel. We can hear the shuttle's engines have already powered up.

AMBASSADOR CEROX:
There. On the dock.

CREIGHTON:
Go!

DUTIFUL EIRAM GUARD:
Ambassador! Over here!

FX: Ambassador Cerox shouts ahead to the guard as she runs the last few steps to the shuttle.

AMBASSADOR CEROX:
(SHOUTING OVER THE ENGINE WHINE)

Get us up to orbit. Quickly. And give the order to deploy our forces. We must be ready for them.

CREIGHTON:
(SHOUTING OVER THE ENGINE WHINE)

No! Ambassador—if you deploy Eiram's forces now, there's no going back. Any chance at peace will be over.

Please. Think about this. Consider the consequences. Think about the people of Jedha who are going to get caught in the crossfire. This isn't what the heirs would want. If we can find a way to contact Xiri and Phan-tu, make them withdraw the E'roni guards . . .

AMBASSADOR CEROX:
(SHOUTING OVER THE ENGINE WHINE)

The heirs aren't *here*! They haven't seen what I've seen.

I'm sorry, Creighton. It's too late. The E'roni are blaming us for the assassination of Tintak. They won't stop. We have no choice. We must defend ourselves.

It's over.

CREIGHTON:
No . . .

FX: The shuttle door hinges shut. The shuttle lifts off as the rioters come around the corner en masse.

AIDA:
Creighton, the mob, they're here.

Creighton.

CREIGHTON:
Right. We need to quell the riot before things escalate. With E'roni and Eirami soldiers on the ground, the civilians will be at risk.

AIDA:
We need Mesook and the Guardians. We can't do this alone.

FX: The rioters are yelling as they charge.

CREIGHTON:
Come on. Let's get back inside.

AIDA:
How?

CREIGHTON:
Remember that speeder?

AIDA:
(NOTE OF WARNING)

Creighton . . .

FX: There's a massive smash as Creighton leaps through a closed window.

AIDA:

(SIGHS)

All right, then, smart-ass.

FX: Aida follows him through.

CUT TO:

SCENE 64. INT. ENLIGHTENMENT TAPBAR

ATMOS: Despite the riots outside, everything is the same in Enlightenment . . .

FX: The door opens and Silandra staggers in, along with P3-7A.

KETH:
Silandra? Pee-Three?

FX: Keth runs over.

SILANDRA:
(RELIEVED)

You made it. I was worried. The streets—

KETH:
—have turned into a riot. I know. It's like the whole world has gone mad. Everywhere except in here. It's always mad in here.

FX: Kradon skitters over to join them.

KRADON:
Never is there any trouble in Enlightenment. Kradon assures all that their worries stay at the door. Here, all are welcome, and all are safe.

KETH:

Come on. There's a drink for you on the bar.

KRADON:

Kradon is generous. Friends' rates still apply.

FX: Kradon skitters off.

P3-7A:

Acceptance is the key to happiness. To exclude others is to lock a little piece of yourself away, every day.

KETH:

Pee-Three—how can I be leaving you out? You *can't* drink. And you're here, aren't you?

FX: Silandra and Keth drop into seats at the bar.

MOONA:

You look terrible, Jedi. But I guess you didn't get yourself killed after all.

SILANDRA:

I'm sorry? You are?

KETH:

This is Moona.

MOONA:

Keth said you went chasing after a guy on a speeder bike who was shooting at you with a blaster. I bet him a drink you weren't coming back.

SILANDRA:

Ah. Well, sorry.

MOONA:

You win some, you lose some.

KETH:

What happened?

SILANDRA:
He got away. He started firing on civilians. I had no choice.

KETH:
Did you get a good look at him?

SILANDRA:
No. That's the strange thing. I can't seem to remember what he looked like. I know he was wearing gray robes. But so's half of Jedha.

KETH:
You probably didn't have time to take a proper look.

SILANDRA:
Hmmm. Maybe.

And you?

KETH:
I looked for you and Pee-Three in the crowds. But when the riot started up, I figured you'd think to meet back here.

SILANDRA:
Good thinking.

FX: Silandra takes a drink and then coughs as it hits the back of her throat.

SILANDRA:
(COUGHS)

KETH:
Do you know what started it?

SILANDRA:
I can't be sure, but it sounded very much like a certain Nautolan zealot was working the crowd into a frenzy.

KETH:
The Path of the Open Hand.

SILANDRA:
And then . . .

KETH:
What?

SILANDRA:
There was something loose in the crowd. An animal, I think . . .

KETH:
Some of those wargarans that escaped from their crates.

SILANDRA:
(UNSURE)

No . . . I . . . I don't think so.

FX: Silandra takes another swig of her drink.

SILANDRA:
Something horrible. Something unexpected. It messed with my head . . . just like the feeling I had in the almshouse, when we spoke to the Mother of the Path.

KETH:
Did you stop it?

SILANDRA:
No. It got away, too. Thank the Light Pee-Three was there. He got me clear before it could . . . well, before it got to me. But there were others. It did something to them. Turned them to *husks.*

KETH:
Husks? Well, I'm glad Pee-Three was around to get you out of there.

MOONA:
A Jedi saved by a droid. Now, there's a tale.

KETH:
But what's all that got to do with the bombs? And the guy on the speeder who attacked us?

SILANDRA:

I don't know. Perhaps nothing. Perhaps everything. But that strange feeling can't be a coincidence. I can't help but think that the Path have something to do with it, but I can't put my finger on what exactly.

(FRUSTRATED)

If I could just make sense of what happened at the spire that day . . .

KETH:
(SHEEPISH)

Ah. Well. There's something I've been meaning to tell you about that. An admission . . .

MOONA:
Oh, here we go. I *told* you not to say anything about it.

SILANDRA:
What is it?

KETH:
(NERVOUS)

It's just . . . I think it might have been my fault.

SILANDRA:
(CONFUSED)

What was your fault?

KETH:
The bomb. Or at least, the fact the droid was able to get inside the spire.

Oh, man. Why is this so hard . . .

SILANDRA:
I think you'd better tell me what's going on, Keth.

KETH:
Just . . .

FX: He glugs the rest of his drink.

KETH:
Okay. Here goes.

MOONA:
Keth . . .

KETH:
Shhh. This is something I have to do.

SILANDRA:
Go on.

KETH:
It started that morning. I told you I was running late. *Very* late. Morton San Tekka was a very understanding man, but even so, I was cutting it fine. And Pee-Three . . . he wanted in.

SILANDRA:
Wanted in?

P3-7A:
There is no differ—

KETH:
(CUTTING HIM OFF)

Not now, Pee-Three.

(TO SILANDRA)

He wanted to come to the ceremony. To see the big event. Of course, I told him no, but he wasn't having it. And so, I figured—what harm could it do?

SILANDRA:
Indeed.

KETH:
And so, when the mediator asked me to fetch a glass of water, I took the opportunity to run upstairs to the next level.

SILANDRA:
And . . .

KETH:
And I opened a window to let Pee-Three in.

SILANDRA:
I see.

KETH:
I was coming back down when the bomb went off.

SILANDRA:
And how is that your fault?

KETH:
I breached security! I let Pee-Three inside. But I left the window open. What if that's how the other droid got in, too?

SILANDRA:
Did you *see* any other droids?

KETH:
Well . . . no.

SILANDRA:
Then it wasn't your fault, Keth.

KETH:
(RELIEVED)

It wasn't?

SILANDRA:
No. The ceremonial droid that carried the bomb was seen talking to someone in the lobby before it was blown to bits. It didn't come in through the window. And besides, it had to

have already been inside for the bomb to go off while you were still coming back down the stairs.

KETH:
Well, I'll drink to that.

Barkeep? Another.

SILANDRA:
The only strange thing is that the descriptions of the person seen with the droid don't seem to match. It's as if everyone saw something different.

But . . .

KETH:
What?

SILANDRA:
You said Pee-Three was there? Inside the conference?

KETH:
Yes. Well. I know he wasn't supposed to be, but—

SILANDRA:
That doesn't matter. What counts is that he was there. He might have seen something.

KETH:
Pee-Three?

P3-7A:
The Force is a constant presence. It guides, and it flows. It is truth incarnate.

KETH:
(WITH DISBELIEF)

You saw them, didn't you?

FX: A hatch opens on the side of P3-7A with a pneumatic hiss.

SILANDRA:
He's giving us access to his databank.

Keth?

KETH:
Unbelievable.

Come here, Pee-Three. Let's see what secrets you're hiding . . .

CUT TO:

SCENE 65. INT. THE SECOND SPIRE—MEETING CHAMBER

ATMOS: The sounds of the riot are carrying on outside, but in here, there's an eerie silence. The fight here is over.

FX: Creighton walks, crunching broken glass with every step. His lightsaber hums.

CREIGHTON:
(GRIM)

Eiram and Eronoh's guards are all dead. All of them.

AIDA:
They blasted away at each other until there was no one left.

(Beat, then SADDENED)

What a terrible, terrible waste.

CREIGHTON:
Soon the whole of Jedha is going to look like this. A graveyard. The peace treaty is as dead as these poor soldiers.

AIDA:
We have to *try* to stop it. If only to protect the civilians. The pilgrims here for the festival. The children. We can't allow them to be caught in the crossfire.

CREIGHTON:
(EMPHATIC)

We *won't.*

FX: Creighton continues to walk through the ruins of the meeting chamber, crunching broken glass.

CREIGHTON:
Why does every attempt at peace end in death and ruin?

AIDA:
Perhaps it's just the *cost* of peace. That it's hard won. That it hurts because it's worthwhile. Worth fighting for. Precious.

CREIGHTON:
We need to be better, Aida. All of us. We need to recognize what we have and help the galaxy cling on to it.

FX: Aida crosses to Creighton and puts a hand on his shoulder.

AIDA:
We will. The Jedi Order, the Republic—we'll find a way. One day, we'll be the beacon of peace that the galaxy needs.

But we're not there yet. In the meantime, we have to do all we can and hope it's enough.

CREIGHTON:
Yes. You're right.

I . . . Thank you, Aida.

(Beat, AND THEN)

AIDA:
Hold on. What happened to the mediator, Tilson Graf?

CREIGHTON:
He's long gone. He was nervous from the start. Kept looking at the windows, drumming his fingers . . .

AIDA:
(SURPRISED)

Surely you can't think he had anything to do with it?

CREIGHTON:
I don't know. I just . . .

We need to find him, either way. Maybe he had something to do with it, maybe he didn't.

AIDA:
Or maybe he was just *scared.*

CREIGHTON:
(FRUSTRATED)

That's just the problem, isn't it? There's too many maybes, and no answers!

AIDA:
There's nothing we can do about it now. We've got more pressing concerns.

CREIGHTON:
All right. You find Mesook or Selik and see how many Guardians of the Whills you can round up. I'll find Bee-Nine and try to get a message through to Coruscant. Maybe they can send support. We're going to need it.

AIDA:
Agreed.

FX: They both run off in opposite directions.

CUT TO:

SCENE 66. EXT. JEDHA MARKETS—MAIN SQUARE

ATMOS: The riot is in full swing. People are fighting, trashing buildings, transports, stalls. Overhead, E'roni military shuttles are coming in to land. Lots of them.

FX: Pela is running, searching for someone to help her in the chaos.

PELA:
(FRANTIC)

Herald?

Mother?

Marda?

FX: The sound of a shuttle landing. The doors hinge open. E'roni soldiers spill from the hold.

E'RONI SERGEANT:
Get back! Everyone! Clear these streets.

FX: People scream. There's a burst of a blaster being fired into the air.

E'RONI SERGEANT:
I repeat: Clear these streets!

PELA:
(SPOTTING THE MOTHER IN THE CROWD, CALLING)

Mother!

There you are.

FX: Pela runs over to her.

THE MOTHER:
(ANXIOUS)

Pela. Thank the Force. You're all right.

PELA:
(SCARED)

I'm *scared.*

What's happening? I was out with the Littles, delivering gifts, when all the people . . . they just seemed to turn on each other. Suddenly everyone was jostling and shouting, and then *fighting,* and then . . .

. . . I saw a man get trampled. And now all these shuttles and soldiers . . .

THE MOTHER:
(SUPERIOR)

The Force is unbalanced. The Jedi have brought this down upon us, Pela. Upon all of Jedha.

The war has come.

PELA:
(SHOCKED)

What should we do?

THE MOTHER:

Get the Littles to safety. Find somewhere close and wait until we come for you.

We'll find a safe way off Jedha. The Force wills it.

PELA:
Right. Yes. I'll head to the almshouse.

THE MOTHER:
No. Not there. I've just come from there.

(FALTERING)

The almshouse has been ... It's been attacked, Pela. In the riots. Damaged beyond repair.

PELA:
(APPALLED)

They attacked a house of healing! But ... all those people.

THE MOTHER:
I know, Pela.

FX: More shots being fired into the air.

E'RONI SERGEANT:
(BARKING COMMANDS IN BACKGROUND)

Eirami forces incoming! Take up positions!

THE MOTHER:
Go, Pela. Protect the Littles. They need you now.

PELA:
I'll find somewhere. But—what about you? And Marda and the others?

THE MOTHER:
Don't worry about us. We'll do what the Path does best—help anyone in need.

And show them all that the Jedi have failed them.

CUT TO:

SCENE 67. EXT. JEDHA SIDE STREET

ATMOS: In the distance we can hear the riot in full swing. Military ships are still deploying all around.

FX: Footsteps hurry down a street, then stop. Knuckles rap three times on a door.

TILSON GRAF:
It's Graf.

Let me in.

FX: For a moment there's no reply, then the door creaks open on badly oiled hinges. Tilson Graf enters the building.

TILSON GRAF:
Well?

FX: When Baarla speaks, it's with the same unnerving, triple-layered voice that we've heard from the Brothers of the Ninth Door before.

BAARLA:
Well, *what?*

TILSON GRAF:
Where's Mytion?

BAARLA:
In the temple. Down there.

TILSON GRAF:
(SURPRISED)

Temple?

You have a temple, *here*? I thought this festering stink hole was where the Brothers of the Ninth Door *lived,* not worshipped.

BAARLA:
It is both our home and our temple.

See for yourself.

FX: Tilson Graf crosses a stone floor, and then starts down some stone steps.

BAARLA:
(CALLING AFTER HIM)

Only . . . watch out for the vines.

TILSON GRAF:
(TO SELF, CONFUSED)

The vines?

FX: He gets to the bottom of the stone steps. Something slithers menacingly.

TILSON GRAF:
(DISGUSTED)

Oh. So *those* are the vines . . .

FX: The vines continue to slither, writhing up his legs, pinning him in place.

TILSON GRAF:
(APPALLED)

Urgh. Get it off me!

(Beat, then CALLING)

Mytion!

(Beat, then ANGRY)

Mytion! Get these damn things off of me!

FX: Footsteps approach. When Mytion speaks, his voice bears the same sinister layering as before.

MYTION:
(LAUGHS)

Mr. Graf. I see you've met our friendly guardians.

TILSON GRAF:
(FORCEFUL)

I said: Get them off of me.

MYTION:
(INDULGENT)

As you wish.

FX: The vines slither away. Tilson Graf brushes himself down. He steps clear.

TILSON GRAF:
What are those things?

MYTION:
Just a little insurance policy to dissuade any unwanted visitors who happen upon our little temple.

TILSON GRAF:
(TESTILY)

And I'm unwanted, am I? Me *and* my credits?

MYTION:
I let you in, didn't I?

FX: They walk into the underground temple, footsteps echoing. We can hear a distant drip of water.

TILSON GRAF:
(SARCASTIC)

I can see why you're so keen to protect the place. It's so . . . cozy.

MYTION:
And now you see what I intend to do with those credits you were so quick to mention, Mr. Graf. I shall build a new lodge for my order. Here on Jedha. A new place of worship amongst the churches and temples of the other religions that call this city their home.

TILSON GRAF:
Assuming there's anything left of Jedha after the riots have ended. E'ronoh's forces are deploying from their orbital transports. This place is going to become a war zone.

MYTION:
The brothers will be on hand to assist in the rebuilding. We shall earn the respect of the people and be duly recognized and accepted by the Convocation as a legitimate sect.

TILSON GRAF:
(MUTTERING TO SELF)

Always the same story.

(Beat, then BRIGHTER)

Well, I hope it all works out for you. But first you have to *earn* those credits, don't you?

Is the Jedi dead?

MYTION:
(HESITANT)

Not yet.

TILSON GRAF:
(ANGRY)

Not yet? Then you'd better get on and finish the job, hadn't you? I want her dead.

And the others, while you're at it. Creighton Sun and Aida Forte. Finish them all. The riots will give you all the cover you need. You can even make it look like they were killed by Eiram and E'ronoh, if you like. I know how you enjoy your little . . . *illusions.*

But finish it *soon.* I want off this rock, and I don't want any unfinished business.

MYTION:
(WITH RISING TENSION)

Watch your tone, Mr. Graf. The Brothers of the Ninth Door are not at your beck and call.

TILSON GRAF:
Oh, but you *are,* aren't you, Mytion? How else are you going to get your new temple, hmm?

FX: Tilson Graf starts to walk away.

TILSON GRAF:
Deal with it *now,* Mytion, and all of our problems will evaporate like rain on a warm summer's day . . .

CUT TO:

SCENE 68. INT. ENLIGHTENMENT TAPBAR

ATMOS: As before, but we can hear the battle outside now, even beneath the playing of the harp.

SILANDRA:
I need to get out there. To help.

KETH:
(CONCENTRATING)

We're almost done . . . Just . . .

FX: There's a series of beeps as Keth fiddles with P3-7A's inner workings. A holoprojector whirs.

KETH:
That's it!

FX: The holo whirs on for a moment.

SILANDRA:
Is that the day of the first bomb?

KETH:
Yes. But earlier.

SILANDRA:

Play it forward. We don't need that much insight into your sleeping arrangements.

KETH:
(EMBARRASSED)

Hold on . . .

FX: More beeping and fiddling.

KETH:

There. That's the Second Spire, where the treaty was supposed to be signed.

And that's me opening the window.

SILANDRA:

Hold on. Roll it back a moment. This is too late. We need to see if Pee-Three saw anything prior to entering the building.

FX: More beeping and fiddling.

SILANDRA:
Stop!

There. That's it! That must be the ceremonial droid that Creighton mentioned.

KETH:

And who's that crouched next to it? That must be the person everyone claims to have seen.

SILANDRA:

Yes. But they're wearing black robes. I can't quite . . .

. . . hold on. Is that a—

KETH:
(FINISHING HER SENTENCE)

—skull mask. *Yes.* And that means it's a—

BOTH TOGETHER:
Brother of the Ninth Door.

SILANDRA:
Like the ones we met in the market, with the backfiring speeder.

FX: Keth starts to close the hatch on P3-7A's outer shell.

SILANDRA:
But it doesn't make sense. No one described seeing a Brother of the Ninth Door. Or even anyone in black robes.

And why would a local sect have any interest in disrupting the signing of an interplanetary peace treaty?

KETH:
Hang on. If anyone will know more about them, it's Kradon. He has his fingers in everything that happens here on Jedha.

(Beat, then CALLING)

Kradon?

FX: Kradon comes skittering over.

KRADON:
Yes, my boy? Kradon is at your service.

KETH:
What do you know about the Brothers of the Ninth Door?

KRADON:
Ah . . . now. Understand that Kradon does not say this lightly, but he does have a *reputation* to maintain. Not to mention a tapbar. An *expensive* tapbar.

So it is that Kradon's generosity must have its limits, even for the dearest of friends.

Of course, for you, my dear boy—and for your Jedi accomplice, preferable rates *do* still apply . . .

KETH:
(SIGHS)

How much do you want?

KRADON:
Now, now, young Keth. Haste has ever been the downfall of the inexperienced negotiator.

Zukkels are not the only currency of interest.

KETH:
Then what is?

SILANDRA:
He wants a favor.

KETH:
A favor?

KRADON:
Most perceptive, my Jedi friend.

KETH:
What sort of favor?

KRADON:
The sort that only one of the Order might extend . . .

SILANDRA:
Name your price, Kradon.

KRADON:
Merely that Kradon would have your word that you will do all in your power—*all* in your power—to protect his young adjunct friend from the imminent danger at our door.

KETH:
(TOUCHED)

Kradon . . .

SILANDRA:
You have a deal. And you needn't have asked. I am a Jedi.

KRADON:
(LIGHTLY)

And Kradon is a barkeep who must ensure his best customers *remain* his best customers. So that they might entertain us all with stories, yes?

KETH:
Thank you, Kradon.

P3-7A:
All things are equal in the Force. A life is a life.

KRADON:
Kradon thinks perhaps your droid is cleverer than we thought, eh boy?

KETH:
I don't doubt it.

SILANDRA:
So, now that's all settled . . .

KRADON:
Yes, yes. A debt of information. Allow Kradon to say this: While all are welcome in Enlightenment, there are those who are renowned for not paying their bills.

SILANDRA:
I hardly think that constitutes—

KRADON:
(SHUSHING HER)

Shhhh. Shhhh.

Do you think that Kradon is not observant? Do you think the Twinkle sisters would allow patrons to leave without settling their tabs?

KETH:
Not a chance.

KRADON:
Mmmm. Indeed.

SILANDRA:
So?

KRADON:
So—it is whispered that these "Brothers of the Ninth Door" have the most remarkable ability. They enter an establishment wearing one face and leave wearing another.

SILANDRA:
(SURPRISED)

Shape-shifters?

KRADON:
No, no. Not quite. More that they have perfected a technique for clouding one's mind. To recall the visage of a Brother of the Ninth Door is to see what one *wants* to see, rather than what *was*.

SILANDRA:
(CONCERNED)

Power like that—it sounds like it could be the dark side of the Force.

KRADON:
As Kradon says—*all* are welcome in Enlightenment . . . provided they pay their bills.

FX: Kradon leaves.

SILANDRA:
That must be it, then. They were the ones behind the bombings.

KETH:

It certainly explains why all the eyewitnesses reported different things.

SILANDRA:

I need to get this information to Creighton and Aida. If they can prove to the ambassadors that neither Eiram nor E'ronoh were responsible, perhaps we can still save the peace process. And Jedha.

FX: Silandra pulls out her comlink. It crackles and hisses with static.

SILANDRA:

Creighton? Aida?

Can you hear me? Creighton, Aida?

FX: The only reply is dead static.

SILANDRA:

It's no use. The comms are still down. I'll have to go in person.

KETH:

But the riots . . .

SILANDRA:

A risk I'm going to have to take.

KETH:
(EMPHATIC)

We're going to have to take, you mean.

SILANDRA:

No. You need to stay here, where it's safe. You heard what I said to Kradon. Things are volatile out there. It could be dangerous.

KETH:

All my life, I've wanted to *do* something, Silandra. Something important, something that made a difference. To be a part of the Force. To grow within the church, to help people. To be someone who *mattered,* to make my time in the galaxy count.

All I do is come here, to Enlightenment, to hear everyone else's stories. To live vicariously through tales of distant worlds and different peoples, of Jedi and monsters and adventure.

And now here I am. *Me.* Helping a Jedi to do the right thing. Trying to stop a *war.*

Do you think I'm about to give up on that now? No matter how dangerous it is, I want to *help.*

SILANDRA:
(SIGHS)

Now you're starting to sound like my Padawan.

KETH:
(BRIGHTLY)

I am?

P3-7A:
Our greatest strength is to recognize that we are not alone. We are all a part of the living Force, and the living Force is part of us. Together, we are stronger.

SILANDRA:
All right. But you stay close. And you do what I say. Okay?

KETH:
Okay.

SILANDRA:
We go straight for the Second Spire. We find Creighton and Aida.

KETH:
Understood.

FX: Silandra and Keth stand up.

SILANDRA:
You'd better settle the bill.

KETH:

(DISMISSIVE)

Nah, Kradon's good to stick it on my tab.

SILANDRA:

Then what was all that about, earlier?

KETH:

(LAUGHS)

He likes to put on a good show . . .

CUT TO:

SCENE 69. INT. THE SECOND SPIRE—BRIEFING CHAMBER

ATMOS: The background hum of the equipment, as before. But now we can hear the battle outside the spire, too. Ships shooting at one another. A distant explosion. Blasters firing. People shouting and screaming.

FX: The crackle of static, followed by the choppy sounds of someone trying to speak.

CREIGHTON:
(FRUSTRATED)

Come on! Come *on*!

GT-68:
(MOURNFUL)

Beedle-do-whooo.

B-9H0:
Geetee-Sixtyate says that he is doing his best, sir. The situation outside hasn't helped matters with the poor communications.

CREIGHTON:
(SNAPPING)

Yes, I *know*, Bee-Nine!

FX: There's a moment of silence. The crackle of more static.

CREIGHTON:

(SIGHS)

I'm sorry, Bee-Nine. It's just . . .

B-9H0:

You're anxious, sir. How about a soothing glass of Munck-jaa juice?

CREIGHTON:

(LEVELLY)

No, Bee-Nine. I'm fine.

FX: The crackle suddenly resolves into speech, but while understandable, it remains broken and choppy:

XINITH TARL:

(VIA HOLO)

—there, Creighton? I can barely hear you.

CREIGHTON:

Master Tarl! Thank the Light.

XINITH TARL:

(VIA HOLO)

You sound anxious, Master Sun. I take it things are not progressing as planned on Jedha.

CREIGHTON:

To say the least. We need urgent support. Any Jedi or Republic troops in the immediate area should be dispatched *now*.

XINITH TARL:

(VIA HOLO)

Creighton—what's happened?

CREIGHTON:

Ambassador Tintak of E'ronoh has been murdered. His people are blaming Eiram. The treaty is in tatters. Both sides are deploying military forces.

XINITH TARL:
(VIA HOLO, WITH DISBELIEF)

To *Jedha*?

CREIGHTON:
I'm afraid the Holy City is now a battleground. And to make matters worse, the people are rioting in the streets. They're going to get caught in the crossfire.

XINITH TARL:
(VIA HOLO)

By the Light.

CREIGHTON:
Aida is rallying the Guardians of the Whills. We'll do all we can to bring things under control.

But Master Tarl—it doesn't look good.

XINITH TARL:
(VIA HOLO)

For Jedha, or for the galaxy.

CREIGHTON:
Please—get help here as soon as possible.

XINITH TARL:
(VIA HOLO)

We'll do all we can.

May the Force be with you, Master Sun.

FX: The holo cuts out.

CREIGHTON:
May the Force be with us all.

FX: There's a brief pause. Then:

CREIGHTON:
Geetee? See if you can contact the Eirami transport ship. I want to speak to Ambassador Cerox.

GT-68:
Boo-dah-deeee.

CREIGHTON:
Just do it, Geetee. I know the signal is still choppy.

FX: There's another burst of static. It crackles for a moment before there's a chime. The line is bad, full of pops and whistles.

AMBASSADOR CEROX:
(VIA HOLO)

Creighton. I'm a little busy. What do you want? And don't tell me you need me to stand my forces down.

CREIGHTON:
I need you to stand your forces down.

AMBASSADOR CEROX:
(VIA HOLO)

I've told you already, it's *too late.*

CREIGHTON:
It's never too late. You could stop this *now.* You hold it all in your hands. One word from you, and we could be back in the spire, talking about *peace.*

AMBASSADOR CEROX:
(VIA HOLO)

No, Master Jedi.

You don't understand. It was too late before we even got to Jedha. Too late a year ago. Too late the moment innocent people like me, all over Eiram, lost their children to this bloody war.

CREIGHTON:

But what about everything we've been trying to build? What about Phan-tu and Xiri, and the union? You were there the day of the wedding. You saw how they persevered through everything that happened, to find a way to claim a future for both planets. To find a path to peace.

AMBASSADOR CEROX:
(VIA HOLO)

You think that matters? You think the people of Eiram care about what those trumped-up royals have to say about *any* of this?

For years they asked us to fight their battles. To sacrifice our loved ones—our husbands, wives, partners, and children—on the altar of their glorious war. And we did so, *willingly.*

We followed them to hell. We pledged our very existence to their cause.

And then, one day, just like that, they tell us to lay down our weapons. That the fighting is over. That there will be no more bloodshed.

As if everything that had gone before could just be *forgotten.* As if we could simply accept our losses and move on. Be friends with the people who killed our loved ones. Perhaps even *marry* them . . .

No one came and asked *us* about peace, Creighton. No one cared how we, the people of Eiram, felt about this so-called union. And we've lost too much to just accept it all without a fight.

So yes. I want them to pay. Pay for what they've done to my world, and my family. I want them all to pay.

And as I told you, back when all this started: There are plenty of others who aren't prepared to forgive and forget. Who want justice.

CREIGHTON:
This is no kind of justice, Lian. Innocent people are dying.

AMBASSADOR CEROX:
(VIA HOLO)

Innocent people have been dying for years.

It's nothing new, Creighton. Even the lauded *Jedi* can't change that.

But maybe now I can finally put an end to it. I can win this war for Eiram.

CREIGHTON:
This isn't the way.

AMBASSADOR CEROX:
(VIA HOLO)

It's the only way.

Goodbye, Creighton.

FX: The holo goes dead.

CREIGHTON:
I'm sorry, Lian.

I'm sorry for you all.

CUT TO:

SCENE 70. EXT. JEDHA STREET

ATMOS: It's chaos outside when Silandra, Keth, and P3-7A emerge from Enlightenment. Not only are people still rioting, both E'ronoh's and Eiram's militaries have deployed into the Holy City. So, we have distant blasterfire, explosions, shouting, screaming—all the myriad sounds of conflict and war.

SILANDRA:
(APPALLED)

By the Light . . . it's a *war zone.*

KETH:
The peace treaty . . . something's gone wrong.

Horribly wrong.

SILANDRA:
Whatever the Brothers of the Ninth Door were planning, it's worked. Those are Eirami and E'roni troops. This is far beyond a mere riot.

FX: The whine of an E'roni mining loader clomping heavily down the street. It's a platform on two stocky legs, designed for lifting hunks of marble, but it's been adapted to add an armored turret and heavy weap-

ons. It turns its turret and fires its cannons. A section of street explodes. People scream.

SILANDRA:

They've deployed ordnance! That's a mining loader. E'ronoh's military must have adapted them for battle.

FX: Silandra's shield flares on.

KETH:

How are we going to get through *this*?

SILANDRA:

Change of plan. We're *not*.

FX: The mining loader stomps on for a moment, then stops. Its head turns again. A woman screams.

DISTRAUGHT WOMAN:
(SCREAMS)

No! My home!

FX: The mining loader's weapons whine as they power up.

ZEALOUS EIRAM SOLDIER:
Get out of the way!

FX: The mining loader fires. A chunk of building explodes. Mortar and rubble rain down. Silandra uses the Force to propel her shield. The rubble bounces off the shield as it blocks the debris from hitting the woman.

KETH:

Whoa . . . your shield . . . How did you throw it like *that*?

P3-7A:

The Force guides the hand of those who would stand in the way of harm.

DISTRAUGHT WOMAN:
(DESPERATE)

Thank you! Thank you!

SILANDRA:
(KIND BUT COMMANDING)

Run, now. Find shelter.

FX: The woman runs.

ZEALOUS EIRAM SOLDIER:
Fire! *Fire!*

FX: Blasters rake the loader. It lurches, then fires again. We hear the Eiram soldier die horribly in a blast.

ZEALOUS EIRAM SOLDIER:
(DEATH SCREAM)

SILANDRA:
This is all-out war. We need to get people to safety. They're going to get caught in the crossfire.

FX: The loader is powering up its weapons again.

KETH:
So are we!

SILANDRA:
Hold on.

FX: Silandra's lightsaber flares to life.

SILANDRA:
(GRUNTS WITH EXERTION, CALLING)

And stand back!

FX: Silandra's lightsaber whooshes as she leaps, rebounding off the side of a building with the scrape of her boots . . .

SHOCKED LOADER PILOT:
Watch out! A *Jedi!*

FX: Silandra's lightsaber cuts through one of the loader's legs with a whoosh. There's a mechanical grind as the loader staggers, missteps, and buckles noisily.

SHOCKED LOADER PILOT:
Bail out! Bail!

FX: The loader crashes loudly into the side of a building, bringing part of the building crashing to the ground as the loader rends it and collapses to a rest.

FX: Silandra lands back beside Keth.

SILANDRA:
There.

KETH:
But . . . I thought the Jedi weren't supposed to be taking sides.

SILANDRA:
The only side I'm taking is that of the innocent people of Jedha. They didn't ask for any of this. It's our duty to protect them.

To be their shield.

FX: There's a hail of blasterfire. Silandra deflects it with her lightsaber. The crowds are still screaming.

KETH:
What about getting to the spire?

SILANDRA:
It'll have to wait. Besides—it's a little late for that now. The damage is done.

FX: We hear the scream of ships zooming overhead, the repeating chatter of their blasters. One of the ships takes a hit and dives into a building, causing the ship to detonate.

SILANDRA:
All we can do now is save as many lives as we can, and hope that Creighton and Aida have a plan.

FX: A crowd of people come charging down the street toward us, screaming in fear. We can hear more mining loaders in their wake stomping and shooting.

KETH:
(STRUCK BY AN IDEA)

The dome.

SILANDRA:
I'm sorry?

KETH:
The Dome of Deliverance. That way.

We can lead people there to take cover.

SILANDRA:
Yes. It's big enough to contain half the population of the city. And the dome should provide shelter from stray fire.

FX: Silandra's lightsaber hums as she bats away more stray blaster shots.

SILANDRA:
Do it.

KETH:
(SHOCKED)

Me?

SILANDRA:
Who else? I'll cover you. Meet you there.

FX: There's a pause as Keth considers. The sounds of fighting and screaming civilians are closing in.

SILANDRA:
You can do this, Keth.

KETH:
All right.

SILANDRA:
Good. Take Pee-Three.

FX: An explosion rocks a nearby building. The fleeing civilians are getting closer, and louder.

SILANDRA:
(VOICE RAISED ABOVE NOISE OF CROWD)

Now *go*, before there's no people left to save!

KETH:
(SHOUTING)

This way! Everyone! This way! Head for the Dome of Deliverance!

MAN IN CROWD:
You heard him! Head for the dome!

FX: The crowd surges after Keth and P3-7A. After a moment, we hear the oncoming whine and clomp and the other mining loaders coming toward us. Silandra twirls her lightsaber so that it hums.

SILANDRA:
(DETERMINED)

Right then.

CUT TO:

SCENE 71. EXT. OUTSIDE THE SECOND SPIRE

ATMOS: The fighting is just as intense here. It's carnage. Ships flit above everything, firing. Explosions rock the streets below.

FX: A lightbow fires in the foreground. An enforcer droid explodes. Creighton comes running.

CREIGHTON:
Aida?

FX: More lightbows fire. Another droid explodes.

AIDA:
Creighton. Eiram has deployed enforcer droids. Scores of them.

CREIGHTON:
Enforcer droids? Where did they get those?

AIDA:
I don't know. But they're coming in hot and fast. Watch out!

FX: Aida throws her lightsaber. It vrooms through the air, bisecting a droid in two. The droid crumples to the ground. She uses the Force to recover her lightsaber and reignites it.

CREIGHTON:
Thanks.

How many Guardians did you manage to round up?

AIDA:
Not enough. Mesook and Selik have done all that they can.

FX: Another lightbow shot fires.

MESOOK:
(CALLING OVER)

We're spread too thin, defending the city *and* protecting the civilians.

CREIGHTON:
There must be others out there, helping Silandra and any other Jedi scattered throughout the city. I left Bee-Nine broadcasting a repeated call for aid. I've not been able to reach any of them because of the problems with the local comm systems, but I'm certain they'll be helping where they can.

MESOOK:
Of course. And some of the other sects are doing what they can, too. But nowhere is safe. E'ronoh has set weaponized mining loaders loose in the streets, carrying heavy ordnance.

CREIGHTON:
(CURSING)

Damn.

AIDA:
There'll be nothing left of Jedha soon if we can't stop this.

I tried reaching the E'roni commander, but he refused to respond. With Ambassador Tintak dead, it seems they're unwilling to talk.

CREIGHTON:

And I spoke to Ambassador Cerox.

AIDA:

You did?

CREIGHTON:

She's not backing down. It's like she was just waiting for the excuse to deploy her troops. As if she never believed in the peace process in the first place.

AIDA:

The heirs will hold her to account.

CREIGHTON:

By then it'll be too late. For Jedha at least.

AIDA:

Did you get through to Coruscant?

FX: Creighton's lightsaber whips, deflecting a blaster shot.

CREIGHTON:

I spoke with Master Tarl. She's sending all the support she can muster. The question is whether we can hold out until they get here . . .

AIDA:

I know. But we must have faith. It's all we have left.

CREIGHTON:

Not quite. We have each other. And the Guardians of the Whills. We can try to take the sting out of their tails.

AIDA:

How?

CREIGHTON:

We split up. You take Selik and a contingent of Guardians and spread into the streets, focus on taking down E'ronoh's war machines. Me, Mesook, and the rest will focus on the enforcer droids. At least that way we might be able to minimize loss of life.

AIDA:
And damage to the city.

CREIGHTON:
Exactly. We don't take any lives. On either side. But we might just be able to take some bite out of the fight. At least until the reinforcements arrive.

If they arrive.

AIDA:
All right.

(TO MESOOK)

Mesook?

FX: Mesook fires his lightbow again. Another enforcer droid explodes.

MESOOK:
Works for me. The Guardians will follow your orders without question.

AIDA:
(UNCOMFORTABLE)

I'm no commander.

MESOOK:
No. But you are a *Jedi.* Your motives are unimpeachable.

AIDA:
Thank you, Mesook.

FX: More ships flit overhead, splitting the sky with screaming engines and raking fire.

CREIGHTON:
Hold on to that faith of yours, Aida.

FX: Creighton rushes off, lightsaber singing, as he cuts through a swathe of enforcer droids.

AIDA:
I will. For both of us.

CUT TO:

SCENE 72. EXT. JEDHA STREET

ATMOS: The battle continues to rage. Ships screeching overhead, the sound of distant explosions. The exchange of distant blasterfire.

FX: Two E'roni loaders lurch down the street, firing. Buildings crumble. Eirami soldiers return fire with regular blasters. Civilians run screaming, some of them close.

OLD CIVILIAN:
(SHOUTING)

No! Please!

Please stop!

FX: And then running footsteps and the sound of a lightsaber whooshing through the air as Silandra leaps, aided by the Force. One of the mining loaders tries to turn. There's a thud as Silandra lands on top of it.

SILANDRA:
(SHOUTING)

Get clear! All of you!

YOUNG PILGRIM:
(SHOUTING)

Look! A Jedi, on the roof of that loader!

FX: Silandra's lightsaber stabs through the roof of the turret, cutting open the hatch. It swings open with a metallic clang.

SILANDRA:
Stand down, now.

SCARED LOADER PILOT:
(TREMULOUS)

I have a blaster. I'll *shoot!*

SILANDRA:
Try it.

SCARED LOADER PILOT:
(TERRIFIED)

I . . . umm . . .

SILANDRA:
Out of the loader. *Now.*

SCARED LOADER PILOT:
(TERRIFIED)

But . . .

SILANDRA:
Out!

FX: The loader pilot scrabbles up out of the loader, hauling himself up onto the turret roof beside Silandra.

SILANDRA:
Now jump.

SCARED LOADER PILOT:
(TERRIFIED)

I can't jump from up here!

SILANDRA:
I'll guide you down.

I assure you, you're not going to want to be standing here in a minute's time.

SCARED LOADER PILOT:
(TERRIFIED)

But . . .

SILANDRA:
(SIGHS)

Why do they always choose the hard way?

FX: She gives him a shove. He tumbles over the edge of the loader.

SCARED LOADER PILOT:
(CRYING OUT)

Whoa! Whoa!

FX: He lands gently on the ground.

SCARED LOADER PILOT:
(SHOCKED)

I'm okay! I'm all right!

SILANDRA:
(CALLING)

Now get up and move!

FX: Silandra drops into the loader through the hatch and stabs the controls with her lightsaber. They fizz and crackle loudly.

SILANDRA:
(SATISFIED)

That should do it.

FX: The loader starts going haywire, servos grinding. It tries to run, but charges straight into the side of a building and destroys itself with a bang.

FX: Silandra lands on the ground with a gentle thud.

SILANDRA:
(GRUNTS AS LANDS)

There. Now for the other one.

FX: The other loader grinds to a halt. Silandra walks over. The hatch opens and the other pilot slowly emerges.

SAVVY LOADER PILOT:
Okay! Okay! There's no need to come up here! I'm coming out!

Just . . . just keep that lightsaber away from me . . .

SILANDRA:
(TO SELF)

Well, that was easy.

FX: The other pilot scrambles down the side of the loader.

SAVVY LOADER PILOT:
There! I'm going! See! I'm going!

FX: He runs. Silandra walks over to the other loader and slices through one of its legs with her lightsaber. It creaks, and then topples to the ground with a massive crash.

SILANDRA:
(SHOUTING)

Now, all of you, *run!* Head for the Dome of Deliverance and stay there until this is over.

YOUNG PILGRIM:
Thank the Force for the Jedi!

FX: The civilians hurry off. After a moment, we hear more mining loaders lurching closer.

SILANDRA:
(SIGHS)

Oh, *great.*

FX: Silandra's lightsaber whooshes as she turns toward the sounds and runs.

CUT TO:

SCENE 73. EXT. CENTRAL SQUARE

ATMOS: The battle is raging all around here, too. The same ships screeching overhead, the sound of distant mining loaders, explosions. The exchange of distant blasterfire, too numerous to count. Those civilians who haven't followed Keth to the Dome of Deliverance are congregating here, including the injured and dying.

FX: A man moans in desperate pain.

WOUNDED NAUTOLAN:
(PAINFUL MOAN)

It . . . it hurts . . .

PHINEA:
Marda—what do I *do*? He's . . . his wounds . . .

FX: Marda hurries over. Other people are crying out and moaning all around.

MARDA:
All we can do now is be with him, Phinea.

WOUNDED NAUTOLAN:
(MOANS AGAIN, LOUDER)

MARDA:
(SOOTHING)

It's all right. It's all right. Soon you shall be one with the Force, and you shall be free.

Rest now. The time is near.

ELDER DELWIN:
(IN BACKGROUND, FULL PREACHER MODE)

The Force *will* be free! It will find its balance. Its natural level!

Those who bend the living Force to their will do so at a perilous cost.

Utilize that power to save a life *here,* and someone else must die *there.* Every action, every small manipulation, will cause a ripple that will spread out through the Force until it becomes a wave. A *tsunami!*

In this way, the Jedi have brought this suffering down upon us. They have unbalanced the Force, and now it seeks to reassert itself.

The Jedi sought to bring peace, but instead they bring only war. They have *failed.* See how, even now, they *fight.* As if their only instinct is toward *violence* and destruction. But the Force abhors violence! The Force seeks only peace!

We must learn to trust in its embrace. We must cherish it enough to set it free! For all our sakes!

FX: A child cries out from nearby.

MARDA:
I must go to her, Phinea. Stay with him, until—

PHINEA:
He has already gone.

MARDA:

Then go tend another. The injured and the dying come among us to find peace. We cannot protect them from the horrors of this war, but we *can* show them the light of the Path before it is too late.

PHINEA:

I understand.

The Force will be free.

MARDA:

Yes. Yes, it shall.

CUT TO:

SCENE 74. INT. THE DOME OF DELIVERANCE

ATMOS: Here, the battle sounds a little more distant. People are spilling into the dome, and the hubbub echoes noisily.

KETH:
(SHOUTING ABOVE NOISE)

In *here*! That's it! Keep going! Make room! Make room!

FX: Silandra comes running. She's out of breath.

P3-7A:
A traveler may go far with the Force at her side, but she will never forget her true home.

KETH:
Silandra.

SILANDRA:
(OUT OF BREATH)

I took down a few of E'ronoh's war machines to prevent more civilians being caught in the crossfire.

Keep the doors of the dome open. There are more people heading this way for shelter.

KETH:
(SHOCKED)

You're hurt.

SILANDRA:
(CATCHING HER BREATH NOW)

Just a scratch. You should see the other guy.

Or at least his mining loader.

KETH:
Here. Rest for a moment.

FX: People continue to file into the dome as they speak.

SILANDRA:
No time. There are still too many people out there.

It's worse than I could ever have imagined.

KETH:
Yes, but you won't be able to help any of them if you're hurt.

SILANDRA:
Keth—stop.

KETH:
No. You need to listen to me, Silandra—

SILANDRA:
(CUTTING HIM OFF, SHOUTING)

Get down!

FX: There's the buzz of three electrostaffs humming to life, whipping through the air. Keth hits the ground, struck by one. It's a knockout blow.

KETH:
(UNGH)

FX: Silandra's lightsaber ignites. When Mytion speaks, it's as we've heard the Brothers of the Ninth Door speak before when using their abilities—multilayered, as if three people are speaking at once.

MYTION:
(WITH DISDAIN)

Hello, *Jedi*.

SILANDRA:
You.

You're the ones who started all of this.

MYTION:
Yes. And now it's time we finished it.

FX: The whoosh of a sparking electrostaff striking a lightsaber.

END OF PART FOUR

Part Five

RECKONING

SCENE 75. EXT. JEDHA STREET

ATMOS: The soundscape is brimming with the roar of battle. The fighting is furious. We're down at street level, where the crump of munitions detonating and buildings collapsing is punctuated by the sounds of running boots and the whine of blasterfire.

HYPED EIRAMI SOLDIER:
(BELLOWING)

Now! Now! Now!

FX: The sound of people arming grenades. The whine and thud of a mining loader.

HYPED EIRAMI SOLDIER:
(BELLOWING)

Bring it down! Bring it down!

FX: Hurled grenades bounce off the metal shell of a loader. The loader's weapons are powering up.

HYPED EIRAMI SOLDIER:
(BELLOWING)

Take cover!

FX: The loader fires. The street erupts in the blast.

HYPED EIRAMI SOLDIER:
(DYING SCREAM)

FX: And then the grenades go off in a sequence of smaller explosions. There's a groaning creak as the loader's leg buckles—and then the loader comes down with an enormous crunch. A building collapses.

FRUSTRATED LOADER PILOT:
(CURSING)

Dammit!

Loader six-three-nine is down. We can't let those Eirami bastards get the upper hand.

Quickly—after them. Take down any survivors.

FX: The sounds of the second loader thudding down the street as fast as it can move. And then:

FRUSTRATED LOADER PILOT:
What was that?

CONFUSED LOADER PILOT:
What?

FRUSTRATED LOADER PILOT:
That blur? Something moved. On the rooftop.

CONFUSED LOADER PILOT:
I can't see anything.

FRUSTRATED LOADER PILOT:
Turn the guns. Quickly!

FX: The whine of the loader's turret turning. And then the thud of feet landing on the roof.

CONFUSED LOADER PILOT:
What the—

FX: The sound of a humming lightsaber bursting through the roof of the loader's turret.

FRUSTRATED LOADER PILOT:
(TERRIFIED)

It's a . . . a . . . a *Jedi!*

FX: A metal disk falls into the loader's turret. Followed by Aida Forte dropping in, lightsaber still humming.

AIDA:
I'd get out now if I were you.

FX: The two pilots scrabble, and then shout as they jump clear.

LOADER PILOTS:
(ARGHH)

FX: Aida thrusts her lightsaber into the loader's controls. They fizz and pop. The loader goes haywire, whining as it wobbles and tries to walk in circles. And then it smashes into a building and powers down with a screech.

FX: Aida jumps clear and lands in the street. Nearby we can hear light-bows firing.

AIDA:
How many is that, Selik?

SELIK:
That's nine. But they just keep coming.

AIDA:
Then we keep going. And we use the city against them.

SELIK:
What do you mean?

AIDA:
Those mining loaders weren't designed for this terrain. So we make it as difficult for them as possible. Push them down narrow streets where they can't maneuver.

SELIK:
Herd them to where we want them.

AIDA:
Exactly.

Tell your Guardians to split into smaller groups. Harry them. Channel them toward the central square.

SELIK:
Consider it done.

CUT TO:

SCENE 76. INT. THE DOME OF DELIVERANCE

ATMOS: There's a terrible hush come over the proceedings inside the Dome of Deliverance. We can still hear the faint sounds of the battle outside, but they're nothing compared with the sounds of the three-on-one electrostaff/lightsaber battle going on inside.

FX: The crackle of the electrostaffs and the lightsaber battering against one another, fast and furious. Silandra is using her shield on her arm, too, to help fend off some of the blows.

SILANDRA:
(GRUNTS WITH EFFORT)

FX: Mytion's voice is layered and sinister as previously.

MYTION:
You fight well, Jedi. I was led to believe you'd be far easier to dispatch.

FX: More furious parrying. But then Silandra goes on the attack. The lightsaber sings. She knocks Baarla back with a bash from her shield...

BAARLA:
(UNGH)

FX: And then spins, her lightsaber whirling as it slices across Inoke's chest...

INOKE:
(DEATH CRY)

BAARLA:
Inoke!

FX: And then Silandra cries out with effort—not anger—as she flips sideways...

SILANDRA:
(RAARGH)

FX: And brings her lightsaber down in a fierce chopping motion, severing both of Baarla's forearms. His electrostaff hits the ground—both hands still attached. When Baarla screams, he also has a strange, layered voice.

BAARLA:
(SCREAMS IN PAIN)

My arms!

FX: Baarla staggers back. Silandra uses the moment to break away, making a dash for the lower level, beneath the dome.

BAARLA:
(WHIMPERS)

Mytion...

MYTION:
(WEARY)

Know that you have failed, Brother. There can be no redemption.

FX: Mytion strikes Baarla hard with his electrostaff. There's a crunch. Baarla gurgles and falls to the floor, dead. Civilians in the Dome of Deliverance scream in horror.

CROWD:
(SCREAMS)

MYTION:
(SIGHS)

I really do have to do *everything* myself.

FX: He sets off after Silandra at a run.

CUT TO:

SCENE 77. EXT. JEDHA STREET—ROOFTOPS

ATMOS: Up here on the rooftops, the sounds of the overhead ship-to-ship battle are even closer and louder. The screech of engines, the squeal of blasters, the explosions of ships in low orbit, and the hail of debris falling on the city below.

FX: Creighton and Mesook stand back-to-back on a rooftop, fighting enforcer droids. Creighton's lightsaber flashes, deflecting shots. One of them catches an enforcer droid, which explodes.

MESOOK:
Creighton!

FX: Creighton uses the Force to fling an enforcer droid into Mesook's line of sight with a whoosh.

CREIGHTON:
(CALLING)

Here!

FX: Mesook's lightbow fires. The shot strikes an enforcer droid, which fizzes and pops electronically, then crashes into the side of a building and slumps.

MESOOK:
(BELLOWING)

Overhead! More droids incoming!

FX: Blaster shots stutter like violent raindrops on the roof tiles.
Creighton's lightsaber swings, returning some, taking out two droids.
But there's more.

CREIGHTON:
(THROUGH GRITTED TEETH)

No. You. Don't.

FX: He uses the Force to slam two of the enforcer droids into each other,
causing an explosion.

ENFORCER DROID:
Stand down! Immediately.

FX: We hear the roar of a shuttle swooping low overhead.

CREIGHTON:
Down? You're going up! Right into the path of that shuttle.

FX: Creighton throws the enforcer droid up just as a shuttle swoops low
over the rooftops. It collides with the droid, smashing it to pieces.

MESOOK:
(CHEEKY)

Why can't you use the Force to toss them all away like that?

CREIGHTON:
If it's so easy, why don't *you* try?

FX: From down below, lightbows are firing in repeating waves. Enforcer
droids are returning fire. We hear several droids explode, but also a
Guardian's death scream:

GUARDIAN:
(DEATH SCREAM)

FX: Creighton's lightsaber whips back and forth, deflecting more blaster shots.

CREIGHTON:
(CALLING)

Mesook?

MESOOK:
(CALLING BACK, WITH EFFORT)

Little busy . . .

CREIGHTON:
(CALLING)

And about to get busier. I think we're surrounded.

FX: Creighton bats another blaster shot away. Enforcer droids stomp into position around them, in all directions. Their eyes whirl and rotate mechanically.

ENFORCER DROID:
Stand down. You are surrounded.

CREIGHTON:
(WEARY)

Yeah, I'd noticed.

FX: Several enforcer droids lock their arms with a mechanical click, presenting their weapons.

ENFORCER DROID:
This is your final warning. Lay down your weapons or you will be destroyed.

CREIGHTON:
(ANGERED)

Destroyed? We're *living beings.*

ENFORCER DROID:
You have been warned.

FX: The droids fire in unison. Creighton's lightsaber flashes multiple times.

ENFORCER DROID:
You shall be destr—

FX: The enforcer droid's speech glitches, buzzes, and crackles out mid-sentence as the droids all fall, destroyed by their own deflected blasts.

MESOOK:
(GRIM)

There are too many of them. And while we're fighting the droids and the weaponized loaders, Eiram's and E'ronoh's troops are closing on the central square.

It's going to be a massacre.

CREIGHTON:
(GRIM)

We'll get there. We'll stop it.

But first we need to buy some more time for the civilians to get clear. The best way to do that is to stick to the plan and take out the worst of the ordnance.

MESOOK:
More droids?

CREIGHTON:
More droids.

FX: A ship roars overhead.

MESOOK:
That's a civilian ship. Someone must have cleared a path to the shuttle docks.

CREIGHTON:
Good.

Then let's keep going.

For as long as we can.

CUT TO:

SCENE 78. INT. EIRAM MILITARY COMMAND SHIP—BRIDGE—JEDHA ATMOSPHERE

ATMOS: The background hum of engines. The whine of shuttles being dispatched outside, and the occasional boom of a ship being destroyed in the dogfights raging in low orbit.

FX: Ambassador Cerox walks onto the bridge, footsteps ringing out on the lacquered floor.

AMBASSADOR CEROX:
How fares the battle, Commander?

WARY COMMANDER:
(WARILY)

Somewhat unexpectedly, Ambassador Cerox.

AMBASSADOR CEROX:
(CONFUSED)

How so? Surely the enforcer droids are making short work of the E'roni military? Or did that damn Graf lie to me about their efficacy?

WARY COMMANDER:

No, Ambassador. Tilson Graf did not lie. The enforcer droids are everything he promised they would be. It's just . . . he hadn't accounted for the fact that they'd be fighting *Jedi.*

AMBASSADOR CEROX:

They're *what*? Jedi! The Jedi are supposed to remain neutral in all of this.

WARY COMMANDER:

Indeed. And yet, Master Sun is apparently on a crusade to take out as many of our droids as possible.

AMBASSADOR CEROX:
(TIGHTLY)

And our soldiers?

WARY COMMANDER:

Just the droids. Reports from the surface are sketchy, but it seems the other Jedi—

AMBASSADOR CEROX:
—Aida Forte—

WARY COMMANDER:

—yes. The Nikto. She's taking down all E'ronoh's war machines with the same zeal. They . . . umm . . . they have the Guardians of the Whills under their command, too.

AMBASSADOR CEROX:
(SIGHS)

Damn Jedi. All they do is *interfere.*

Tell the droids to execute them on sight.

WARY COMMANDER:
(SHOCKED)

Execute the Jedi?

AMBASSADOR CEROX:
Yes. We've wasted enough time and enough lives here already.

WARY COMMANDER:
(UNSURE)

But . . . surely killing the Jedi will bring the Republic down on our heads . . .

AMBASSADOR CEROX:
(SNAPPING, IMPATIENT)

Just do it, will you? Before there are no droids left to carry out the damn order!

CUT TO:

SCENE 79. INT. THE DOME OF DELIVERANCE

ATMOS: Inside the Dome of Deliverance, there's a terrified hush. The murmur of the gathered civilian crowd is low, and we can hear the roar of battle outside. There's no sound of Silandra and the brothers, however—all is mysteriously quiet on that front.

FX: P3-7A gives the unconscious Keth a little zap of electricity. Keth twitches but doesn't wake up.

P3-7A:
Only the sleep of the righteous is undisturbed.

FX: P3-7A gives Keth another zap. He twitches again.

KETH:
(GROANS)

P3-7A:
And when he awoke, he saw that all his mighty works had come to naught, and the enemy were close at the door.

KETH:
(GROANS LOUDER)

Pee-Three?

FX: P3-7A gives Keth a third zap.

KETH:

Oww! I'm awake! I'm awake! What time is—

(Beat, then CONFUSED)

—where am I?

FX: People come hurrying over.

CONCERNED TOGRUTA:

You're alive! Here. Careful.

(CALLING TO OTHERS)

Someone find a medic!

FX: The civilian helps Keth to sit up, while someone else starts seeking a medic in the crowd.

PANICKED CITIZEN:

(CALLING IN BACKGROUND)

We need a medic here! Any medics?

KETH:

(GROANS AGAIN)

My *head.*

CONCERNED TOGRUTA:

We thought you were . . . well, dead, like *him.*

KETH:

A Brother of the Ninth Door.

The dome . . .

(WINCES SHARPLY)

My head . . .

CONCERNED TOGRUTA:

You took quite a blow. There's . . . ummm . . . you should be careful. You're still bleeding.

KETH:

I'm . . . I think I'm all right.

Where's . . . Where's Silandra?

(REMEMBERING)

Oh, Light! They came for her, didn't they!

CONCERNED TOGRUTA:

One of them hit you, then they all ran off. I'm not sure where.

(SOOTHINGLY)

But they've gone now. You don't have to worry. Just relax while we wait for the medic.

P3-7A:

To reflect on one's nature is to learn of one's true place in the Force.

KETH:

(STILL GROGGY)

What? I don't know what you're talking about, Pee-Three.

CONCERNED TOGRUTA:

I take it this is your droid.

KETH:

Yes.

CONCERNED TOGRUTA:

It's . . . *unusual.*

KETH:

Don't I know it.

P3-7A:

What one sees in a mirror is not a true reflection of the self; it is merely a mirage, an impression of the person you really are.

You must look beyond the mirror to find what you truly seek.

KETH:

(CONFUSED)

What are you—

(REALIZES)

Mirrors! Reflections! You mean Silandra and the brothers are down there, in the Hall of Reflection?

P3-7A:

Finally, the young man came to the Light.

FX: Keth starts to get to his feet.

CONCERNED TOGRUTA:

No. No—wait. You can't get up! You need to wait for the medic.

FX: Keth pushes them gently off.

KETH:

No. What I need to do is help my friend.

CONCERNED TOGRUTA:

You're in no condition to help *anyone.*

KETH:

You don't understand. I *have* to do this.

FX: Keth starts to hurry off, with P3-7A at his side.

CONCERNED TOGRUTA:

(CALLING AFTER HIM)

But your head . . .

KETH:
Thank you, Pee-Three. You're the only one who really gets me, aren't you? I never appreciated that before, but . . .

. . . *thanks.*

P3-7A:
And at long last, he found faith in the Force, and all was right in the galaxy.

CUT TO:

SCENE 80. INT. HALL OF REFLECTION— CONTINUOUS

ATMOS: It's quiet down here amongst the Kyber Mirrors. We can't hear any of what's going on above, or the battle raging outside. Voices echo down here, and the brothers continue to have their strange, layered voices.

FX: Footsteps as Mytion walks between the mirrors, seeking Silandra.

MYTION:
Seeking to hide in a hall of mirrors may not have been the wisest of choices, Master Sho.

FX: Silandra's lightsaber ignites as she leaps out from behind a mirror.

SILANDRA:
I wasn't trying to hide.

FX: Mytion swings his electrostaff up to meet her lightsaber. They crackle together.

MYTION:
Ah. Of course. The civilians. You merely wished to avoid any collateral damage.

FX: There's a flurry of blows, Silandra working hard to defend herself from the brutal attack.

MYTION:
You needn't have worried. The Brothers of the Ninth Door respect the sanctity of innocent life. We are, in fact, a most peaceful sect. Indeed, many of our order are out in the city now, assisting those who need safe harbor.

FX: More lightsaber/electrostaff exchanges, along with Silandra battering away blows with her shield (which is on her other arm).

SILANDRA:
(GRUNTS WITH EXERTION)

And what about the people you killed with your *bombs*?

MYTION:
Do you really believe any of those politicians or soldiers were *innocent*? Do you believe *you* are?

SILANDRA:
They didn't deserve to *die*.

MYTION:
The Force deemed otherwise. We are guided by its hand.

SILANDRA:
(FIRM BUT CONTROLLED)

Do not presume to speak for the Force.

FX: Silandra makes a big push, whipping her lightsaber around furiously, using one of the mirrors to push herself into a flip over Mytion's head. But he counters her flurry of blows, and she lands, lightsaber humming.

MYTION:
(AMUSED)

I merely sought to fulfill certain *obligations*. That is all.

SILANDRA:
Obligations to *whom*?

MYTION:
(GENUINELY SURPRISED)

You really don't know, do you?

We all have masters, Jedi. Those who would see us do their bidding for the right price. Or perhaps the right cause.

SILANDRA:
Who?

MYTION:
(LAUGHS)

SILANDRA:
Who?

MYTION:
(WRYLY)

Let me see if I can remember his exact words. . . .

FX: When Mytion speaks, it's with the same triple-layered effect, but now his voice is emulating Tilson Graf.

MYTION:
(AS TILSON GRAF)

So, the bomb will detonate at the appointed time?

Excellent. Make sure Morton San Tekka catches the brunt of it, will you? He's been a thorn in my family's side for years.

(Beat, then AS IF OFF THE CUFF)

Oh, and there's another Jedi, too. Silandra Sho. She might prove troublesome. See to her, too, will you?

(Beat, then AIRILY)

I'm not a bad person, you know. You must understand that I'm only looking out for my interests. My *family's* interests. A . . .

umm . . . a friend has shown me how I might win back their affections, you see. Would be churlish not to try, wouldn't it?

FX: Silandra staggers back, breathless.

SILANDRA:
(APPALLED)

Him.

Tilson Graf.

He's the one who hired you to carry out the bombings.

FX: Mytion's voice is back to its usual creepy self.

MYTION:
Some people, it seems, believe conflict to be a more sustainable and profitable state for the galaxy than peace.

Personally, I do not care.

FX: While Silandra is disoriented, Mytion comes on strong, with a series of fast, vicious attacks with the electrostaff. One of the blows gets through Silandra's defenses, pushing her back with a snarl of pain.

SILANDRA:
(SNARL OF PAIN)

FX: But then she kicks out in response. The kick connects with Mytion, pushing him back against one of the mirrors.

MYTION:
(UNGH)

FX: There's a moment of silence as both Mytion and Silandra take this in.

MYTION:
It seems both of my brothers somewhat underestimated you, Master Sho.

Not I, however.

FX: Mytion growls as he launches a string of attacks.

MYTION:
(GROWLS ANGRILY)

FX: Silandra counters furiously. This is epic lightsaber/electrostaff dueling. They're weaving in and out of the mirrors, boots crunching on loose stone, flipping and jumping, whipping their weapons back and forth with humming and sparking as they clash. And then:

MYTION:
(ROARS)

Just die, Jedi!

You're testing my patience.

FX: Mytion batters aside Silandra's shield with brute strength, his electrostaff sparking furiously. He blocks a down cut from Silandra and knocks her lightsaber hand wide, and then jabs her, hard, with the sparking end of the electrostaff, knocking her back against one of the mirrors.

SILANDRA:
(CRIES OUT)

FX: Silandra tries to bring her lightsaber down with a humming swipe, but Mytion steps closer, swinging his electrostaff and bringing it down hard on her wrist.

SILANDRA:
(UNGH)

My saber!

FX: The lightsaber tumbles away onto the ground and extinguishes. Mytion strikes her again, hard, and she falls back against one of the Kyber Mirrors.

SILANDRA:
(OOMPH)

MYTION:
Perhaps Tilson was right, after all.

Perhaps you *are* easy to kill.

FX: Mytion grasps Silandra around the throat, pushing her back.

SILANDRA:
(CHOKING SOUNDS)

FX: When Mytion speaks next, he's using Tilson Graf's voice again, but it's still weird and multilayered.

MYTION:
(AS TILSON GRAF)

I'm only looking after my family interests.

FX: Mytion is now back to using his own voice.

MYTION:
They are, after all, my brothers . . .

FX: Very faintly, in the background, we hear P3-7A's thrusters.

SILANDRA:
(CHOKING)

No . . . No . . . *Don't* . . .

CUT TO:

SCENE 81. EXT. JEDHA STREET

ATMOS: The battle continues to rage.

FX: Aida is running down the street, breathing raggedly with the exertion.

AIDA:
(BETWEEN RAGGED BREATHS, TO SELF)

Come on. Come on. Keep following me, you bucket of industrial junk.

FX: We realize an adapted loader is giving chase. It's thundering down the street at speed, servos whining. It fires, and an empty market stall explodes, burning.

AIDA:
Come *on*!

SELIK:
(VIA COMM, ALSO RUNNING)

Aida? We're coming to the first junction now.

AIDA:
Keep going. They're hot on my tail, just as we planned.

CUT TO:

SCENE 82. INT. INSIDE THE MINING LOADER— CONTINUOUS

ATMOS: As previous scene, but muffled. Equipment beeps and hums, and the whining of the servos is louder.

DETERMINED LOADER PILOT:
Damn! We nearly had her!

TRIGGER-HAPPY LOADER PILOT:
Prepare for another shot! We're gaining on the Jedi!

CUT TO:

SCENE 83. EXT. JEDHA STREET—CONTINUOUS

ATMOS: As previous.

FX: Aida is still running. She leaps over an obstruction . . .

AIDA:
(GRUNTS)

FX: . . . and lands, still running. We can hear the loader's weapons powering up again.

AIDA:
(STILL BREATHING HARD)

Nearly . . . nearly . . .

FX: The loader fires again. A section of wall crumbles with the rending of split stone. It slides to the ground . . . but Aida is still running.

AIDA:
Too . . .

(HUFF)

. . . close.

FX: We can hear the thundering footsteps of another loader in the near distance.

SELIK:
(VIA COMM, ALSO RUNNING)

Coming in hot, Aida. I can hear your loader now.

AIDA:
Stick to the plan. Wait for my signal.

We have to wait until the last minute, make it impossible for both loaders to slow down.

SELIK:
(VIA COMM, ALSO RUNNING)

Are you *sure* this is a good plan?

AIDA:
Bit late to be worrying about that now!

CUT TO:

SCENE 84. INT. INSIDE OF MINING LOADER— CONTINUOUS

ATMOS: As previous.

DETERMINED LOADER PILOT:
You missed her *again*!

Do you know how many of our loaders she's brought down? We'll get a damn medal for finishing her off. Now *concentrate*!

TRIGGER-HAPPY LOADER PILOT:
I'm trying to! But she's a bloody *Jedi*!

Just—*speed* up!

DETERMINED LOADER PILOT:
I'm giving it everything she has!

FX: The whining of the servos increases to a near-unbearable level as the loader approximates a run, feet thudding . . .

CUT TO:

SCENE 85. EXT. JEDHA STREET—CONTINUOUS

ATMOS: As previous.

FX: The sound of the other loader is growing, and it's moving almost as fast as the one pursuing Aida.

AIDA:
Come on, Selik. Come on.

FX: We hear the thudding footsteps of someone else running now, but toward us. And the other loader is lurching around the corner in pursuit.

AIDA:
(SHOUTING)

Selik! Here!

SELIK:
I see you!

FX: More running, and then:

AIDA:
Take my hand . . .

FX: Aida roars with effort . . .

AIDA:

(RAAAGHHH)

FX: ... as she leaps, using the Force, she propels them both out of the way as ...

CUT TO:

SCENE 86. INT. INSIDE OF MINING LOADER—CONTINUOUS

ATMOS: As previous.

FX: We can hear the thudding of the other loader coming straight at us.

TRIGGER-HAPPY LOADER PILOT:
Druk! That's loader seven-four-three! It's coming straight at us. It's a trap! Stop! Stop!

DETERMINED LOADER PILOT:
I can't stop! I can't . . . Shi—

FX: The two loaders collide with a massive boom and the grinding of metal. They sway together for a moment, and then topple, burning, their legs buckling.

CUT TO:

SCENE 87. EXT. JEDHA STREET—ROOFTOP

ATMOS: The battle rages on.

SELIK:
(CATCHING HIS BREATH)

And another two loaders down.

Looks like the pilots made it. They're scrabbling for their lives down there.

AIDA:
Good. There's been enough needless death.

FX: There's another explosion of twisted metal close by.

AIDA:
And another one falls.

I'm sorry, Selik.

SELIK:
For what?

AIDA:
For the losses you've suffered here today, and those who might still suffer. For the people who won't be as lucky as those pilots.

SELIK:
Aida . . .

AIDA:
A few days ago, Creighton said something. I thought he was just brooding, but maybe he was right.

SELIK:
What?

AIDA:
He said we'd brought the war to your doorstep. That none of you wanted it, but we'd brought it here anyway.

I told him we'd brought *peace*—the signing of a treaty that would finally end the conflict . . .

But he was right, wasn't he? We did bring the war here.

And now *look* at it. Look at what we've done.

SELIK:
Aida . . . you were *right*.

This isn't on you, or Creighton, or the Republic. Nor is it a mere failure of diplomacy. You aimed for peace. What could be more important than that? Isn't that what the Force wills? Isn't that our true purpose, be us Jedi, Guardian, or disciple?

What's happened here is the fault of Eiram and E'ronoh for starting this war in the first place. And it's on the shoulders of whoever was behind the bombings and assassinations.

They carry the responsibility for all these deaths, and more.

AIDA:
Perhaps. But the Jedi will not forget what happened here easily. And we shall help with the rebuilding . . . if the Convocation allows us.

SELIK:

(CHUCKLES)

First, we have to make it out alive.

FX: A flurry of blaster shots fills the streets around them, down below.

AIDA:

The Eirami troops. They'll be converging on the central square soon.

SELIK:

Then we should go. Most of the adapted mining loaders are down. We can leave the rest to the other Guardians.

FX: Ships flit overhead, firing on one another and swooping.

AIDA:

All right. I just hope Creighton and Mesook have managed to slow those enforcer droids. Otherwise, the central square is set to become a kill box.

SELIK:

Have faith, Aida. They know what they're about.

CUT TO:

SCENE 88. EXT. CENTRAL SQUARE

ATMOS: The fighting is getting closer as the battle in the streets progresses. The sounds of fighting, screaming, dying, explosions, and blasterfire can all be heard close by. But in the foreground, we have the tears and moans of the wounded, dying, and dispossessed, who are still gathering here.

FX: Someone comes running, carrying a heavy burden.

DAD:
(SCARED AND DESPERATE)

Help me! Help me, please. My child. A piece of shrapnel . . .

PHINEA:
Over here, quickly.

STENNIE:
(SOBS)

FX: The man hurries over.

PHINEA:
Lay them down. Just there. That's right. We need to bind the leg. Give me your shirt.

DAD:
(CONFUSED)

My . . . shirt?

PHINEA:
Do it, man! For the bindings!

STENNIE:
(SOBBING)

Dadda . . .

FX: The man tears off his shirt.

DAD:
Here.

FX: Phinea rips the shirt into strips.

PHINEA:
Help me. Hold him still. I need to tie it around the leg.

STENNIE:
(WHIMPERS)

DAD:
It's all right, Stennie. It'll be okay. Dad's here. And this lady is going to help us.

PHINEA:
I am. The Path of the Open Hand helps all in need.

DAD:
Right. Yes. Thank you. Thank you.

FX: Phinea finishes tying the bindings.

PHINEA:
There, now. That'll do until we can get you proper medical attention.

STENNIE:
(CONCERNED)

That's it?

PHINEA:
It's the best we can do. Now stay with him.

FX: Phinea leaves.

DAD:
There now, Stennie. There now.

FX: Elder Delwin's preaching starts up again in the background, but gets louder as we follow Phinea, walking toward him.

ELDER DELWIN:
(IN BACKGROUND)

You have the Jedi to thank for your pain! For your suffering! For it is they who have brought this down upon us. They who have so abused the living Force that they have unbalanced the natural order of all things!

FX: The preaching continues as Phinea spots Marda in the crowd.

ELDER DELWIN:
(IN BACKGROUND)

Consider this—would you ever trust a Jedi again? All they know is lies and obfuscation. All they *do* is lie!

PHINEA:
(CALLING)

Marda! Marda!

MARDA:
Phinea.

PHINEA:
(WORRIED)

What are we going to do, Marda? These people—they're coming to us for help. But we're so few, and we have no medical equipment, no water, no shelter. The fighting is so close now . . .

MARDA:
I understand your fear, Phinea. But we must trust in the Force. The Force will show us the way. It will guide us—no matter the danger.

PHINEA:
You really think so?

MARDA:
(REASSURING)

I know it.

Now go. There are others who need our help. Continue the good work. Show these people that the Path is strong, and the Jedi weak.

PHINEA:
Yes. Thank you, Marda.

FX: Phinea leaves.

ELDER DELWIN:
(IN BACKGROUND)

Those who use the Force for their own gain—they are criminals. They would take something that is sacred to all life, and they would twist it and bend it to their will. The consequences of such despicable behavior are felt throughout the entire galaxy. In doing this, they harm us *all.*

The Path of the Open Hand believes such practices should be stopped. Outlawed! That the Force should, and will, be *fre—*

FX: A blaster shot goes off, hitting Elder Delwin in the head with a splich, cutting him off in the middle of his speech. His body hits the ground hard.

MARDA:
(APPALLED)

Elder Delwin!

FX: Marda starts over to his body, but more blaster shots sound nearby, stopping her in her tracks. Civilians start screaming and running. Chaos erupts all around.

PATH DISCIPLE:
(PANICKED)

Soldiers! They're here! They're coming!

MAN 2:
(URGENT)

Everyone run!

DAD:
(DESPERATE)

What about my boy? My boy!

MARDA:
Oh no. No.

Force protect us.

Not like this.

FX: More blaster shots are fired. They're still distant, but they're coming closer.

MARDA:
(SHOUTING)

Everyone run! *Run!*

FX: Marda joins the crowds of people fleeing the oncoming conflict.

CUT TO:

SCENE 89. INT. HALL OF REFLECTION

ATMOS: It's still quiet down here in the cavern beneath the main building. Quiet and eerie.

FX: Mytion is choking Silandra in the background. P3-7A's thrusters fire in the foreground, along with some hurried steps.

KETH:
(HUSHED)

Silandra!

Pee-Three—stay low. And fetch me that lightsaber. Quickly.

P3-7A:
In times of great difficul—

KETH:
(CUTTING HIM OFF, HUSHED)

Not now, Pee-Three!

Just do it! The lightsaber. *Hurry!*

FX: P3-7A's thrusters fire gently. Closer now, Silandra is gasping in Mytion's iron grip.

SILANDRA:
(GASPING, PAINED)

No ... Do ... Don't ...

MYTION:
(SIGHS)

You disappoint me, Master Sho.

To beg in such a fashion is somewhat unbecoming for a Jedi, is it not?

SILANDRA:
(GASPING, PAINED)

K ... K ... Ke ...

MYTION:
Kill you?

If you insist ...

FX: A lightsaber ignites.

MYTION:
What? Who are y—

FX: The lightsaber pierces Mytion's chest as he turns, cutting off his words.

MYTION:
(GURGLES)

KETH:
My name is Keth. Keth Cerapath.

SILANDRA:
(GASPS FOR BREATH)

KETH:
Silan—

FX: Mytion wheels, spinning his electrostaff. He shoves it, hard, right through Keth's stomach.

KETH:
(SCREAMS IN PAIN)

FX: The lightsaber powers off. Keth drops it and staggers back, gurgling blood. Mytion sinks to the ground, laughing, then dies.

MYTION:
(LAUGHS WETLY)

Goodbye . . . Keth . . . Cerapath.

(ISSUES A LONG DEATH SIGH)

SILANDRA:
(STILL GASPING)

Keth. *Keth.*

FX: Silandra falls to her knees beside Keth. He's coughing up blood and wincing in horrible pain.

SILANDRA:
Oh, no. Keth. No.

KETH:
(COUGHING WETLY, PAINED)

I . . . I . . . got him.

SILANDRA:
(KINDLY)

You did.

You did.

You saved me.

KETH:
(BETWEEN CHOKING SPLUTTERS)

Like a . . . like a Pada . . .

FX: Keth can't finish his words for coughing up blood.

SILANDRA:
(CHOKING BACK A SOB)

Yes. Just like a Padawan.

KETH:
(BETWEEN CHOKING SPLUTTERS)

I couldn't ... couldn't let ... him ...

SILANDRA:
The peace treaty. I know. You wanted people to hear the truth.

I'll make *sure* they hear it, Keth. I promise. All of it.

KETH:
(GROWING WEAKER)

No. No ... Not that. I couldn't ... let ... him ...

... hurt ...

... my *friend.*

FX: Silandra lets out a massive sob.

SILANDRA:
(SOBS)

KETH:
(WEAKER STILL)

Hey. It's ... okay ... it ...

FX: Keth coughs up more blood.

SILANDRA:
It's all right, Keth. You can rest now. You don't have to say anything else.

KETH:
But ... but ...

(SIGHS WETLY)

... at least ...

(JOYOUSLY)

... at least I got to ... live my story ... in the end, didn't I?

Piralli won't belie—

FX: The last breath burbles from Keth's lungs. Silandra eases his body down to the ground.

P3-7A:
Shed not a tear for the dying, for the moment has been prepared for, and with the passing of the light all become one with the Force.

FX: Silandra gives the start of a sob, and then catches herself and takes a couple of deep breaths to compose herself.

SILANDRA:
(MUFFLED SOB, THEN STEADIES HERSELF)

I'm sorry, Keth. I let you down.

This should never have happened.

P3-7A:
A pilgrim must find their *own* path to the Force. Sometimes it is surprising. But it is always *their path,* and only they can choose to walk it.

SILANDRA:
I know, Pee-Three. I know.

And I promise you, Keth—your story will be heard. You won't be forgotten, and what you've done here on Jedha will *count.*

It *must* count.

P3-7A:
Where one story ends, another must begin. The Force flows ever on without cease.

FX: Silandra gets up, dusting herself down.

SILANDRA:

Will you stay with him, Pee-Three? Until this is over. Until we can send someone to bring his body back to the temple.

P3-7A:

In vigil do we find peace.

SILANDRA:

Thank you. You are a good friend to him.

FX: Silandra recovers her lightsaber and shield.

SILANDRA:

No one else dies today, Pee-Three. Not if I have anything to do with it.

Not if I can be their shield.

FX: Silandra's shield flares on. After a moment, her lightsaber ignites, too. She walks away, footsteps echoing as they fade.

P3-7A:

May the Force be with you.

CUT TO:

SCENE 90. EXT. JEDHA STREET

ATMOS: The buildings in the area are on fire. Blaster shots fill the air. We can hear people marching—lots of them. Some of them are shouting indistinctly.

FX: The sound of a damaged ship, screaming out of the sky. It crashes into a building in the near vicinity, and both are destroyed in the ensuing explosion.

FX: Creighton grunts as his lightsaber swings back and forth, bisecting enforcer droids that spit and fizz with electricity. Each of his following words are punctuated by another droid being destroyed:

CREIGHTON:
(UNGH)

So. Many. Droids.

FX: We can hear Mesook's lightbow firing repeatedly as he takes down waves of droids, too.

MESOOK:
And they seem more interested in killing *us* than the E'roni troopers.

CREIGHTON:
(WRYLY)

I'd noticed.

FX: Another burst of rapid lightbow fire. Several more droids detonate.

MESOOK:
It's working, though. We're holding them off, thinning their ranks.

CREIGHTON:
While the troops continue to march on the central square. And each other.

We need to get over there. Rendezvous with Aida. Stop the battle before it turns into any more of a massacre.

FX: There's a low, deep, rumble, like the ground itself is heaving—like a groundquake.

MESOOK:
What the—

FX: The wail of rending stone, like the sky itself is cracking. The sound blocks out everything else.

CREIGHTON:
Over there. The statue.

(Beat, then AWED)

By the Light . . . No . . .

FX: A massive thud that shakes the entire city. The immense statue of a Jedi—the Protector—has come crashing down outside the city walls. A sudden hush comes over the city.

MESOOK:
(APPALLED)

The Protector . . .

CREIGHTON:
(SHAKEN, WITH DISBELIEF)

It's fallen.

The Protector has *fallen.*

MESOOK:
(CRUSHED)

How could this have happened? How could we have fallen so far?

That statue . . . it was Jedha itself. The very core of who we are. The symbol of the Holy City. Without it . . .

Without it we are just thugs fighting in the streets while the city crumbles.

CREIGHTON:
(SOLEMN)

It's the reason we came here, to Jedha. A place of peace. A place where we could show two warring worlds what peace could look like. What it was to be protected and cherished by a community, rather than give yourself over to hate and mistrust.

And now this. This is what we have wrought. Destruction and death.

FX: The scream of a ship flying low overhead pierces the silence, bringing us back to the fight. Distant explosions.

CREIGHTON:
Jedha is never going to recover from this.

MESOOK:
We must take heart. The Force will sho—(GAHKH)

FX: Several blaster shots catch Mesook in the chest, causing him to stumble back, cut off mid-sentence.

CREIGHTON:
Mesook!

FX: The flash of Creighton's lightsaber as he quickly dispatches the droids that had come for them while they were distracted.

CREIGHTON:
(ROARS IN FRUSTRATION)

FX: The droids crumple. Creighton runs over to Mesook.

CREIGHTON:
Mesook.

Mesook.

FX: But there's only silence in reply. It lingers for a moment. We can hear only the background sounds of the battle, still raging.

CREIGHTON:
(SOFTLY)

I'm sorry, Mesook. I wish . . .

. . . I would have liked to have known you better.

May the Force embrace you.

FX: Creighton hefts his lightsaber.

CREIGHTON:
(WITH RESOLVE)

Now. Time to end this.

CUT TO:

SCENE 91. EXT. JEDHA STREET

ATMOS: It's chaos on the ground. People are running, screaming. Weapons are discharging. Buildings are crumbling. We can still hear the occasional whine and clump of a mining loader, the thudding of its cannons. Ships still do battle overhead.

THE MOTHER:
Come on, Qwerb. And you, Jukkyuk. Keep walking. And remember, we *must* locate the Leveler. At all costs. The Herald has been gone with it for too long.

FX: The noise of the crowd is almost unbearable. In the foreground, we can hear three sets of footsteps: the Mother and her two guards, Qwerb and Jukkyuk. They hurry past desperate people:

DAD:
(DESPERATE)

My boy! Where's my boy?

WOUNDED TALPIDDIAN:
(WAILS IN PAIN)

My leg! It's trapped. I can't feel it! Please!

ANXIOUS MOTHER:
(ANXIOUS)

Ginnith? Ginnith?

INJURED MAN:
(TEARFUL)

Help me, *please.* Why won't anyone help?

DISTRAUGHT TWI'LEK:
(HOPELESS)

My home . . .

CONFUSED CHILD:
(CONFUSED)

He's not moving. None of them are moving.

FX: The Mother and her guards keep on walking.

JUKKYUK:
Rwraaaaaghh!

QWERB:
(CONFUSED)

So many people. Shouldn't we stop, Mother? Try to help them.

THE MOTHER:
(FIRM, EMOTIONLESS)

We keep walking.

QWERB:
But the tenets of the Path—

THE MOTHER:
(CUTTING HIM OFF)

Are what *I* say they are. Remember your orders. Find me the Leveler. I must know where it is, for all our sakes.

JUKKYUK:
(UNSURE)

Waaahhrrooo.

THE MOTHER:
(SIGHS)

Yes, yes. I understand.

(LIP SERVICE)

And it pains me to walk on past these poor people, too, so much I can hardly bear it.

But we *must* keep moving. How can we help others if we do not help ourselves? How can we continue our work if we, ourselves, become victims of this terrible conflict? If we are unable to locate our most treasured weapon?

QWERB:
But the others—they're still out there, tending to the injured.

THE MOTHER:
Such is their dedication to the faith. But Marda is with them, and she will guide them to us.

QWERB:
At the shuttle docks?

THE MOTHER:
Marda knows what to do. With the almshouse destroyed, we must return to the *Gaze Electric*. Our time on Jedha is over.

We head for my shuttle as planned. Once the Leveler has been retrieved.

FX: Up ahead of them, we hear two enforcer droids battling E'ronoh soldiers: an exchange of blasterfire, flaring energy shields. Shouting soldiers.

ANGRY E'RONOH SOLDIER:
(URGENT, BELLOWED)

Take them down! Now! Fire! Fire! Fire!

FX: A hailstorm of blasterfire.

ENFORCER DROID:
The enemy will be destroyed.

FX: More blasterfire, followed by the sounds of people dying.

ANGRY E'RONOH SOLDIER:
(SHOUTS IN PAIN)

No! No!

FX: Another blaster shot, a single one, finishes him. The enforcer droids turn and start marching toward the Mother, Qwerb, and Jukkyuk.

ENFORCER DROID:
All enemies will be destroyed.

THE MOTHER:
(PLACATING)

No, no! We are not your enemy. We are peaceful followers of the Path of the Open Hand.

ENFORCER DROID:
All enemies will be destroyed.

FX: The enforcer droids continue to march closer.

THE MOTHER:
(WORRIED)

Qwerb . . .

QWERB:
Get behind me.

FX: Qwerb raises his blaster and shoots. The shot glances off one of the enforcer droids. It returns fire. There's a sizzling sound, followed by a thud.

QWERB:
(URRK)

(DYING)

Mother . . .

JUKKYUK:
Rrrawwwwaggghh!

FX: Jukkyuk charges the two droids. They fire wildly, but he collides with them, slamming them together.

ENFORCER DROID:
All enemies will be—

FX: Jukkyuk tears the head off the speaking droid, causing a shower of sparks.

JUKKYUK:
(FIERCE, ANGRY)

Wraaaghh rwwwooo!

FX: More slamming sounds as he beats the other one against the side of the building. We hear more enforcer droids closing in.

ENFORCER DROID:
(COMING CLOSER)

All enemies will be destroyed.

JUKKYUK:
Arrrwwwaaghhhh!

FX: The Mother backs slowly away down the street.

THE MOTHER:
(TO SELF)

That's it. Keep them busy, Jukkyuk.

FX: She turns and runs. Her footsteps fade out as she runs away.

CUT TO:

SCENE 92. EXT. CENTRAL SQUARE

ATMOS: We're at the heart of the besieged city. The civilians have fled. Blasterfire rings out in the streets. Ships scream overhead, but fewer now. The two forces of troopers—Eiram and E'ronoh—are marching on the square from two sides of the city. They're going to meet here at any moment.

FX: Creighton comes running.

CREIGHTON:
Aida!

FX: Creighton skids to a halt.

AIDA:
(RELIEVED)

Creighton. You made it.

SELIK:
Mesook?

CREIGHTON:
I ...

... I'm sorry, Selik. He's one with the Force.

SELIK:
(PAINED)

May the Force embrace him.

CREIGHTON:
It already has. I know it.

(Beat, then TO AIDA)

The loaders?

AIDA:
Most of them are downed. Thank the Force.

And the droids?

CREIGHTON:
We did our best. It'll have to be enough.

FX: The marching of boots is getting louder, and closer on both sides.

CREIGHTON:
Where are the rest of the Guardians? You were twice this number when we began.

AIDA:
This . . . this is it, Creighton.

SELIK:
The battle has taken a heavy toll.

But we few stand for Jedha. Until the end.

GUARDIANS:
(ALL)

For Jedha! For the Force!

CREIGHTON:
(GRIEF STRUCK)

I . . . I don't know what to say. I'm sorry. So sorry . . .

SELIK:
There is no need. We stand side by side, Guardian and Jedi.

In the name of peace.

AIDA:
No word from the Jedi Council?

CREIGHTON:
No.

AIDA:
Then it looks as though it's just us.

FX: The marching boots stop.

SELIK:
Both armies are here.

CREIGHTON:
And we're stuck out in the open between them. Just the seven of us.

FX: We hear the forces of E'ronoh present their blasters.

DETERMINED E'RONI SERGEANT:
(CALLING)

Stand aside, Jedi. The E'roni will not go around you.

CREIGHTON:
(CALLING)

You know we can't do that.

PROFESSIONAL EIRAMI SERGEANT:
(CALLING)

Soldiers of Eiram! Present!

FX: The Eirami forces on the other side of the square present their blasters, too. It's a standoff, with the Jedi and Guardians in the middle.

CREIGHTON:
(CALLING)

This war has to end. It has to stop *now*. *Here*.

PROFESSIONAL EIRAMI SERGEANT:
(CALLING)

Out of the way, Jedi. Or stand there and die.

You took sides the moment you engaged our droids.

AIDA:
(CALLING)

We took *no* sides. We tried to protect the civilians.

DETERMINED E'RONI SERGEANT:
(CALLING)

By destroying our war machines.

It's *your* fault we're here at all.

Troopers!

AIDA:
(TO SELF, APPALLED)

No . . .

DETERMINED E'RONI SERGEANT:
Ready arms!

AIDA:
Creighton . . .

END OF PART FIVE

Part Six
SALVATION

SCENE 93. EXT. JEDHA STREET—NEAR SHUTTLE DOCKS

ATMOS: Explosions are still going off throughout the city. Ships are still tearing up the sky, dogfighting, raking the streets with fire and debris. Buildings are on fire.

FX: Running footsteps.

TILSON GRAF:
(CALLING)

Mother!

(Beat, then CALLING)

Mother, stop!

FX: More running.

TILSON GRAF:
(EXASPERATED CALLING)

Mother!

FX: The running stops.

THE MOTHER:
You?

TILSON GRAF:
(BREATHLESS)

I *thought* I'd find you around here somewhere.

I need your help getting off this hellhole.

THE MOTHER:
(WITH DISDAIN)

And why would I help *you*?

TILSON GRAF:
(CATCHING BREATH)

Because we're partners. Because of the mutual respect—not to mention the *debt*—that stands between us.

THE MOTHER:
(DISMISSIVE)

We have never been *partners,* Tilson Graf. That implies equality. You were always a means to an end.

TILSON GRAF:
Business associates, then. Whatever you want to call it.

All the same—I can see you're heading for your shuttle.

I'm coming with you.

THE MOTHER:
No. It's too risky. Even being seen out here, talking to you, puts my position in danger.

TILSON GRAF:
(GETTING ANGRY)

I don't care how *uncomfortable* it makes you. We had a deal. I provided you with a shipment of enforcer droids to protect your people. They're already stashed safely on your ship.

(Beat, then LOWERS VOICE)

Not to mention all that unsavory business with the Brothers of the Ninth Door.

(Beat, then NORMAL VOLUME AGAIN)

I've played my part. Now it's time for you to make good. In credits, *and* in helping me get off this rock. Have you seen what's going on out here? Have you?

We did this, Elecia. We started *all of this.*

THE MOTHER:
(FIRMLY)

I said *no.*

I stacked the deck in your favor with the Republic, didn't I? I put one of our doddering Elders forward as a replacement mediator so that even *you* would look enticing as an alternative. That's enough. My debts are paid.

Now find another way offworld. You can afford it.

TILSON GRAF:
(FURIOUS)

In case you hadn't noticed, no one's taking bookings for flights right now.

(SIGHS, TRIES TO BE REASONABLE)

Look, I'll stay out of the way. Hide me away in a little compartment on the *Gaze Electric* if you have to. No one will even know I'm there. You can drop me off at your first port of call, wherever it is. I'll see myself right from there. I just . . .

. . . things are a little too *hot* here.

THE MOTHER:
And if I don't?

TILSON GRAF:
(SIGHS)

Don't make me say it, Elecia. We both know it doesn't pay to leave loose ends lying around. Especially if you insist on causing bad feeling between us . . .

THE MOTHER:
(FEIGNING RESIGNATION)

You're right. You're right.

I can't risk anyone finding out about our little "connection," can I?

TILSON GRAF:
(RELIEVED)

Good. Thank you. I knew you'd see sense.

THE MOTHER:
I always do in the end, Tilson.

FX: The Mother pulls a blaster from under her robes and shoots Tilson Graf dead at close range.

TILSON GRAF:
(PAINED)

But . . .

(DYING GASP)

FX: His body slumps heavily to the floor.

THE MOTHER:
I always do.

CUT TO:

SCENE 94. EXT. CENTRAL SQUARE

ATMOS: The sounds of battle have stilled momentarily. You could cut the tension with a knife.

CREIGHTON:
(BELLOWING)

Don't fire!

FX: The sky fills with the ominous drone of a massive transport ship sliding in above the city.

PROFESSIONAL EIRAMI SERGEANT:
What in the name . . .

FX: Cargo ramps release from the side of the ship with a series of three pneumatic hisses. And then people jump out.

AIDA:
(RELIEVED)

They came.

CREIGHTON:
Master Tarl came through.

FX: Around twenty people thud to the ground, landing perfectly despite the height of the drop. Lightsabers ignite along the line. The Jedi are here.

CREIGHTON:
Master Vohlan. Master Har'kin.

All of you . . .

(Beat, then HEARTFELT)

Thank you.

MASTER HAR'KIN:
(LIGHTLY)

Don't thank us yet, Creighton. There's still a hell of a mess to tidy up.

CREIGHTON:
To say the least.

MASTER VOHLAN:
We brought a platoon of Republic peacekeeping troops along for the ride, just in case. I'm only thankful that Jedha is part of the Republic. If this had been neutral territory like Eiram or E'ronoh, we'd never have been able to intervene.

CREIGHTON:
I know.

Now, *surely*, it must be over.

AIDA:
They're not lowering their weapons.

CREIGHTON:
(SHOUTING)

All of you. Lower your blasters. The battle is over.

MASTER HAR'KIN:
They don't look so sure . . .

PROFESSIONAL EIRAMI SERGEANT:
Troopers! Present arms!

FX: A line of soldiers readies its blasters.

CONFUSED EIRAMI SOLDIER:
(IN BACKGROUND)

But sir! The Jedi!

PROFESSIONAL EIRAMI SERGEANT:
(BARKING)

Damn the Jedi! Get ready to fire! Our enemy are just on the other side of this square. We will *not* show them our bellies this day!

For Eiram!

EIRAMI SOLDIERS:
For Eiram!

CREIGHTON:
They're not listening . . .

FX: On the opposite side, E'ronoh's soldiers also re-present their arms.

DETERMINED E'RONI SERGEANT:
Soldiers of E'ronoh! On my command!

MASTER VOHLAN:
The E'roni soldiers, too . . .

AIDA:
(SHOCKED)

What are they *doing*? They're going to . . .

DETERMINED E'RONI SERGEANT:
Fire!

PROFESSIONAL EIRAMI SERGEANT:
Fire!

FX: A hailstorm of blasters and heavy munitions fire in a massive cascade, from both sides of the square. The soundscape is filled with the shots.

MASTER VOHLAN:
(CALLING)

Together! Now!

FX: And then the shots just . . . stop. The sound of them ceases completely. None of them land or strike anything. There's a strange flickering sound, like a thousand indistinct whispers being spoken at once.

AWED EIRAMI SOLDIER:
The blaster shots . . .

They're just . . .

SHOCKED EIRAMI SOLDIER:
. . . *hanging* there.

PROFESSIONAL EIRAMI SERGEANT:
(BELLOWING)

Fire again! Keep firing!

FX: Another barrage of shots from the Eiram side. But they, too, just . . . stop.

MASTER VOHLAN:
(STRAINING)

Creighton . . . we cannot . . . hold this for long . . .

CUT TO:

SCENE 95. EXT. JEDHA STREET—NEAR SHUTTLE DOCKS

ATMOS: The atmosphere in the city has changed. The sounds of fighting in the streets seem more distant now, but not over.

MIRIALAN MAN:
(SHOUTING)

Get out of here! Clear the docks! Incoming!

FX: A ship zips past overhead, its blasters opening up, and two shuttles in the docks explode on their landing pads.

SILANDRA:
(BELLOWING)

Those are civilian ships! These people are trying to flee!

FX: The offending ship is already zooming away. Silandra runs toward the burning wreckage. People are running in the opposite direction.

SILANDRA:
(CALLING)

Is anyone there?

Hello? I'm here to help!

INJURED HUMAN WOMAN:
(CROAKING)

Please . . . It burns.

FX: Silandra hurries over to the woman.

INJURED HUMAN WOMAN:
(UNCERTAIN)

Oh, no. No.

SILANDRA:
It's all right. We can bind the wound. It's serious, but if we can get you treatment, it'll be—

INJURED HUMAN WOMAN:
(INSISTENT)

No. You're a Jedi.

SILANDRA:
Yes, but—

INJURED HUMAN WOMAN:
The Jedi have done *enough.* Leave me alone. Leave me!

FX: Silandra backs away.

SILANDRA:
(CONFUSED)

But I'm only trying to help.

INJURED HUMAN WOMAN:
It's all your fault. I heard those people in the square. They said it was *your* doing. The Jedi!

You brought this down on us.

SILANDRA:
But . . .

FX: A man comes running over.

MIRIALAN MAN:
It's all right. I'll help her. You go.

SILANDRA:
Surely—

MIRIALAN MAN:
(FIRM)

Just go. You're upsetting her. *Go.*

SILANDRA:
I'm sorry . . . I . . .

FX: Silandra backs away.

FX: The ship comes around for another pass, firing on the shuttle docks again. There's another explosion.

SILANDRA:
(SHOUTING)

Stop it! Just . . . *stop*! These docks are not a military target!

FX: Silandra walks a bit farther toward the burning wrecks.

SILANDRA:
What—

Tilson! Tilson Graf!

FX: Silandra runs over to where Tilson Graf's body lies in the ruins.

SILANDRA:
Oh, no.

Not you, too.

Not before you faced justice for what you've done.

FX: Silandra kneels for a moment in the wreckage. It crunches beneath her weight.

SILANDRA:
(QUIET, SEPULCHRAL)

This is what you wanted, isn't it?

Chaos and death.

People blaming the Jedi—*anyone* but *you*—for what was happening.

And what did you get out of it, hmm? Profit? Respect? A way to buy the affections of the people who were supposed to love you anyway?

No. What you got was a blaster shot through the chest in a ruined side street. An anonymous death.

And where's the justice in that? Where's the justice for *Keth*?

Tell me that, Tilson Graf.

(Beat, then WHISPERED)

Tell me that.

CUT TO:

SCENE 96. EXT. CENTRAL SQUARE

ATMOS: *The strange warbling, whispering sounds continue as the assembled Jedi work together to hold back the shots from both sides of the square.*

DETERMINED E'RONI SERGEANT:
(BELLOWING IN BACKGROUND)

Fire *again*!

UNCERTAIN E'RONI SOLDIER:
But sir ...

DETERMINED E'RONI SERGEANT:
Just do it!

FX: *More shots, but it's a halfhearted volley this time. They stop as per before. But this is not easy on the Jedi ...*

MASTER VOHLAN:
(UNDER IMMENSE STRAIN)

Creighton ...

CREIGHTON:
Yes, Master Vohlan.

FX: *Creighton walks out into the open.*

CREIGHTON:
(RAISED VOICE)

My friend Aida will tell you I'm about as cynical as a Jedi can get.

I came to Jedha worried that things were going to go wrong. On my first day here, I looked up at the sky, at the sight of those transport ships hanging low over the city, and my heart sank.

But Aida—she didn't see what I saw. She didn't see those ships as symbols of hate, and pain, and blood and death.

She saw the fact that both sides were *here.* That you had come together to put a final end to this messy, belligerent conflict. That you were willing to talk about *peace.* She reminded me how remarkable that was.

And we *tried.* We all tried, *so hard.* Your own royal families shared our dream of peace and unity. They came together to make that dream a reality. They showed us all how *love* could triumph over hate, how we could all strive for a better future.

Yes, there were people who stood against us. Those who *wanted* us to fail, no matter the cost. Who stand to gain from a long and bitter war.

And I know that some of you aren't yet ready to forget. I *understand.* You've all given up so much. You've all lost people you loved to this most devastating of wars. You've learned to despise your enemy. The war has been long, and it has come to define your lives.

And I understand that you are *scared.* That you fear by letting go of that burning hatred, that need for revenge, that you'll also be letting down those you have lost. That by laying down your weapons, you'll have failed to find them justice. By moving on, you're leaving them behind.

But that is not true. That is not what they would want. For any of you. You know this in your hearts. You know that those loved ones would want you to *live*. To carry on living, and find peace again.

Yes, there are those who were so damaged, so hurt by what has already passed, that they lash out in bitterness, and cannot see beyond their need for revenge. That they would have you all return to the killing fields and take up arms against those who now seek to call you kin. Tirelessly, they lead you astray to satisfy their own need for vengeance.

And the truth is, today, we let *them* win. Because they are the only winners here. The *only* ones.

FX: Creighton paces while he talks. All the while, the blaster shots are being held back by the Jedi's combined use of the Force.

CREIGHTON:
No matter how many of your so-called enemies you kill, no matter how proud you feel to be standing there, holding a weapon under the flag of your people—by engaging in this battle, you've *lost*.

Every death, every single person you kill, or hurt, or maim— they become a stain upon you. A stain that will *never* wash away.

Those people, the ones who planted those bombs, who wanted us to be here now, at each other's throats—they know that divided, *we are weaker.*

Look up. See what's become of all your blaster shots and missiles. The Jedi have achieved this by *working together.* By uniting against those who would tear us down.

Isn't it time you did the same?

FX: Creighton extinguishes his lightsaber.

CREIGHTON:
Lay down your weapons. Do it because it's the right thing to do. *Please.* Prove Aida right.

No matter what you do now, this battle is over. We Jedi are the shield that will *not* buckle. In that transport ship is a platoon of Republic peacekeeping troops.

I say it again.

You. Cannot. Win.

Choose wisely, with your hearts.

FX: Someone throws down a blaster. Then another follows. And another, and more, and more.

DETERMINED E'RONI SERGEANT:
Pick up those weapons! Now! You shall be court-martialed! Pick them up, now!

FX: But more blasters are being dropped on both sides. And people start to walk away.

DETERMINED E'RONI SERGEANT:
Get *back* here!

FX: There's a massive release, like a held breath being expelled, and all of the blaster shots being held in stasis shoot skyward and away.

AIDA:
Creighton . . .

CREIGHTON:
(WEARY)

You were right, Aida. Despite everything.

AIDA:
(LAUGHS)

I usually am.

CUT TO:

SCENE 97. EXT. JEDHA STREET—NEAR SHUTTLE DOCKS

ATMOS: As previous. The ships are still circling above the shuttle docks, still dogfighting. The troopers in the central square might have laid down arms, but the battle hasn't been formally called off.

FX: The crackle and fizz of a comlink. It chimes. Silandra scrabbles to get it out of a pouch, then answers it. The connection is clear and bright.

SILANDRA:
Creighton? Aida?

CREIGHTON:
(VIA COMLINK)

Silandra! Thank the Light. We feared the worst. Are you all right?

SILANDRA:
(HESITANT)

I . . .

(Beat, then TAKES DEEP BREATH)

Yes. I'm okay.

How did you get the comms working?

CREIGHTON:
(VIA COMLINK)

A Republic ship. We're amplifying through their relays.

Masters Har'kin and Vohlan are here, along with others from the Order.

Where are you?

SILANDRA:
By the shuttle docks. It's carnage, Creighton. They're destroying civilian ships.

CREIGHTON:
(VIA COMLINK)

The Republic negotiators are speaking with representatives of the warring planets now. They're trying to effect a withdrawal.

SILANDRA:
It can't come soon enough. The scale of death . . .

CREIGHTON:
(VIA COMLINK)

I know.

SILANDRA:
It was Tilson Graf. I tried to reach you, to warn you . . . He was the one behind the bombings. Him and a local sect called the Brothers of the Ninth Door—or at least some people within that sect.

CREIGHTON:
(VIA COMLINK)

I'll get an alert out. We'll try to stop him getting offworld.

SILANDRA:
(GRIM)

No need. He's dead. I found his body by the docks. Shot with a blaster.

CREIGHTON:
(VIA COMLINK)

Damn.

It could have been anyone in this chaos. Even a stray shot.

SILANDRA:
Perhaps.

CREIGHTON:
(VIA COMLINK)

Look, we're gathered in the central square. Head over here when you can.

SILANDRA:
On my way. I'll just—

FX: Silandra cuts the link.

SILANDRA:
(SHOUTING)

Get down! That ship is going to fire on us!

FX: A ship screams overhead. Blasters fire. A shuttle on a nearby landing pad explodes. A woman screams.

SILANDRA:
(SHOUTING)

Here! With me!

FX: Silandra's shield flares. We hear shrapnel striking the shield. We can hear the wrecked shuttle burning in the background.

SILANDRA:
Are you hurt . . .

THE MOTHER:
(RAGGED BREATHS)

SILANDRA:
(SHOCKED)

Mother . . .

THE MOTHER:
(STEADYING HER BREATHING)

Master Sho. It seems I owe you my life.

FX: Silandra powers off her shield.

SILANDRA:
You owe me nothing.

Here, let me help you—

THE MOTHER:
(ABRUPT)

No. No. I can manage.

FX: The Mother gets slowly to her feet.

SILANDRA:
You were heading for your shuttle.

THE MOTHER:
Yes. Yes, I was trying to reach our ship. To oversee the evacuation of my people. Our almshouse was attacked. The riots . . .

SILANDRA:
I'm sorry. It's been a . . . *trying* day.

THE MOTHER:
Where's your young friend? The adjunct?

SILANDRA:
(CHOKED)

He's . . .

He didn't make it.

THE MOTHER:
Poor boy. So young. I fear there'll be many such stories when the dust has settled.

I only hope our own Littles have survived the ordeal unscathed.

SILANDRA:
I hope so, too.

What will you do now? The Republic will likely arrange emergency transport for those who've been stranded or displaced. Although it might take some time.

THE MOTHER:
No. No—I must find Marda Ro, our Guide.

SILANDRA:
Do you know where she might have gone?

THE MOTHER:
Knowing Marda, she'll be close to the thick of things, trying to help or protect the Littles.

SILANDRA:
In that case, come with me. We'll see if we can find her together. I know you don't approve of Jedi, but perhaps you can stomach my company for a little while, just until you reach the safety of your people?

THE MOTHER:
My thanks to you, Master Sho.

CUT TO:

SCENE 98. INT. ABANDONED CELLAR

ATMOS: The sound of the fighting has abated outside, save for the now-distant crump of the occasional explosion. There are several people down in this old cellar, and we can hear their breathing. It's claustrophobic.

FX: A scrabble of feet, and then a hatch being slightly opened with a grating sound. After a moment:

NADDIE:
I think the fighting has stopped.

PELA:
Naddie! Come down from there! You're still injured! You'll open your wounds.

NADDIE:
I'll be all right, Pela. My face still hurts, but I'll be careful.

FX: The grating sounds again as Naddie pushes the hatch a little farther open.

TROMAK:
Is it over, Naddie? Can we go outside again now?

PELA:
(SIGHS MOROSELY)

I know hiding down here in the dark is scary, Tromak, but it's *safe*. I promised the Mother I would protect you.

NADDIE:
I'm going to take a look.

PELA:
(WARNING)

Naddie . . .

FX: Naddie wriggles up through the hole. There's a moment of silence in the cellar. Then:

TROMAK:
(WORRIED)

What if she doesn't come back?

FX: One of the other Littles sniffs. Another starts to cry.

PELA:
(SOOTHING)

Shush. Shush, now. She'll be back.

FX: Another moment passes, and then the grating sounds again, louder this time, as Naddie drags the hatch completely clear.

NADDIE:
(SHOUTING)

It's okay! You can come out now. The fighting's over.

(Beat, then LESS SURE)

I think.

PELA:
(CALLING UP)

What can you see?

(Beat, AND THEN)

NADDIE:
(SHOUTING)

Broken houses. And dead people.

PELA:
(WORRIED)

All right. I'm coming up, too. Don't look at them, Naddie.

NADDIE:
(SHOUTING)

I won't.

FX: Feet clang as they climb iron rungs, and then Pela grunts with effort...

PELA:
(GRUNTS WITH EXERTION)

FX: . . . as she pulls herself out of the hatch, emerging to:

SCENE 99. EXT. JEDHA STREET—CONTINUOUS

ATMOS: It's still and quiet, aside from distant, indistinct shouting.

FX: Pela emerges from the hatch and dusts herself down.

PELA:
(SHOCKED)

Force be with us. It's . . .

NADDIE:
(REVEALING HOW SCARED SHE REALLY IS)

Horrible. It's *horrible*.

FX: Pela gathers Naddie up in a hug.

PELA:
(CARING)

Don't you worry, Naddie. I'll get you out of here. All of you.

We'll find the other members of the Path and we'll go somewhere safe. Back to the *Gaze Electric*.

NADDIE:
Back home to Dalna?

PELA:
(HESITANT)

I ... ummm ... maybe. I don't know. But somewhere away from here.

NADDIE:
Okay, Pela. I trust you.

PELA:
Good. Now, do you feel up to helping me fetch the others out of that cellar?

NADDIE:
Mmmm-hmmmm.

PELA:
Great. The let's help them up and we can all go look for Marda and the Mother.

Okay?

NADDIE:
(RESOLUTE)

Okay.

FX: We hear footsteps coming up the iron rungs from below.

CUT TO:

SCENE 100. EXT. JEDHA STREET

ATMOS: As per previous scene. The streets are beginning to settle as the violence abates.

FX: Silandra and the Mother walk together, feet crunching on spilled rubble and dust. They continue walking under:

SILANDRA:
Help me to understand. What is it the Path of the Open Hand hate so much about the Jedi?

THE MOTHER:
It is not the Jedi that we dislike, Silandra Sho—it is what you *do.*

SILANDRA:
You truly believe we're damaging the living Force?

THE MOTHER:
I *know* it.

Consider this—every action has its consequences, does it not?

SILANDRA:
(UNEASY)

Well . . . yes.

THE MOTHER:
And the Force seeks balance in all things. Would you agree?

SILANDRA:
To an extent.

I do believe that balance in the Force is essential to finding an equilibrium in the galaxy.

THE MOTHER:
Then we are not so different after all.

But now think on this: A person is in danger. You act to save their life. You manipulate the Force to do it.

Let's say . . . you use your shield to defend someone from the explosion of a shuttle on a landing pad.

SILANDRA:
(WARY)

Go on . . .

THE MOTHER:
Then as we have already established, there must be consequences for that action, correct?

SILANDRA:
(LEVEL)

There *are* consequences. You're still alive.

THE MOTHER:
And I'm grateful for that. But also saddened by what it implies. What it *means*.

SILANDRA:
What do you think it means? That you're somehow indebted to me for saving your life?

That's not how the Jedi work.

It's not how *I* work.

THE MOTHER:
No, no. You misunderstand. The Force. It must seek balance. You saved my life . . .

SILANDRA:
. . . so you believe that, as a consequence, another person will die in your stead?

THE MOTHER:
Precisely.

SILANDRA:
(NOT CONVINCED)

But—that's not how the Force works.

THE MOTHER:
Can you be certain?

SILANDRA:
I have seen no evidence of what you describe. *Ever.*

THE MOTHER:
And yet here we are, walking through the rubble of an unnecessary and unwanted war.

SILANDRA:
(UNCONVINCED)

You cannot really believe that this conflict is the result of the Jedi's misuses of the Force.

THE MOTHER:
All things must find their balance, Silandra.

SILANDRA:
I reject that. I reject every implication of that theory.

THE MOTHER:
Of course you do. You're a Jedi.

SILANDRA:

So, what? You believe the Jedi should be destroyed? Wiped out? That you will do so by any means necessary?

THE MOTHER:
(SHOCKED)

Of course not.

SILANDRA:
(KNOWING)

But I heard your Herald in the crowds, stirring up the people. If it hadn't been for him, for those incendiary words, the riot might never have started. And all of *this* might have been avoided.

THE MOTHER:

The Herald has, I am ashamed to say, taken matters into his own hands. His views have become increasingly extreme. I've been worried about him for some time.

SILANDRA:

And the assassination attempts on Eiram and E'ronoh? Others in the Jedi Order have uncovered evidence that people connected to your sect were involved.

You might almost put the two things together and believe that the Path were attempting to *frame* the Jedi . . . To overturn the peace process and undermine all those who had worked so hard to bring it about.

THE MOTHER:
(APPALLED)

I know nothing of these assassination attempts, or of such *evidence.* I would see it.

But if the Herald *was* involved in such a terrible scheme, I shall see to it that justice is carried out. The Path see to their own. We will not tolerate such elements within our family.

We are a peaceful people.

SILANDRA:
(KNOWS THE TRUTH, BUT CAN'T PROVE IT)

I see.

FX: We hear a fight up ahead in the street. Silandra's shield flares to life.

SILANDRA:
Wait here.

THE MOTHER:
I'll be right behind you.

FX: Silandra runs toward the fight.

CUT TO:

SCENE 101. EXT. CENTRAL SQUARE

ATMOS: The last of Eiram's and E'ronoh's troops are now with-drawing from the central square. The explosions have stopped. We can hear the steady hum of the Republic transport ship hanging above the square.

FX: The static crackle of a comm.

MASTER HAR'KIN:
(TO COMLINK)

I see. Excellent. Thank you, Commander.

FX: Master Har'kin walks over to join Creighton and Aida.

AIDA:
What did they say?

MASTER HAR'KIN:
It's over.

For now. The two forces are in full retreat. They shall return to their own transports and then exit Jedha orbit immediately.

The Republic troops are monitoring the withdrawal and will then begin the relief effort on the streets. As will the Jedi.

CREIGHTON:
(EMPHATIC)

We'll help.

MASTER HAR'KIN:
You'll do no such thing.

CREIGHTON:
But—

MASTER HAR'KIN:
You'll *rest.* Both of you.

What happened here—you need time to meditate. To commune with the Force. To come to terms with what you've witnessed.

FX: Another set of footsteps approaches.

MASTER VOHLAN:
And to make a full report to the Jedi Council. Not to mention the Republic.

There's an ill wind blowing, and I fear we've just witnessed the start of an impending disaster.

AIDA:
Of course. We'll do everything we can to help uncover the truth of what happened here. And to get the peace process back on track.

MASTER VOHLAN:
It may be a little late for that. I believe we're about to see the war between Eiram and E'ronoh reignite on an unprecedented scale. There's been too much conspiracy. Too much subterfuge. The will of the heirs has been undermined. The actions of Ambassador Cerox and the military commanders here show that peace between Eiram and E'ronoh is no longer entirely

under Xiri and Phan-tu's control. The factions that wish to return to war are too strong.

Unless we can somehow find a way to contain it, what happened here today was the opening salvo of a fresh conflict between those benighted worlds.

CREIGHTON:
(CRESTFALLEN)

I'm sorry . . . we . . .

MASTER VOHLAN:
Did what *any* of us would.

FX: Master Vohlan claps Creighton on the shoulder.

MASTER HAR'KIN:
No matter how hard we try, Creighton, we cannot hold back the tide. The waves wash over us all eventually.

This is not your fault.

MASTER VOHLAN:
Your quick reactions saved lives today. Both of you. Hold on to that. This could have been so much worse.

AIDA:
And what you said, Creighton. That speech . . .

MASTER VOHLAN:
Was truly inspired.

CREIGHTON:
I . . .

Thank you.

MASTER VOHLAN:
(KINDLY)

Now go. Rest. Tend to your wounds.

CREIGHTON:
Soon.

First, there's someone I still need to see . . .

CUT TO:

SCENE 102. EXT. JEDHA STREET

ATMOS: As previous.

FX: The scuffle is still going on. There are three rioters attacking Marda and another disciple of the Path. A fourth rioter lies dead nearby. Two of the rioters are kicking the Path disciple on the ground.

PATH DISCIPLE:
(OOMPH)

FX: Silandra throws her shield out with the Force. It strikes one of the rioters, and he rebounds noisily, hitting the ground.

GLEEFUL RIOTER:
(UNGH)

FX: Silandra's shield hums as it returns to her arm.

SCARED RIOTER:
A Jedi! Run!

FX: The three rioters run away. Silandra comes closer.

SILANDRA:
(TO MARDA)

Are you hurt?

FX: There's a pause. Then:

THE MOTHER:
(FROM BACKGROUND, COMING CLOSER)

Marda?

MARDA:
Mother?

Mother! You're alive. You're alive!

FX: Marda runs and bundles the Mother into a hug. The Mother bristles and grunts.

THE MOTHER:
(UNGH)

FX: Marda releases her and steps back.

MARDA:
(WORRIED)

Are you hurt?

THE MOTHER:
(REASSURRING)

I am *safe,* Marda, thanks to Silandra Sho.

A true servant of the Force.

FX: Silandra stoops to examine a body in the street.

SILANDRA:
(SUSPICIOUS)

This body . . .

What happened here?

MARDA:
(WORRIED)

I . . .

FX: The Path disciple stirs on the ground, slowly getting up.

PATH DISCIPLE:
We found the poor brute lying on his back.

(GROANS)

Marda tried to revive him, but to no avail.

SILANDRA:
(LEVELLY)

A lightsaber through the heart will do that.

FX: *The Path disciple gets to his feet.*

PATH DISCIPLE:
Then those . . . *monsters* jumped us. Blaming us for what has . . .
has . . .

FX: *The Path disciple starts to topple over again. Marda rushes to catch him.*

MARDA:
I've got you.

THE MOTHER:
Your poor injuries.

PATH DISCIPLE:
I will recover. By the will of the Force.

THE MOTHER:
The Force will deliver us all. That I can promise you.

MARDA:
(FIRM)

We should go.

Master Jedi, I thank you for delivering the Mother to us, but
now we shall get her to our ship.

SILANDRA:
(LEVELLY)

I shall accompany you.

FX: Marda takes a step forward.

MARDA:
(HARD)

No.

(Beat, AND THEN, SOFTER)

I mean to say, it is our responsibility. I am the Guide of the Path of the Open Hand.

SILANDRA:
You are?

MARDA:
(SUPRESSING ANGER)

I will get my people to safety.

FX: Silandra's comlink crackles. She answers it.

SILANDRA:
Sho here.

CREIGHTON:
(VIA COMLINK)

Silandra? Where are you? We're expecting you back at the Republic transport ship in the central square.

SILANDRA:
I was escorting the Mother of the Path of the Open Hand to her craft.

THE MOTHER:
(RAISING HER VOICE TO BE HEARD OVER THE COM-
LINK)

A task she performed admirably, Master Jedi.

But now that I am back in the hands of my people, Master Sho
should return to her duties, with our thanks.

SILANDRA:
(SUSPICIOUS)

Are you sure?

THE MOTHER:
Please. While we may never agree over your use of the Force, I
can never—*will never*—deny the importance of your work.

Jedha needs you, Silandra. Go, with my blessing.

SILANDRA:
Very well.

(TO COMLINK)

Creighton—I'm on my way.

FX: Silandra stashes her comlink.

SILANDRA:
(TO MOTHER)

May the Force be with you and your people.

FX: Silandra hurries away.

THE MOTHER:
It always is.

CUT TO:

SCENE 103. INT. EIRAM MILITARY COMMAND SHIP—BRIDGE—JEDHA ATMOSPHERE

ATMOS: The background hum of engines. The whine of shuttles coming in to land.

AMBASSADOR CEROX:
(IMPATIENT)

Has the evacuation of our troops been completed, Commander?

WARY COMMANDER:
Almost, Ambassador. The final shuttles are bringing them to orbit now, and the remaining enforcer droids have been recalled for transit.

AMBASSADOR CEROX:
(SCORNFUL)

A full retreat. Forced by the Jedi.

I can hardly credit it.

WARY COMMANDER:
(WARILY)

Does this mean it's over?

AMBASSADOR CEROX:
(ANGRY)

Over?

No. It's not over, Commander. The actions of E'ronoh's forces here on Jedha will not be allowed to stand.

WARY COMMANDER:
But the heirs—

AMBASSADOR CEROX:
(ANGRY)

Damn the heirs! Damn them and their union!

Too many people have died. Too many. This will not be over until Eiram has been vindicated, and the people of E'ronoh have paid for their crimes.

Do you understand?

WARY COMMANDER:
Yes, Ambassador. I understand.

AMBASSADOR CEROX:
(SUDDENLY REASONABLE AGAIN)

Good.

Then we have an understanding. I'd hate to have to consider you a traitor.

WARY COMMANDER:
(WARILY)

No, Ambassador.

AMBASSADOR CEROX:

Then make the final preparations for our departure. I wish to be away from this dreadful moon within the hour.

WARY COMMANDER:

Right away, Ambassador.

Right away.

CUT TO:

SCENE 104. EXT. CENTRAL SQUARE—SOON AFTER

ATMOS: Republic peacekeeping troops are now deploying in shuttles from the transport ship that's still hanging over the city. Shuttles flit to and fro, some coming in to land and people disembarking. Under:

SILANDRA:
(CALLING)

Creighton? Aida?

CREIGHTON:
(CALLING, PLEASED)

Silandra! Over here!

FX: Silandra walks over to join Creighton and Aida. The sounds of the deploying peacekeepers carry on around them.

SILANDRA:
So, the backup arrived?

CREIGHTON:
And just in time.

FX: Creighton and Silandra embrace.

SILANDRA:
You're a sight for sore eyes.

CREIGHTON:
You too.

SILANDRA:
Aida. It's good to see you.

FX: Silandra and Aida embrace, too.

AIDA:
I'm sorry. This wasn't the pilgrimage you'd planned.

SILANDRA:
I was where the Force needed me to be. That's enough.

Mesook? Is he here? I saw the Guardians were fighting in the streets.

FX: There's a long pause.

CREIGHTON:
(QUIET, SERIOUS)

I'm so sorry, Silandra.

He didn't make it. He gave his life fighting for peace.

FX: Another pause.

SILANDRA:
(QUIET, SERIOUS)

As he would have wanted.

There was still so much I wished to say.

AIDA:
Words don't seem enough. For any of this.

SILANDRA:
(QUIET)

May the Force embrace him.

CREIGHTON:

I'm sorry to ask, Silandra. But what can you tell us about Tilson Graf? We need to make sure the Council knows the truth. If the warring parties can be made to understand . . . perhaps there's still a slim chance for peace.

SILANDRA:

I'll tell you everything I know. But . . .

CREIGHTON:

Silandra? What is it?

SILANDRA:

(SIGHS REGRETFULLY)

I was too late. If we'd known sooner . . .

CREIGHTON:

No. It's like Masters Har'kin and Vohlan said—we did everything we could.

You did everything you could.

SILANDRA:

It's not just that. I made a promise.

AIDA:

To whom?

SILANDRA:

To the young adjunct, Keth Cerapath.

To his friends . . .

AIDA:

(SADDENED, GENTLY)

He didn't make it?

SILANDRA:
No.

He . . .

He saved my life.

CREIGHTON:
Silandra. You've lost so much.

SILANDRA:
We all have.

AIDA:
He's one with the Force now, Silandra. Take comfort in that.

FX: There's a moment of silence, when we can just hear more Republic peacekeeping troops unloading crates from shuttles.

CREIGHTON:
What about the Path of the Open Hand? Did anything come of Gella's suspicions?

SILANDRA:
Their so-called Herald was instrumental in starting the riots here in the square, working the crowd with vile anti-Jedi propaganda. But there's more than that. I just . . .

AIDA:
What?

SILANDRA:
Nothing I can put my finger on. There's no *evidence*.

But the Mother . . . something's off about her. And that Guide of theirs, too—the young woman called Marda Ro. I think we need to keep a close eye on them. If they weren't involved in the bombings, they were certainly up to *something* here on Jedha. I just don't know what it was.

CREIGHTON:
We'll inform the Council.

SILANDRA:
There's more. A creature . . .

CREIGHTON:
We know. Some wargarans were brought in for the festival and got loose. Several people died when they went on the prowl in the markets.

The Path of the Open Hand were instrumental in bringing them under control.

SILANDRA:
No, not them. This was different. It happened just after the riot started. There was *something* loose in the crowd. Something horrible. It killed two people—reduced them to *husks*. I went after it, but it got away.

CREIGHTON:
(APPALLED)

What did it look like?

SILANDRA:
That's just it—I never managed to get a good look at it. Just being near it . . . it was like it somehow interfered with my connection to the Force.

AIDA:
(SHOCKED)

Your connection to the *Force*?

SILANDRA:
I know how it sounds, but I was overcome. I couldn't go after it, and then with everything that happened after . . .

AIDA:
And you think this had something to do with the Path of the Open Hand?

SILANDRA:
(HESITANT)

I don't know for sure. Only—I had a similar, but weaker feeling when I visited the Mother in the Path's almshouse.

CREIGHTON:
It can't be a coincidence.

But what *was* it?

SILANDRA:
I wish I knew. It was the worst thing I've ever felt. Just this yawning emptiness, and a deep, horrible *hunger.*

CREIGHTON:
(CONCERNED)

Look, I think it's best you come with us, back to Coruscant. Get some rest. When you feel ready, you can talk to the Council, too, tell them what you saw, and your suspicions about the Path.

I have a sense that we're close to something very dangerous here. We need the Council's help to find out what it is.

SILANDRA:
All right.

But first, there's one last thing I need to do.

CREIGHTON:
What can we do to help?

CUT TO:

SCENE 105. INT. TEMPLE OF THE KYBER—CHURCH OF THE FORCE SECTOR—LATER

ATMOS: It's quiet in here, as before. Voices echo, and we can hear the soft chanting of sung prayers in the background.

PREFECT SAOUS:
It is kind of you to return him to us, Master Sho. We will see to it that he is honored for the part he played in helping to save the people of Jedha.

SILANDRA:
Thank you, Prefect Saous. Keth deserves that and more. All those civilians who sat out the worst of the battle inside the Dome of Deliverance—they owe their lives to him.

As do I.

I only wish that things had been different.

PREFECT SAOUS:
Do not mourn for what might never be, Master Sho. Celebrate what has already been. In life, Keth wished only to make a difference.

What he never understood is that he *did* make a difference, every day. He touched the lives of all of us here in the church.

Yes, he swept the floors and changed the water and lit the candles—but in their own way, those small acts had a huge impact upon the lives of the people here. Likewise, his friends.

We all of us leave more of an impression upon our small corner of the galaxy than we know.

It is clear to me that Keth made a very special kind of impression upon you, and you on him. He was so excited to become a part of your life, your story.

That his own story has now come to an end means only that he is complete. That his tale is written, and he has chosen how he wished to be remembered.

Isn't that all any of us can hope for?

SILANDRA:
Wise words, Prefect Saous. I thank you for them.

PREFECT SAOUS:
And I thank you, Silandra Sho. You and those like you, who stood as a shield against the horrors of war and refused to give ground. You honor us, and you honor the Force.

SILANDRA:
I must go. Please, tell his friends . . .

Tell them . . .

PREFECT SAOUS:
Tell them?

SILANDRA:
No. Don't worry. I'll tell them myself.

FX: Silandra leaves, her footsteps echoing.

CUT TO:

SCENE 106. INT. THE JEDI TEMPLE ON CORUSCANT—PRIVATE CHAMBERS—DAYS LATER

ATMOS: The constant hum of the traffic lanes outside. The burble of a fountain.

AIDA:
I'd forgotten how hectic things were on Coruscant.

CREIGHTON:
And how quickly the time passes when your days are filled with meetings and reports.

Jedha already seems like a lifetime ago, and it was only a matter of days.

AIDA:
There's a part of me that wishes we *could* consign it to the past.

CREIGHTON:
As recent events have conspired to remind me—the unresolved past always has a way of coming back to haunt you. Look at Ambassador Cerox, for instance, and how little she was prepared to forgive and forget.

FX: Doors swoosh open and B-9H0 enters the room.

B-9HO:
May I offer either of you some cooling refreshments?

CREIGHTON:
No, thank you, Bee-Nine.

B-9HO:
Jedi Knight Forte?

AIDA:
I'm fine, thanks, Bee-Nine.

B-9HO:
(SLIGHTLY HAUGHTY)

Very well. If I am not required, I shall loiter in the adjoining room until needed.

FX: B-9HO leaves. The doors swish again behind him.

CREIGHTON:
I'm sure he gets worse.

AIDA:
Leave him be. He only wants to help.

CREIGHTON:
There you go again.

AIDA:
What do you mean?

CREIGHTON:
Being optimistic. Seeing the best in people.

AIDA:
Creighton—he's a *droid.*

CREIGHTON:
All that means is he's even worse at hiding his derision.

AIDA:
(SIGHS)

How did it go with the Council today?

CREIGHTON:
They were the Council. You know what they're like.

AIDA:
Creighton . . .

CREIGHTON:
All right. All right.

FX: Creighton gets up and paces to the window. The sounds of the traffic get louder.

CREIGHTON:
It's just—Coruscant always makes me feel a little . . .

AIDA:
(LIGHTLY)

Grumpy?

CREIGHTON:
I was going to say *reflective*.

AIDA:
Oh, I see. *Reflective*.

CREIGHTON:
Before you say it, I'm not—

AIDA:
(CUTTING HIM OFF)

Brooding?

CREIGHTON:
(CHUCKLES)

Well, perhaps a little. But there's good reason.

Master Vohlan was right. We stand on the precipice of a disaster. Communications around Eiram and E'ronoh were restored for only moments before they were destroyed again, meaning we can't be clear what's happening there. Chancellor Mollo may find himself amid escalating danger with nowhere to turn. And I fear the heirs may be unable to contain the crisis.

AIDA:

If Ambassador Cerox is in any way an exemplifier of how people on either planet feel about the peace process . . .

CREIGHTON:

Then the heirs have a battle of hearts and minds to fight, as well as the rising potential for further conflict. Not to mention the pirates that are reportedly making the most of the chaotic situation by mounting a series of raids on the vulnerable settlements of both worlds.

AIDA:

Pirates? That's all they need at a time like this.

CREIGHTON:

Still, it seems our testimony to Master Yoda and Chancellor Greylark has been duly considered and the matter has been escalated. Master Roy and Padawan Keen are to set out for Eiram and E'ronoh immediately, to see what can be done about the situation—and to reach out to Chancellor Mollo and ensure his safety.

And Chancellor Greylark is debating a closure of hyperspace lanes to try to contain any danger to the neighboring systems.

AIDA:

It's a mess.

CREIGHTON:

The truth is, we're back to where we started.

AIDA:

Not quite.

CREIGHTON:
We're not?

AIDA:
No. Because we *tried.*

And surely trying and failing is better than not trying at all.

CREIGHTON:
Yes. I think perhaps you're right.

AIDA:
(LAUGHING)

I usually am.

And besides—what happened in the square, what you said to those soldiers—that was no small triumph, Creighton.

They *laid down their arms.*

CREIGHTON:
Yes. And now every single one of them has probably been court-martialed.

AIDA:
They knew that when they made the choice to follow your lead. Can't you see that? They knew what would happen and they *did it anyway.* Because you helped them to believe in peace.

CREIGHTON:
Yes. You're right. I just . . . I wish the ambassadors had been listening.

AIDA:
Tintak would have believed in what you said.

CREIGHTON:
There was a time when I would have said the same about Cerox, too. But as she deployed those enforcer droids . . . well, she said there were those who couldn't let go of the pain they'd suffered during the conflict. Perhaps I should have known.

AIDA:
Known what?

CREIGHTON:
That she was one of them. She never really wanted peace. She wanted *revenge.*

AIDA:
And it twisted her into something bitter and broken. Such is the way of war.

CREIGHTON:
An investigation into the wrecked enforcer droids showed that they were of Graf manufacture. We now think she must have been approached by Tilson Graf. He sold her the droids, and probably persuaded her to help sabotage the peace process.

AIDA:
It doesn't sound as if she needed much persuading.

CREIGHTON:
No. I don't suppose she did.

Anyway, all we can do now is hope the heirs can rally their people once again. To find a way back to peace. Xiri and Phantu have such profound resolve—I know they'll remain committed to settling this conflict, once and for all.

FX: Creighton crosses the room to a chair and sits down.

CREIGHTON:
Are you prepared for our journey to Dalna in the morning?

AIDA:
As prepared as one can be for such a mission. I'm grateful the Council gave us leave to follow the Mother and the Path after they fled Jedha in such a hurry. It now appears that many on Jedha blame the Path for starting the riots. And for releasing the wargarans in the first place. With their Herald taken into

custody for looting, it seems public sentiment has now turned against the Path of the Open Hand.

But what could they possibly want on Dalna? Do you have any notion of what we might find?

CREIGHTON:
Honestly? No. I'm as much at a loss as you.

Except . . . everything Silandra told us on Jedha, plus the fact that Axel Greylark was likely tied up with them . . . it points to them being involved in all this, *somehow.*

I just wish we had more to go on. Investigations of the wreckage of the almshouse on Jedha revealed nothing. And Silandra led a sweep of the city, but found no sign of the creature she encountered. We're not any clearer about where it came from, except that she was certain it was somehow linked to the Path, after what she'd felt when she visited the Mother at the almshouse.

Still, I sense that the answers await us there, on Dalna. The answers to all of this.

AIDA:
I hope so.

Have you seen Silandra?

CREIGHTON:
No. I believe she's already on her way back to Batuu to collect her Padawan, Rooper.

AIDA:
Good.

CREIGHTON:
Well, there's nothing more for it. I think I'm going to have to ask Bee-Nine for one of those drinks after all.

AIDA:
(GENTLY TEASING)

You just want to make sure he feels useful, don't you?

CREIGHTON:
(WITH MOCK SURPRISE)

Me? No . . .

(CALLING)

Bee-Nine! Bee-Nine!

CUT TO:

SCENE 107. INT. ENLIGHTENMENT TAPBAR—
SOMETIME LATER

ATMOS: Things are back to normal in Enlightenment. The harpist is playing. The banter is back to its regular hubbub. The clink of glasses and the glug of liquor.

FX: Footsteps enter the bar.

PIRALLI:
Camille. Delphine.

CAMILLE:
Piralli.

DELPHINE:
Piralli.

PIRALLI:
Don't mind my friend here. He promises to be on his best behavior.

FX: Piralli heads to the bar. We hear the subtle sounds of P3-7A's thrusters in the background.

KRADON:
Ah, Piralli! Kradon is most pleased to see you.

MOONA:
(TEASING)

See, Piralli. Not *everyone* hates you around here.

PIRALLI:
Then I clearly need to work harder at it.

P3-7A:
To cultivate hate is easy yet leads only to the dark side; to cultivate love is a far greater challenge, yet infinitely more rewarding.

KRADON:
As adroit as ever, Pee-Three.

FX: Piralli pulls out his stool. It scrapes on the floor. He sits down.

KRADON:
What is Piralli drinking this most delightful of evenings?

PIRALLI:
Blue Mappa. And whatever she's drinking.

MOONA:
(SURPRISED)

Feeling generous today, are we?

PIRALLI:
No. But I figured it'd help you stick around for a while. I . . .

Well, I could do with the company.

MOONA:
(LAUGHS)

As if I have anywhere else to be.

FX: Kradon pours the drinks. The door swings open again, and footsteps enter.

MOONA:

Hey, Piralli. It's that Jedi. The one who was hanging around with Keth.

SILANDRA:
(HESITANT)

Umm, hello again.

PIRALLI:

Moona—before you start—

MOONA:
(CUTTING HIM OFF)

Hey, Kradon?

KRADON:

Yes, my dear?

MOONA:

See that Jedi? Pour her a strong drink, would you? On me.

KRADON:
(AMUSED)

Indeed! Indeed!

SILANDRA:
(SURPRISED)

Thank you.

PIRALLI:
(SIGHS WITH RELIEF)

So, you *like* Jedi now, do you, Moona?

MOONA:

Any friend of Keth is a friend of mine. And besides, everyone's welcome in Enlightenment. Isn't that right, Kradon?

KRADON:

Kradon couldn't put it better himself.

PIRALLI:

Then you'd better pull up a stool, Master Jedi.

FX: Kradon puts Silandra's drink on the bar with a clink. Silandra pulls out a stool and sits down.

SILANDRA:

Thank you.

I . . . I just . . .

PIRALLI:

We know why you're here.

SILANDRA:

You do?

PIRALLI:

Yeah. You've come to pay your respects. To Keth.

SILANDRA:

In a manner of speaking. I've come to tell you a story.

MOONA:

What story?

FX: Moona takes a swig of her drink. The glass clinks as she places it back on the bar.

SILANDRA:

A story that's full of adventure. Of friendship under pressure. Of a young man trying to do the right thing while even the world seems to be against him.

MOONA:

You've been watching too many holodramas, Jedi.

KRADON:

Ah. Kradon understands. Kradon thinks he knows this story.

You should listen well, Moona. It is a good one.

MOONA:

(CONFUSED)

Okay, but if you already know it ... ?

KRADON:

Kradon would be happy to hear it again.

Please, Master Jedi. Let us begin.

SILANDRA:

(A BIT CHOKED)

Okay. Yes.

Well, it starts with a young adjunct from the Church of the Force. He'd never really done a lot with his life, but he was well loved by his friends and had a good heart. He worked at the Temple of the Kyber, sweeping floors, and every day, while performing his chores, he dreamed of adventure ...

FADE TO OUTRO MUSIC.
THE END

Acknowledgments

No story is written in isolation, and that's particularly true of a Star Wars story, for which the humble creator stands upon the shoulders of giants. The Star Wars universe is huge, and beautifully diverse, and so many people have helped to shape it over the years, not least my co-conspirators in The High Republic: Cavan Scott, Justina Ireland, Claudia Gray, Charles Soule, Daniel José Older, Tessa Gratton, Lydia Kang, and Zoraida Córdova. My thanks to you all. What a team.

Sincere thanks are also due to Michael Siglain, Jennifer Heddle, and the whole team at Lucasfilm for their ongoing patronage and support. To the team at Del Rey, and in particular Tom Hoeler for his keen editorial eye. To my agent, Charlotte Robertson. And to my family, who always have my back. Know that I appreciate everything you do.

About the Author

George Mann is a *Sunday Times* bestselling novelist, comics writer, and screenwriter. He's the creator of the Wychwood supernatural mystery series as well as the popular Newbury & Hobbes and Tales of the Ghost series. He's written comics, novels, and audio dramas for properties such as *Star Wars, Doctor Who,* Sherlock Holmes*, Judge Dredd, Teenage Mutant Ninja Turtles,* and *Dark Souls,* and was recently part of the writers' room on several adult animated television shows.

George lives near Grantham, England, with his wife, children, and two noisy dogs. He loves mythology and folklore, Kate Bush, and chocolate. He is constantly surrounded by tottering piles of comics and books.

About the Type

This book was set in Hermann, a typeface created in 2019 by Chilean designers Diego Aravena and Salvador Rodriguez for W Type Foundry. Hermann was developed as a modern tribute to classic novels, taking its name from the author Hermann Hesse. It combines key legibility features from the typefaces Sabon and Garamond with more dynamic and bolder visual components.